A Blow to the Heart

MARCEL THEROUX

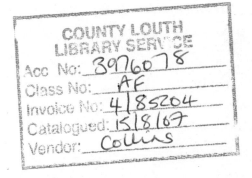

faber and faber

First published in 2006
by Faber and Faber Limited
3 Queen Square London WC1N 3AU

Typeset by Faber and Faber
Printed in England by Mackays of Chatham, plc

A CIP record for this book
is available from the British Library

ISBN 978-0-571-22951-2
ISBN 0-571-22951-4

2 4 6 8 10 9 7 5 3 1

A BLOW TO THE HEART

One

Daisy Polidoro was seven when she saw her first boxing match. The television set was an old black and white one that her father sometimes thumped to improve the reception. He was a gentle man: his way with mutinous appliances the only hint of violence in their orderly world. The interest in boxing was not foreshadowed by anything in his character. Daisy saw a squared ring crackling between bursts of static, a beaten fighter, head sagging in defeat. It was no more than a glimpse. Daisy's father spied her at the door in her nightie and dispatched her quickly back to bed. It would be twenty-five years before she saw another.

Her father died a year later. That image – him twiddling the recalcitrant aerial, the picture fizzing with electric snow – was one of a handful that sustained his memory into her adult life. Some others: the smell of his Irish stew; creosoting the shed; dragging Daisy unwillingly round garden centres on Sunday afternoons; her hugging him after he came down from the loft and her shock at the vicious prickle of fibreglass insulation in his jumper; the vertiginous swoop when he lifted her up to carry her on his shoulders.

Nothing had prepared her for his death. Loss is a stranger sometimes to the only child. Even games of ludo had been weighted miraculously in her favour. 'She doesn't like losing.' Who did?

Daisy took it well, they said; her mother less so. She never remarried. Daisy grew up bright, precociously adult, a little closed. Her sharp tongue intimidated potential suitors. She thought her glasses were the problem.

Someone once told Daisy she was too beautiful for public transport. She didn't believe it. She didn't have that kind of face or body. But on any given day she could be beautiful enough to feel a curious alteration in men's attitudes to her: the unfocused attentiveness and clumsy passes that are the hazard and birthright of the beautiful.

Daisy was thirteen at the time of her first encounter with the hereditary privileges of the very beautiful. On a French exchange in Toulouse she shared a room with Lindsey, a statuesque and prematurely buxom blonde girl who made a big impression on the host family. '*Daisy est jolie*,' Madame Boissoneault cooed over the breakfast table, '*mais Lindsey est belle.*'

Lindsey looked uncomprehendingly at Daisy.

'She said I'm pretty, but you're beautiful,' Daisy explained. She resented the observation, but not as much as she resented having to translate it for Lindsey, whose French was rudimentary.

Lindsey brightened. 'Oh, I think you're beautiful too, Daisy.'

'It's not my opinion. I'm just translating,' said Daisy.

'*Merci*,' said Lindsey. '*Mais, Daisy avoir* . . . How do you say "lovely skin", Daze?'

It was strange how good looks conferred a special status on Lindsey: dim, lazy Lindsey, who missed home, couldn't speak French, and pretended to be ill in order to avoid Madame B's garlicky cooking. The prerogatives of her beauty even survived Madame B's discovering her in her room, stuffing her face with a tin of spaghetti hoops that she had bought on a secret and uncharacteristically resourceful trip to the hypermarket.

Life is unfair, Daisy wrote precociously in her journal. She knew already that contrary to everything that adults implied, people didn't start, compete, or finish equal. God had given some his equivalent of a trust fund: a big bust, blonde hair and a retroussé nose. And how was it possible to worship the beautiful without diminishing the plain? Everyone, surely, was entitled to feel beautiful. And in her life, Daisy did feel beautiful at times – though not at those times around Christmas when drunk men in suits approached her on the Underground with inane chat-up lines, of which 'you're too beautiful to travel by public transport' was the most memorable.

Daisy Polidoro was thirty-two; when she thought of feeling beautiful, she thought of her husband Stuart twisting her hair into a thick, soft rope, or marvelling at the lightness of her step as she moved noiselessly over the creaky wooden floorboards of their bedroom, or praising her figure.

'My dad said small breasts are the secret of a long and happy marriage,' he said once, cupping hers in his hands as she sat brushing her hair before the mirror.

'He's right,' said Daisy. 'I wouldn't fancy you with big ones.'

Stuart chuckled and rubbed his nose against her neck. '. . . because they stay beautiful for ever.'

'But wasn't it your dad who said that if you get the chance to sleep with a woman you should always take it? And always to try and pick up waitresses?'

'He's a red-blooded Sardinian male,' said Stuart, 'and a product of his upbringing, but he was right about the breasts.'

Daisy and Stuart met at university. She noticed him in Freshers' Week at a party in their hall of residence. Stuart struck her as the only grown-up. She loved his good-humoured calm, his intelligence and sobriety. He was big, virile, serious, balding like a young Brando, with an equine combination of strength and tenderness.

Stuart was studying medicine and wanted to be a psychiatrist, he said. That struck Daisy as the only false note about him. After knowing him for twenty minutes, Daisy felt it was a bad choice: he was too sane, too open. All health, no darkness; how could he understand the blighted inner worlds of his future patients? So Daisy was pleased when Stuart changed his mind and decided to specialize in haematology.

They married very young for their time and class, at twenty-four, but delayed having children while they each secured a foothold in their respective careers. Daisy had trained as a journalist and was doing casual shifts at a national newspaper, where her fluency and humour were impressing her superiors. After a while, she got a rolling one-year contract to work for the political desk at a salary that struck both her and Stuart as astronomical.

After several years of marriage, she continued to be surprised by the varieties of happiness in her life. At the office party one Christmas, Stuart arrived late and stood uncomfortably in the corner with his coat over his arm, and an orange juice, waiting for her to finish her conversation with the editor. Daisy knew he was impatient to leave, but still she lingered, so proud of him, wanting to show him off, conscious of his love in the room like a private sun which shone only for her.

They never argued about it, but she knew it irked Stuart that she used her maiden name on her byline. 'My family think it's weird,' was all that Stuart would say. She found it hard to explain to him why she chose not to use her married name: 'Daisy Adams', the name she had borne through school and university and journalism school, seemed to keep faith with a younger self whose ambitions she was finally beginning to fulfil.

That was the only source of friction – that, and the pressure to have children that she knew Stuart was under from his family. Stuart shielded her from it on the whole, but his parents dropped not-so-subtle hints whenever they went round to visit, especially if Stuart's prolific younger sisters (two children each and counting) were there. And then, three months after her thirtieth birthday, Daisy got pregnant. She hadn't really intended to, but they had grown less and less vigilant about birth control in a way that did seem to be tempting fate.

Daisy took the pregnancy test in her lunch-hour and walked around the block for ten minutes with the indicator in her bag. When she looked at it in the privacy of a toilet cubicle, she was taken aback at the unambiguousness of the blue line that marked the threshold of this new world.

There were practical obstacles: the timing ruled her out of covering the party conferences; they had a garden but no spare room; she wondered how they would manage on just Stuart's salary. But when she got home that evening, Stuart was cooking and she felt so full of love for him, and so excited by the extraordinary effect her news would have on him, that it spilled out of her with none of the coy preamble she had been rehearsing on the tube. Stuart wanted to call his parents immediately.

'We have to wait twelve weeks, Dr Polidoro,' said Daisy.

Stuart scrunched up his face with the imagined effort of bottling up the news. 'What if someone asks? You know I can't tell a lie.'

Daisy pinched him. 'Why would anyone ask, unless bigmouth was dropping hints?'

Stuart, who was protective at the best of times, started to behave as though Daisy was the sole and haemophiliac heir of an important dynasty. If he could have carried her around on a cushion like a rare and fragile egg, he would have. He sent her flowers at work – but mainly, she knew, so they would absorb radiation from her computer screen; he urged folic acid supplements on her, scrutinized potatoes for eyes, vetoed sushi because of worries about mercury levels, and kept her out of smoky rooms. Most astonishingly, he stuck to his word not to tell anyone. Daisy knew what this cost him. His open nature was not designed to keep secrets.

Finally, they were ready. They decided to make the formal announcement at Stuart's parents' house over Sunday dinner. It was the ninth of January. The anticipation of the inevitable scenes of melodrama (Mrs Polidoro in tears; Mr Polidoro probably in tears as well; endless advice and anecdotes – and no chance of a drink to make the time go faster) gave Daisy a reprise of her morning sickness and she stayed in bed. 'I'll get up in a minute,' she said half-heartedly. Stuart pulled on a polo-neck sweater. 'What's the hurry?' he said and went to get the papers.

He was gone so long that she made herself a forbidden cup of coffee and was drinking it in the kitchen when the front door bell rang. Stuart had forgotten his keys. Daisy briefly considered dumping the coffee in the sink, but she decided to brazen it out and went to the door with the cup in her hand. She liked the rituals of loving chastisement which were part of his protective nature, and anticipated another, a telling-off so tender it would resemble a caress: 'Coffee? At least tell me it was decaf', and, shaking his head, Stuart would push past her with the papers: 'Well, at least I hope you made me one too.'

Daisy pulled the door open.

'Mrs Polidoro? May I come in? I'm afraid I have some bad news. Would you like to sit down? There's been an accident. Your husband was badly hurt. He was taken by ambulance to hospital, but the doctors were unable to do anything for him.'

The ground lurched. 'There must be a mistake. He just went out to buy the papers.'

'We've identified the body.'

'The body?' Daisy felt an immense emptiness, the sensation of a coin dropping into a bottomless well. Something heavy seemed to clang shut inside her. 'I want to see him.'

The police officers accompanied Daisy to the morgue. They pulled back the sheet. Stuart smelled of the soap with the plastic goldfish inside that his nieces had given them for Christmas: sweet and rainwater-fresh. He seemed unmarked. Daisy searched his big sculpted body for the fatal injury and could see only a small round hole to the side of his left nipple, as though a tiny bead had entered his chest.

'That killed him?'

'Instantly.'

In the week after Stuart's death, Daisy lost her baby. She was glad she had told no one. She burned the pictures from the twelve week scan in the fireplace along with the indicator she had saved from the pregnancy test. As she watched the flames blister the chemicals in the images, it seemed to her that a natural law which kept the quantity of happiness constant over

6

time was asserting itself, and she was now paying for all those years of unconscious contentment with her husband.

Daisy spent the whole funeral feeling overwhelmed by Stuart's huge and boisterously grieving family. Daisy's own mother tried to be supportive, but Daisy protected her, as she had always done, from the depth of her sadness, conscious that her fragile, overburdened, anxious mother would sink under the weight of Daisy's grief. So Daisy bore it alone.

She went with her mother-in-law to every day of the trial of Stuart's killer. He was seventeen years old, skinny, and pale as a seagull. He wore a tracksuit and trainers to court and was accompanied by someone from Social Services.

In his testimony he described how, on the day of Stuart's death, he had been drinking and taking amphetamines. Walking down the street that morning, he had been vandalizing cars when Stuart confronted him. Faced with a larger, angry man – Stuart, the defence counsel reminded the jury, was six foot three and had played rugby for his university team – the boy panicked and stabbed at Stuart with the Phillips head screwdriver he had been using to scrape paint off vehicles.

Stabbed *at* him: the defence barrister was careful to draw attention to the preposition. 'Was it your intention to inflict an injury on Mr Polidoro?'

'No. I was afraid he was going to do something to me.'

Drugged up, jumpy, surprised in the act of committing a mindless but minor offence, menaced by the terrifying bulk of Stuart Polidoro, the barrister implied, who wouldn't behave as young Joel Heath had behaved?

Daisy resented Stuart's demotion from 'Dr' to 'Mr'. It was his job to be calm in a crisis. She thought: *Stuart angry?* He was a pillar of cool self-assurance. He would have confronted the boy with gentle authority, asked him what he was doing, why was he doing it? Whose anger was the boy blinded by? Not Stuart's.

Heath's mother came to court for the verdict. She was not

7

much older than Daisy; not unattractive either, but weary-looking, pinched and pale. With her was a girl of about six, Heath's sister, who carried felt-tips in a pink plastic handbag. As they waited in the corridor, Heath's mother bent her head to supervise her daughter's colouring, and stopped her own bronchitic cough with her fist.

Daisy concentrated on remaining poised, but she wanted to scream at the boy's mother: this thing you call your *life*, a broken sewage pipe spilling into other people's lives.

Mrs Polidoro was more confrontational. 'Scum,' she muttered audibly.

'What did you say?' screamed Heath's mother, in a voice that was surprisingly deep and raw for her slight frame. She made as though to fly at them, but was easily restrained by the ushers.

Joel Heath was found guilty only of manslaughter. He received a two-year sentence in a young offenders' institution and was ordered to attend a drug treatment programme.

For a while, Daisy kept in touch with Stuart's family, but their meetings were too unsettling. Her presence in their house was in fact unwelcome, an image of Stuart's murder; and she and the elder Mrs Polidoro, who had at first consoled one another, were like a pair of mirrors, reflecting each other's grief in an infinite arc, until they were forced to turn away from each other.

Two

After the trial, Daisy sold the home she had shared with Stuart and moved to a smaller flat in another part of the city. She bought the first property she looked at. The move generated an unintended windfall of money: never had she wanted so little, yet never had she been so well-off.

Her new flat was sparely furnished. Daisy gave away or sold many of their joint possessions. Things that were too precious to give up she stacked in boxes in the tiny cloakroom that the estate agent had euphemistically called the study-bedroom. Then Daisy took a sabbatical from her work, and went away to Sri Lanka for a month.

It was the low season and the hotel she stayed in was empty except for a young German man who was also travelling on his own. She could feel his glance on her at mealtimes. One evening, fortified by beer, he plucked up courage to sit with her. He had just come from Goa. He had a design consultancy in Munich. She guessed he was twenty-six. She let him buy her a drink, but when he put his hand on her knee, her body tensed. 'I'm a widow,' she said. She felt him shrink from her.

The next day, in the afternoon, she borrowed one of the rickety hotel bicycles. Five minutes away from the hotel, the road snaked through rice fields. Men were working in the heat, barebacked, making bricks by hand. Beyond the fields, wild elephants ambled at the fringes of the forest. *I am a widow*, she thought, but the heat and the strange surroundings seemed to have erased her pain and her sense of self. There was hope here, in spite of the friends who had advised her not to come away alone. Living in an unthinking present in an unfamiliar place, eating, sleeping, swimming in the pool – the hotel manager warned her about the seasonal rip tides that made the beach too hazardous for swimming – Daisy began to feel that some kind of life without her husband was recoverable.

But when Daisy returned home, she discovered that she had simply left the feeling part of herself behind, and that her grief and pain were waiting for her, concealed like loose change in a thousand odd receptacles: the sympathetic smile of a colleague who had covered Heath's trial, or the sound of a baby crying, or the rare cards she got from Mrs Polidoro.

Daisy found that she could no longer do her job. To write even the kind of articles she had been writing, she had to reach into herself, inhabit her soul a little, but she found it too painful. Whatever she was writing, she dredged up memories of her dead husband and child; her ambition, which had preceded even her love for Stuart, vanished; and the blistering image she had burned in the hearth of her old flat haunted her like an emblem of lost hope. She quit and took a job at her local library. It was less than half a mile from her flat, a purpose-built Edwardian building with books spread over two floors – reference section in the basement – and a separate children's library housed in another building. By the issues desk were shelves of videos and CDs, like an anxious assertion of relevance, but the bulk of the borrowers wanted romantic novels, books on learning English, or simply to study at the desks in the reference library.

Now Daisy walked to work, she stamped and stacked books, she walked home and ate and went to bed. A year passed.

How did she cope? Barely. Sundays were the worst.

It made perfect sense to Daisy, an agnostic, that Christians worshipped on a Sunday: Sunday was the day that everyone needed God. Sunday was a tyrant, a psychopath who could be bribed to sweetness for an hour or two by a trip to a gallery, or lunch with a friend, or a walk, but when it got you alone after seven p.m. its expression changed, turned cold and hard, and it told you to wipe the smile off your face: it's too late, you're too old, too lost, to start again.

One of Daisy's friends told her about their cure for Sunday: the Valley Hall steam baths. On a Sunday evening, she said, the intense heat of the hot rooms and the freezing water of the plunge pool seemed to turn the blood in your legs to marble and purge the worst of your gloom.

Daisy disagreed. She'd been there with Stuart and couldn't bear them any more. The ghostly shapes in the steam-room were a too-literal afterlife, and the shabbiness and smoking and smells of fried food in the changing area, while tolerable with Stuart, were too close in texture to the hopeless melancholy that nibbled at the circumference of her reduced existence. She missed Stuart all the time, but she missed him most on Sundays.

It was March again. London bathed beneath an unseasonal Tuscan sun: the city gilded, its sky turquoise. The big supermarket by the canal was empty. Daisy shopped there every Friday in her lunch-hour. She was examining a shopping list she'd found in a trolley in the car park.

On a scrap of torn exercise book, a woman's hand had written in blue biro: *tampax, cauliflower, teabags, lemons, jif, things for kids lunches.* Since Stuart's death, Daisy had acquired an odd tic: whenever she found a shopping list, she used it. Over a six-month period, this strange rule had disclosed an unexpected taste for silverskin onions and cockles; confirmed her hatred of melons, brown sauce and tinned steak-and-kidney pudding; and revealed a predictable dislike of nicotine chewing gum which, as a non-smoker, she had no incentive to try and enjoy.

The random items on this list gave a glimpse of someone else's life: the life of a busy and organized mother with school-age children. Its brevity implied a kitchen replete with the things that the woman didn't need to mention, the way the best lives were full of understatement and meanings grasped without effort: the terracotta tiles, and the door opened out on to the garden, the laundry room fragrant with soap powder and the musky smell of husband on the sheets in the basket, and Daisy was dangerously close to the eternal Sunday at the heart of her being, an endless Sunday, as dark as the tiny hole that had whistled the life out of Stuart's body.

Daisy took her shopping home and filed it in the cupboards of her kitchen. There was so little to do. There was so little she wanted any more. As she opened the bathroom cabinet to put away the toothpaste, she avoided meeting her own gaze in the mirrored door. She had shocked herself on more than one occasion by her youthful appearance, and by the confusion she felt, seeing her own image and being momentarily unsure which body she inhabited.

'It's called "depersonalization",' said the bereavement counsellor who contacted her six months after Stuart's death. 'It's really not that unusual as a symptom of depression. You've suffered a tremendous blow.'

Daisy nodded. 'Not unusual.' And she thought: *I am empty. I am entirely lost.*

At the far right of the bottom row of shelves, an amber plastic bottle stood with its label turned to the side: the sleeping pills she'd husbanded from the ration her GP had given her after she complained of insomnia. They were a secret thought, an emergency hammer glazed behind the thin wall of the mirror. They were a permanent cure for Sunday.

As part of the borough's policy of social inclusiveness, the library was obliged to show that it was making an effort to serve the area's ethnic minorities. There were large sections of books in Farsi, Urdu, Cantonese, as well as European languages. Simon Black, the senior librarian, whose patrician accent, ginger beard and Oxford First made Daisy's overqualification for the job seem less anomalous, encouraged his staff to take advantage of the opportunities for language courses. It would help safeguard the library against budget cuts and was, he implied, a form of unofficial paid holiday.

Daisy wasn't really interested. She could never escape the feeling that there were too many words in the world. Words weren't worth what they used to be when they were set by hand in a printer's forme, letter by letter, or scratched on parchment with recalcitrant ink, or stamped in clay with carved wooden wedges, or bashed on to the platen of a manual typewriter. The library groaned under the weight of words, and the ether was crammed with words too, words that would yield under the faint pressure of a keystroke. And yet, nowhere could she find the words she needed: the words that would console her, or better still, the *talitha cum* that would bring Stuart back to life. She longed for the day when all the words would blow away at last like dandelion clocks, leaving a world of things to be named afresh.

But Simon Black was persistent and officious. In the end, she ticked a box at random on an application form he gave her and found she had signed up for four separate weeks of sign-language classes at Conway Hall.

With its handouts, and homework, and the prospect of a final exam, the course felt like being back at school. Daisy had been a conscientious and ambitious student all her life, so it was particularly liberating to undertake something so half-heartedly, knowing that its outcome was of no importance to her whatsoever. Her initial prejudice was that it wasn't even a language at all, but a sophisticated kind of semaphore. But as the weeks passed, and they went deeper into the language, it became clear that it had its own grammar, a word order unlike English, and a population of native speakers for whom its handshapes and movements were not just a practical link with reality, but their only means of expressing hope, or regret, or shame, or love, or anguish.

Most of the other students worked in the healthcare industry, but there was also a Japanese housewife called Michiko, and a man called Steve who just liked learning languages. In the weeks off, the students went to signed performances of plays and to deaf clubs, where they were largely shunned by the deaf members.

All of them passed their exam and on the last night, they took their deaf tutor out to an Italian restaurant in Soho and drank too much cheap red wine. Daisy drank moderately, but looking around the table she surprised herself by feeling that she would miss the superficial, chance relationships that she had made with these people, and she envied them their full, carefree lives, their appetites, their sense that ordinary things still mattered: *lemons, jif, things for kids lunches.*

But in spite of them all exchanging emails, none of them stayed in touch with each other. And Daisy never had an opportunity to use her sign language.

After she had unpacked her shopping, Daisy cycled back to the library. Jorge, a gay man from Catalonia with a wispy beard and piercings, told her that Simon had gone home with a migraine. Simon had been due to lead Reading Hour with a group of primary-school children and their teacher in the Junior Library. Jorge insisted that he would not do it, so Daisy took over.

Daisy was supposed to read to the children from *The Happy Prince*, a book that their teacher dismissed in their presence as 'crypto-Christian propaganda'.

'It's only short,' Daisy said, and she began reading, the children rapt, cross-legged, in a semicircle around her.

Daisy was curious about the reverse alchemy that would eventually turn these polite and friendly children into the hooded morlocks who started fires behind the shelving, the shameless youths who only Simon Black had any luck confronting. She had puzzled over it and guessed that the problem was men themselves, hardwired for trouble and violence. Because until they became men, at that indeterminate age when they were indistinguishable from girls – so much so that they feigned revulsion from girls as a badge of difference, because they *were* girls – they sat quietly. And Daisy wondered about Joel Heath as an eight-year-old, before the dose of testosterone that had had fatal consequences for Stuart.

Daisy read on: '"Who hath dared to wound thee?" cried the Giant; "tell me, that I may take my big sword and slay him." "Nay!" answered the child; "but these are the wounds of Love."'

And before she knew what was happening, the words had blurred and the room span. She must not, she must not betray herself by the catch in her voice. She must not weep in front of these children. And she dug her thumbnail hard into the side of her hand.

Afterwards, they discussed the story, the children all eager to say the right things. 'Miss, the giant was bad because he wouldn't share!' 'You shouldn't play in other people's gardens!' And though their teacher looked on disapprovingly, Daisy explained the allegory. 'One way of understanding it, is that it's a fable and the child is Jesus.' The children became thoughtful and seemed very satisfied by this explanation: 'That's right, because Jesus made the weather, didn't he, miss?'

At the end of the hour, the children left the library. Daisy watched them holding hands unselfconsciously, swinging each others' arms, jumping the four-inch drop from the edge of the kerb as though into a canyon: riotous, elastic, gentle.

Daisy closed up the library alone that evening at seven. Jorge had asked her to cover for him so he could leave early. He left, excited and happy, looking forward to whatever appointment awaited him. Daisy watched Jorge leave and thought: *he's right to make an effort, to allow himself moods and passions* – and she resolved to behave as though things did matter for a change. She had an invitation of her own. She took a cab across the river, to the mansion block in Battersea where Imogen lived, and clomped to the door in her heels, clutching the bottle of wine that she had taken ten minutes to choose. She was right to come out, right to push herself into real life. Imogen answered the door in greasy hair and pair of shapeless sweat-pants. 'We're having a girls' night in,' Imo announced. 'Eat what we like, wear fat-suits, no make-up, and talk about boys.'

Although her appetite for life had deserted her, Daisy found it perversely heartening to know that there were certain things she didn't want. And she didn't want this. She sat in an armchair. Someone came into the room carrying a tub of ice-cream. She introduced herself as Brigid. Brigid seemed affronted by Daisy's smart appearance. 'Have you been somewhere? Didn't Imo tell you? It's dress-down Friday, isn't it, Imo?'

Pizza, ice-cream with melted Mars bars, crappy television: the food and behaviour were infantile. But Daisy understood that for Imo and her friends it was also reassuring. These women with plenty of their own worries and difficult jobs were allowing themselves to regress. Meanwhile, Daisy was dressed for a cocktail party. It was shaming, and she felt that the other girls – Brigid, Helen, Tricia, Becca – resented her for it; until she went to the loo. When she came back, she knew that Imogen had briefed everyone on her sad history, and she sensed the warming in their attitudes to her now that she was no longer a competitor, but a charity case.

The girls swapped war stories. 'I had a blind date last week. I went to Whistles and went mad with my credit card, and he turned up in jeans and a fleece!'

'That's why I want to do speed-dating. You only spend three minutes with each person.'

Imogen filled Daisy's glass. 'Are you dating yet?' ventured Helen, emboldened by wine to prod Daisy for an intimacy.

'Not really.'

'Recovering . . .' said someone. The conversation faltered. Daisy wondered: is it my fault? Did she walk around with a perpetual rain-cloud over her head? But the silence was filled, eventually, without too much difficulty until, half-cut, Imo trapped Daisy in the kitchen.

'How are you, Daisy?' And then: 'How *are* you?' Daisy

stared at the washing-up, wondering why they couldn't have had this conversation when they were sober.

'You're so pretty, Daisy. You should be out snogging boys, enjoying yourself. It's been, what, two years almost? Seize the day. Is this what Stew-pot would have wanted?' Imo looked at her unsteadily, eyes pink with wine, gesticulating with her glass, maudlin in her shapeless beige tracksuit.

Daisy felt a lightning bolt of anger surge through her and take shape in bitter words. 'Don't tell me what I *should* do. I was married for eight years to someone I was in love with. All I hear from people is that they're confused, they can't commit, that relationships are so, so difficult. Well, my relationship was the easiest thing I ever did in my life. It's just everything else that's impossible.' Imogen's eyes filled with tears. Daisy knew she had gone too far and she began to apologize.

'No, I had no business . . .' Imogen dabbed at her eyes with a piece of kitchen towel. Helen came into the kitchen, appraised the situation and retreated. Daisy felt like the school bully: vile, isolated and hateful. She couldn't leave on such a sour note. So she sat with them for another hour, until the sitcoms ended, and the wine was drunk, and Imogen dug out of a cupboard some Hungarian liqueur in a round green bottle that someone had brought back from Budapest.

The girls shrieked. 'It looks like Baby-Bio!' 'Or poison!' And Daisy found herself laughing too, at Imo, who was pretending to be indignant, but really wringing out all the comic possibilities of her unwanted liqueur. 'It's this or lighter fluid!'

Imogen hugged her for a long time at the door when Daisy finally left. Daisy got into her cab thinking that, in the end, coming out had been the right decision.

The next day, she bought a card and spent a long time trying to compose a note to Imogen to apologize for her outburst and to thank Imogen for her continued friendship. It was odd, she wanted to say, but since losing her temper, she had noticed a change in herself. Something faint but unmistakable had happened: the sensation of new life, the tingling of blood returning to a withered limb. However frailly, she felt once more in contact with her own desires, and she caught the scent of life again, like woodsmoke in the air, like the indistinct music of a far-off celebration. In the end, it felt too difficult and perhaps too dangerously premature to put all these feelings on paper, but she posted the note with a sense of gratitude, pausing at the pillar box – then, as she turned away, she found herself looking into the eyes of Joel Heath.

Three

The post box was set into a wall beside the station entrance, and alongside it was a patch of brickwork that had been covered over with generations of flyposters. One of the newer ones announced a boxing match that was going to take place in a leisure centre in Elephant and Castle. There was a hierarchy of names descending from the biggest draws to the virtual unknowns in small print at the bottom. Someone had decided that Heath was important enough to merit a photo. There he was, in the bottom right-hand corner, posing in a low crouch.

He had a new physique, a new, confident look about him, and a new haircut, close cropped and segmented with three or four short lines at one side of the brow.

'Making his long-awaited professional debut,' ran the blurb above his name. 'Joel Heath, Canning Town.' At the bottom of the poster was a list of names and mobile phone numbers for people who wanted to buy tickets in advance: Heath's was among them.

Daisy froze as she recognized his face. It was like being threatened in daylight by a creature from a nightmare. She stood rooted to the pavement, drinking in every detail of the poster, knowing everything about it was toxic to her: the suggestion of braggadocio in the posture, the muscled confidence, the tough guy haircut. 'Look at me,' the photo seemed to say, 'I promise spectacular violence.' But to Daisy it also said something else: 'Look at me, your life's in ruins. Look at me – you widowed, childless mess.' ('stabbed *at* him, your honour.') 'Look at you, weeping in front of those children at something you read in a book' – could he even read? – 'buying other people's crap when you go shopping because you've got no crap of your own to buy. A stupid job, no friends, no life to speak of. Is *that* what Stew-pot would have wanted?'

She turned aside from the picture. Her sense of revulsion was physical: a punch in the solar plexus. She felt breathless, winded. She saw Heath shuffling out of the dock. Already free. Again, the image of that tiny wound, absurdly little on Stuart's big body. It must have been no larger than the punctuation marks on the poster. Around her, the world looked just the same: the same traffic under the same clouds, indifferent to her misery.

That night, it took a sleeping pill to silence Heath's voice and knock Daisy out, but she woke at three a.m., unable to breathe. Daisy had asthma, but it had been so many years since her last attack that she didn't have an inhaler in the house. She tried to control her breathing using a technique she'd learned when she'd taken up yoga in the first weeks of her pregnancy. And inevitably, the associations of that – yoga, pregnancy, Stuart, Stuart's death – took her back to Heath.

'He really should have minded his own business,' said the sneering voice. 'I'm a professional fighter, Daisy. I made mincemeat out of that big lump, your husband. That big ex-husband, your lump. That ex-lump. Stew-pot. I was very confused at the time. Stabbed *at* him, your honour. All my feelings go out to the relatives. It's great how life gives us a second chance if we want it. Six months of metalwork in Feltham and, open sesame, I'm a pugilist-specialist. Wicked. Are you happy, Daisy? Are you happy for me?'

Something had come alive in her, a jeering, disdainful being that she recognized in her more lucid moments probably didn't even resemble Heath, but which had emerged fully formed from somewhere inside her brain. It was a shadow image of everything she valued. It spoke in a voice of power and contempt; a voice that was all the more awful because the things it said had the force of harsh truths.

Daisy sat for two hours on the side of the bed that night, breathing into a paper bag to control her asthma. Even with the window of her bedroom open, she felt feverishly hot. Heath's face on the poster rose up in the darkness, more vivid than it had ever been outside the station. His mouth flexed into a sleepy grin. The telephone number beside his name seemed to move and glitter like the digits on an electronic tickertape. Daisy hadn't failed to notice, with a certain grim satisfaction, that Heath was scheduled to fight in just over a week's time: on a Sunday.

The next day, Daisy read the sports sections of all the broadsheets and searched the internet. She found two cursory mentions of Joel Heath, one on a website belonging to his promoter, Ron Costello. But she turned up nothing that described Heath or mentioned his history. Nothing that would give her a clue, that would help answer the questions that had begun to obsess her. Who was he? And *why*? Why had this stranger turned her life to dust? The idea of Joel Heath had burned itself on to her brain like the after-image of the sun on closed eyelids.

On Sunday night, again unable to sleep, Daisy picked up the handset beside her bed and punched in the numbers of Heath's mobile phone. After half a dozen rings, she heard a sleepy 'Yeah?' She was silent. 'Who is it?' the voice asked. Daisy said nothing. Heath – if it was him – was too tired and discombobulated to be irate. 'Darrell? Is that you? Fucking . . .' he muttered grumpily and hung up.

Daisy was surprised at how little she felt. It was disappointing. The voice at the other end had been too blurred with sleep, too confused, too unlike the voice she heard in her head to bear any of the significance she wanted to attach to it.

The following Sunday, Daisy went alone to the venue in South London where Heath was scheduled to fight. She paid twenty pounds for her ticket and four for the glossy programme. The programme notes said: 'Costello Promotions are proud to present the first professional bout of this talented

21

youngster of whom we'll no doubt be hearing more of. After a promising amateur career, Joel has been away for a while, but now he's focused on the job in hand and hopes to make a career fighting without the vest.' The words meant very little to Daisy. *Of whom we'll no doubt be hearing more of.* The wonky grammar seemed of a piece with the crowd of neanderthals who'd come to watch men inflict legal brain damage on each other. Of many injustices, what struck her most was that not once during the course of the trial had any mention been made of Heath's boxing. It turned out that the fearful little vandal presented to the court by the defence had actually been trained to fight.

Heath's was the second bout of the afternoon. His opponent entered the ring first, with no fanfare. There was no mention of his name in the programme. He was in his thirties, with a creased, babyish face. Two trainers accompanied him into the ring: a tall, stoop-shouldered white man and a shorter, light-skinned black man, who took up positions at the edge of the ring. There was a flurry of interest from the crowd as the lights dipped and Heath made his entrance to a hip-hop track. He wore a satin robe and was flanked by cornermen in matching shirts. The auditorium was two-thirds empty. Heath vaulted the ring rope to the shouted encouragement of half a dozen youngish fans; no sign of his mother.

As the referee gave his final instructions, Heath stretched his waist and gyrated. Daisy looked at his body, white and free of blemishes, and thought of Stuart's body, big and cold and stretched out on the mortuary slab.

Heath won his fight on points over the scheduled six rounds and was cheered out of the ring by his handful of support. Whatever Daisy was hoping to find, she hadn't found it. There was something barbarous and depressing about the whole spectacle: the preening of the young men in the audience, their tarty girlfriends, the unmistakable musk of violence in the air. And the contest itself had looked one-sided. Heath's baby-faced opponent seemed content to run away and let Heath chase him. Daisy left immediately after Heath's fight. She had seen enough.

And yet, when Heath fought again, Daisy was again among the spectators. It wasn't the vividness of the contest, the surrender to the mass will of the crowd, or the expectation of blood that drew her back. Somehow she *had* to know, had to see him. There was a furtive compulsion in her behaviour. After that fight, she told herself it would be the last, and then she found herself making a mental note of the time and venue of the next, calculating how long it would take to get there. The third time, she set off on a impulse without a ticket, leaving it to chance and the traffic to determine her fate.

Each time, Heath won a quick victory. As his opponent dropped unconscious to the canvas, or was saved on his feet by the referee's intercession, hurt and bewildered, sometimes still protesting, Daisy felt a spasm of agony, and then a kind of relief, as if her unexpressed pain had found an outlet. Afterwards, she would be overwhelmed by shame and swear never to return. Then, as the next date drew near, the itch would start again. She couldn't understand the reason for her compulsion or the mysterious, short-lived catharsis it brought her. Her guilt about her odd behaviour isolated her. She glimpsed her own strangeness and it was frightening. After Heath's sixth victory, Daisy felt the split inside her had become intolerable, and she made up her mind to confront him in person.

Four

'There's no excuse for boxing,' said Ron Costello, hoisting his legs on to the top of his empty desk so that the soles of his goatskin boots were pointing at Daisy's face. 'Surprise you, doesn't it?' The shoes were clearly handmade. Their unmarked leather soles gleamed. 'I'm the first to say it. There's enough tears and pain in the world already.'

Ron slid open a drawer and took out a framed photograph. 'When a fighter comes to me and tells me he wants to make it as a professional, I always show him this.' He handed the picture to Daisy. It was a flash photograph of a boxer with his face squashed up like the ribs of an accordion from the impact of a punch. 'Jersey Joe Walcott. I ask you: how can a man take the face his mother gave him, fed, nursed, pressed to her bosoms, kissed all over, wiped clean with spit on a hankie, and subject it to *that*?' Ron Costello shook his head disbelievingly. 'I'm tennis, me. There's a sport: two men going at it *mano a mano*, all the mind games, all the athleticism and kidology, all the competition, none of the brain damage. What did you say your paper was?'

Daisy touched her spectacles and named her old employer.

Ron sighed. 'But banning things never did any good. What you've got now is a brutal, cruel, bloodthirsty, regulated sport. Banning it – where does that get you? The bareknuckle situation: a brutal, cruel, bloodthirsty, *un*regulated sport. And believe me, I know the unlicensed game. It's ten times worse than professional boxing. You can't just ban what's ugly in human nature. Think about it: where does it all go? It's nature. Human nature. How can nature be illegal?'

Something reminded Ron of something. Without a break in his flow of words, he got up, ambled to the door, handed a piece of paper to his cowed secretary and returned. 'It was an old-fashioned sport when I came into it. Run by a load of old farts. The golf club lot. I brought in a bit of flash and pizzazz. I'm a showman: light shows, music and, yes, topless promotions. Whatever it took to get tickets sold and television interested. I'm the major player in the sport right now. Those old gits who told me I was vulgarizing the game – where are they now?'

Ron pulled a packet of nicotine chewing gum out of his breast pocket and popped one of the squares out of the blister pack. He was physically imposing, green-eyed, courteous and certainly not stupid. What was left of his black hair was cropped close to his bullet head. Ron chewed his gum. 'So how can I be of excellent service?'

'As I told you, I'm researching a book on boxing. An anatomy of the sport.'

'An anatomy of boxing.' Costello nodded. He savoured the taste of the words like an expensive cigar, and she could tell he liked it. 'A woman's angle.'

Daisy was about to correct him. Then it occurred to her that being a woman in Ron's world was the best thing she could be. It put her beyond suspicion. In Ron's world, women were girlfriends or wives, or they put on fishnet tights and held numbered cards in the air between rounds.

'I want to do it as a series of profiles,' said Daisy. She gave him the list of people she was proposing to interview. 'I was keen to talk to you and one of the fighters you manage, Joel Heath.'

'Heath,' muttered Ron, as though the name was unfamiliar to him, eyeballing the list. 'Shouldn't be a problem.'

In spite of the rumours that circulated about Ron Costello, Daisy felt unafraid of him. He was too verbose, too flash, too self-consciously colourful for her to find him intimidating. At the moment of their meeting she had shaken his big hand and glanced at the enormous gold Rolex that encircled his wrist like a miniature version of a championship belt. 'Rolex,' he said. 'I've always loved them. Some wise guy started calling me Rolex Ron and the name sort of stuck.'

The time that Daisy had asked for in her letter was up, but Ron showed no desire to end the meeting. 'I've always wanted to write a book about boxing myself.'

'The promoter's angle?'

Ron shook his head. 'The psychological angle. I've done a lot of reading about this.' He leaned forward and stabbed a fat finger at Daisy. 'How many brains do you think you have?'

'Just the one, I imagine,' said Daisy.

Ron smiled. 'Three,' he said. 'Three.' Now he was enjoying Daisy's puzzled look. 'You've got your mammal brain, right, but inside that is your fish brain, and inside that is the oldest brain of all, the reptile brain. Because of evolution.'

'Right,' said Daisy. 'And what's that got to do with boxing?'

'Everything. You're an educated, well-brought-up person. But in part of your brain, you're still a crocodile.' Ron looked pleased with himself. 'People are always saying to me: I hate what you do, Costello, glamorizing violence. But guess what? Violence is glamorous. Always has been. Know why?'

'The reptile brain.'

'Bingo, Daisy. People want to see a man get beaten into a pulp. They identify with the winner. All that sweet science stuff is rubbish: no one really comes to boxing to see a defensive genius. A craftsman racking up a lead in points. They come for a ring war: two men knocking ten bells out of each other. And here's why.' Costello grabbed a handful of forms from his in-tray. 'VAT, income tax, another audit, medical reports. They're killing me with bits of paper. I'm just a simple deal-maker, and look at it. We're not designed for this nonsense, most of us. The reptile brain is simple: fear, hate, rage, boredom, hunger, thirst, winning, losing. Take you – you don't know what a bolo punch is, or a cross counter, or even a left hook, but you know what it means to see a man on all fours, dazed and groping about for his gum-shield. People are tired of shades of grey, paperwork, trying to obey the law all the time. They want certainty. They want to *know*: victory, defeat, winners, losers, life, death, black, white. You follow me? They want things that make sense of it. That's why, legal or not, this business will go on for ever.'

Daisy got to her feet. 'I've used up enough of your valuable time.'

'It's been a pleasure,' said Ron. 'Daisy . . .?'

'Adams.'

Daisy's hand was swallowed up in Ron's big paw.

'Married, Daisy?'

Daisy shook her head.

'Got a boyfriend?'

'No.'

'I hope you don't mind me saying this, but you're a very attractive woman.'

Daisy glanced down at her trapped hand in consternation, trying not to look panicked.

'You'll let me know if there's anything else I can do for you?'

She nodded mutely and Ron let go of her hand. 'Nice to meet you,' he said.

Five

Late October: a swirl of copper leaves clattered up the steps of Valley Hall and collapsed in a pile by the entrance, where they rustled like discarded money under the parade of footwear passing through the swing doors.

Daisy entered the foyer, bright and draughty and filled with the faint but heartless smells of beer, cologne, detergent and autumn streets. Just ahead of her, Ron Costello stopped by the merchandise stand and Daisy almost collided with him. Over his tailored dinner jacket hung a long black coat of Italian leather with a collar of pale fur from which the rain had coaxed a sharp, feral smell. Ron was counting out pound coins with his big scrubbed fingers, but the vendor was only too happy to give him the programmes for nothing. This was Ron's kingdom: if it had had a currency of its own, it would have had Ron's head on it.

'Mr Costello?'

'Hello, Daisy. Programme?'

'Yes, please.'

Ron handed a programme to Daisy and one to his girlfriend Janice, who accepted it without thanks or interest. She swept Daisy with her fixed smile and hostile eyes.

Daisy took it as a compliment. She had dressed carefully in the clothes she had worn when she worked as a journalist. Stuart had loved her newsroom outfits: something executive about them appealed to his secret desire to be dominated. Her shoes raised her two inches. No glasses tonight: everything about Daisy suggested poise and authority. She looked beautiful.

Ron, Janice and Daisy decamped to the bar. Janice sipped an alcopop and looked on with a sour expression as Daisy took out her tape recorder.

'Another easy fight?' asked Daisy.

'There are no easy fights at this level,' said Ron, bringing his bottle-green eyes to bear intensely on Daisy's. 'He's the champ, everyone's looking to chill him.'

'The champ?'

'Southern Area, yeah.' Ron was enjoying Daisy's interest. 'Joel's had his shares of ups and downs. Boxing's given him a second chance like it did me. I see a lot of myself in the lad.'

'What kind of thing was he in trouble for?' asked Daisy.

'Small stuff mostly. You can ask him yourself.'

'I will,' she said.

Janice excused herself to go and circulate.

As Daisy bent her head over her drink, Ron gave her an appraising glance. Her story hadn't quite checked out. She hadn't written anything for the newspaper for over a year. He wondered exactly what she was doing here, in his dark and crooked world of false certainties.

'How do you like your work?' he asked.

Daisy looked up. Something about his tone made her uncomfortable. 'I have to be honest with you,' she said. 'I haven't actually been working as a journalist for some time.'

'A fib?' Costello's eyes were ice-cold.

Daisy kept her composure. 'I was on the political desk for several years. I went freelance.'

'To the library.' There was menace in his voice.

'You've done some research.'

'I like to know who I'm dealing with.'

'I downshifted. I had some personal problems. The stress at work wasn't helping.'

'What sort of thing?'

'I prefer not to talk about it.'

'I'm sorry to hear it,' said Ron, suddenly all smiles. 'Here, look who's decided to show up.'

Daisy turned in the direction of his pointing finger and saw Joel Heath in the middle of a press of people, moving through the auditorium. He wore a baseball cap, headphones and a green satin tracksuit which gleamed and rustled like balloon silk.

A large black-haired man in a suit approached Ron and whispered something into his ear. 'Daisy Adams,' said Ron, 'my associate, Terry Menswear.'

Terry Menswear, real name Nicodemus Mansour, was a Maronite Christian from Beirut who shared with his boss a taste for sharp tailoring.

'Boss,' said Terry, 'we've got a situation with Dodson.'

'Dodson?' asked Daisy. 'Isn't he Heath's opponent?'

Terry shot her a suspicious glance.

'I'll deal with it,' said Ron. 'Excuse me, Daisy.'

Aaron Dodson was waiting in his dressing room. He was a former Olympic silver medallist, but his professional career had stalled after a series of points defeats. He was said to have a suspect temperament. Even so, he had done enough in the amateur ranks to think well of himself, and it rankled with him that he was billed as the underdog against Heath. Then at the weigh-in there had been two further unpleasant revelations. The first was that the match had been made at a heavier weight than he had trained for. The second was that Heath was earning considerably more for the bout than he was.

With just over an hour to go, Dodson sat in his tiny dressing room, refusing to get changed until some of the discrepancy between his and Heath's purse had been rectified.

Ron found his way to the dressing room and opened the door to see Dodson sitting on the massage table in his Olympic tracksuit with his trainer, Billy Schwinn, standing anxiously beside him.

'Not getting changed, Aaron?' said Ron, running his hand over his pate. 'I'm getting reports from Terry Menswear that you're not happy.'

'That's putting it a bit strong, Ronnie,' said Billy Schwinn, keen to mollify Costello.

'Is it? This looks unprofessional to me, Billy.'

'Not happy,' said Aaron, with a hint of petulance. 'Wrong cut of the purse. Wrong weight. Wrong everything. I'm not going in for less than a third of what he's getting.'

'Money isn't everything,' said Ron.

While Aaron was fit and trim, Ron was enormous, a brutal silverback of a man. He stood over the sitting boxer, menacing him with his sheer bulk.

The trainer intervened. 'Aaron's point isn't well put, Ron, but he feels we've come here, you've told us . . .'

'What have *I* told you? I've told you nothing.'

'*Someone*'s told us the wrong weight, so he's giving away the best part of ten pounds, and now you're . . .'

'What am *I*?' asked Ron, bridling at the choice of pronoun.

The trainer groped hopelessly for something less controversial. 'I . . . someone . . . it's . . . He's being shorted on the purse, he feels.'

'But you had tickets, Billy. How many did he sell?'

'Come on, Ron, he's not a big ticket-selling fighter yet, and an FA Cup night and everything – who's going to come down here for Aaron when they can watch football on the telly for free?'

'Boxing fans, that's who. Now get changed,' said Ron. 'Don't make me ask you again.'

Dodson's pride, his Olympic silver, his past eighteen months on a treadmill of disappointments, spoke for him then. 'Fuck yourself,' he said in a weary voice.

'Wrap his hands, Billy,' said Ron icily, 'or I'll do it myself.'

The trainer moved nervously towards his fighter with the bandages, dropping one of them in his haste to obey; it unspooled across the floor like a party streamer. He turned apologetically to Ron, and froze, paralysed by his own ineptitude.

Ron stepped quickly across to the massage table and

trapped Dodson in a headlock, then splayed out the fingers of Dodson's left hand and broke the fingers at the knuckle with a snap that sounded like a pencil breaking. Dodson's fingers jutted out at an obscene angle and the boxer howled in agony while Ron Costello retreated a step to observe, not for the first time in his life, how like an animal's is the face of a man in pain.

Daisy waited at the bar while the auditorium filled up. This was her first visit to Valley Hall for the boxing. It wasn't actually Victorian (foundation stone laid in 1904 by Mayor Stanley Tett), but the building, which included public baths, a lending library and an indoor arena for sporting events, was totally Victorian in its befuddling association of books, baths and boxers: an ethos of self-improvement as quaint as Stanley Tett's chain of office, as pretentious as the Latin names in the different chambers of the steam rooms, as optimistic as . . . As what, really? What in Daisy's neurotic times could compare with the magnificent confidence of those Victorian aldermen?

Daisy had lost weight. Her face had a hollowness, an angularity from eating less and not sleeping which suited her and set off the intensity of her blue eyes. Though she looked more frail, something in her was stretched taut by the anticipation of meeting Heath. She had entered his world in disguise. She had deceived Ron Costello. She felt an inward exultation at those small victories. Now she would meet her husband's killer and sit in judgement on him. Her multiple deceptions had restored her sense of her own power.

But the truth was stranger still than the story she told herself. Her behaviour puzzled even her. Every encounter with Heath brought fresh pain. She knew this one was unlikely to come to good. What was the chance that Heath would express genuine remorse? What could he possibly tell her that might make sense of her loss? Did she want to see contrition in his eyes? Something to humanize him? Possibly. Find something in him to forgive, something that would stop that tiny wound from which she continued to bleed? 'Stabbed *at* him.' Did she want reconciliation? Truly, the answer was no. She had already made her choice. She had chosen hate. She hated him already. Always had done.

The truth was this: for a moment, a brief window that day outside the station, at a level of consciousness that didn't even seem to involve her participation, Daisy had been faced with a choice: to move on, or to move back. Faced with the imminence of change, she stuttered, stumbled and fell back into hating.

Daisy dreamed of a desert: an arid landscape of cliffs and dry valleys that gleamed coldly in the moonlight. Out of the cleft in a rock grew a single flower: a rose with thorns as big as bullets.

At the basest level, Daisy knew she was still alive because she woke up every day in pain.

Ron appeared at the bar and ordered a drink. He looked agitated and sweaty, and smelled of something metallic. 'Dodson pulled a muscle warming up,' he told Daisy.

'What does that mean?' asked Daisy. 'Is the fight off?' She felt a stab of disappointment. Would the interview be cancelled as well?

'We have to find a replacement.'

'Now? How do you do that?'

'Terry Menswear's on it.' When Ron hunched over his drink a big boulder of flesh formed on the back of his neck. Now he cadged a cigarette off the barman and smoked it greedily, looking round him for any sign of Janice. 'Don't want the missus to see,' he said.

Something was clearly preoccupying Ron. He bought himself another drink, and another fizzy water for Daisy, paying with a fifty-pound note from a bundle that splayed in his fist like a lady's fan. Terry suddenly loomed up behind him.

'And?' Ron enquired.

'You'd better come.'

'Problem?'

'He's got a fighter but Tate doesn't want to use him.'

'Tate?' Ron's tight frown relaxed into a smile. 'Tate?' He glanced across to Daisy, seeming to include her in the joke. 'We'll buy him a drink, then. We'll buy him two. Tate likes a drink.' He clapped Terry on the back. 'Let's go have a word with them.' He finished his drink and nodded at Daisy. 'You come too. This'll be good for your book. Sammy and Tate's boys are rather special.'

'How's that?' Daisy couldn't help noticing that Ron's mood had lifted. He had grown quite animated as they negotiated the abrupt turns of the long corridor that led to the arena's changing area.

'They're losers.'

'All of them?'

'Losers aren't that easy to find,' said Ron, nodding his head in greeting at a shadowy face in the corridor. 'Yeah, you can stick gloves on any bozo and push him into a boxing ring and he'll lose. But a specialist loser? An artisan? Someone with experience and ringcraft, who'll put up a good show, perhaps bring the prospect along a little, let him find out something about himself and, on top of that, not win? Not so easy to find.'

Costello paused at the door of the dressing room. 'Ready?'

Daisy nodded. She had expected more time to prepare herself. She followed him into the changing room. It was bright and noisy. Someone was playing rap music on a boom box. Boxers were in various states of preparation for their bouts, while the noise of the shower suggested that for one or two at least, the night's work was already over. Every eye in the room swivelled in Costello's direction. Behind him, Daisy felt invisible.

Costello hailed a tall, balding man who Daisy recognized from her previous visits to boxing. 'Good news,' said Costello.

'Terry told us,' said the man. 'What happened to Dodson?'

'Didn't warm up properly. Put his arm out. Now there's a

34

shot at the big time going begging for one of your lot.' There was a pause as the whole dressing room seemed to take in his words.

'Where's Heath?' said Daisy.

Costello turned back to her. 'You what?'

'Where's Heath?'

Costello's face broke into a big grin. 'Did you hear that, Sammy? "Where's Heath?"'

The man called Sammy looked at Daisy for the first time since she'd entered the room. 'You won't find him in here, love. This is the losers' dressing room.'

Daisy looked at the boxers behind him. There was no indignation in their faces. It was a statement of fact.

Sammy offered Daisy his hand.

Broad-backed, balding, pallid, always overdressed because he disdained central heating, Sammy exuded the distinctive but not unpleasant smell of knitwear and fried breakfasts. He had a singular nose, especially for an ex-fighter, which flattened slightly at the end as though pressed up against a windowpane. He had uneven teeth and a surprisingly delicate complexion – Sammy Kimball almost never drank – and he could have been forty-five or sixty. He went to bed late and got up early. 'Don't need it at my age,' he would say, leaving people to wonder whether a diminished appetite for sleep was a property of his relative age or youthfulness.

'Who's it going to be, Sammy?' said Ron.

'You've put us in a tight spot,' Sammy said. 'If we'd known earlier. Wesley's the right weight, but he's not come to fight, he's come to support the other lads.'

'What's it going to take to make him change his mind?' asked Ron.

Sammy hesitated, as though adding numbers in his head. 'It's not that simple. Tate's not happy about him fighting.'

Daisy saw Tate look up at the mention of his name. He was a slim, light-skinned black man sitting quietly on one of the wooden benches. He was fortyish. His big scarred knuckles

35

gave away his former trade, as did his striking left eye – its iris flashed silver as though it had been sealed over with a fish-scale.

Many times before, Daisy realized, she had seen Tate and Sammy lead their losers to and from defeats in the ring.

'Wesley's not ready,' said Tate. 'He's never fought ten rounds.'

'Well, get him ready,' said Ron, deliberately misunderstanding Tate's words.

Now some whispered consultations took place, first between Ron and Sammy, then between Sammy and Tate. Sammy grew more animated as he tried to make his points. Tate shook his head emphatically. 'He's not ready,' Daisy heard him say. There was an edge of frustration in his voice.

'When he's ready,' said Sammy, 'they won't want him for Heath.' His voice tailed away into a whisper as he talked pounds and purses, the wisdom of the cash in hand over the slow and unlikely path to championhood.

Daisy could see that Sammy, blustering, full of words, was the senior partner. Tate had no power to resist his arguments. And yet the aura of melancholy around Tate, and the way the young boxers glanced towards him as he sat shaking his head, gazing at his scarred hands, made it clear to her that he was talismanic in some way to them.

'I'm waiting,' said Ron.

'It's done,' said Sammy. He nodded at Wesley to get changed.

Daisy was at ringside as Sammy led Wesley into the ring, carrying a first-aid kit in a plastic box like a packed lunch, with a jar of cotton buds balanced on the top. Aficionados nudged one another. In his way, Sammy was as famous in this world as Ron Costello. Tate followed Wesley, ushering him gently forward as the public address system blasted out 'Eye of the Tiger'.

Then there was a delay. Heath had arranged a more complicated entrance involving dry ice and his own choice of music, but the dry ice wasn't working and he kept them all waiting while it was sorted out. The lights dimmed and he emerged into a spotlight, the hood of his robe raised, acknowledged the crowd and trotted to the ring.

At the opening bell, Wesley started fast, knowing that his best chance to win would come early.

In spite of his minimal preparation, Wesley looked loose and confident. There was no pressure on him and he took Heath by surprise, flicking out hurtful punches that made the other man back up. Wesley bossed him, bore down, cut down the ring, arrogant now, picking his punches, a matador.

Daisy felt a surge of energy in the crowd that matched her own excitement. This was the hardest match Heath had faced. His supporters called out advice – 'Come on, Joel, he's not your quality!' 'Double up the jab!' – and there was a rustling as impressed neutrals tried in vain to find Wesley's name in the programme.

At the end of the first three minutes, Wesley returned to his corner with a slight swagger and shared a smile with Tate. Tate removed the gumshield and dropped it in the bucket. Daisy watched as Tate towelled Wesley's face. There was something astonishingly tender both in his movements and in the look of concern as he examined the boy's face for damage.

Sammy pushed Tate aside. 'What are you playing at? There's nine more rounds of this. Slow down. Have a walk round. Save energy.'

'He's doing fine, Sammy. Let him fight his fight,' said Tate.

'A minute ago, you didn't want him fighting at all.'

Tate and Sammy bickered as the seconds ticked by. The argument disconcerted Wesley and all three of them were caught by surprise at the round bell. They had to heave Wesley back on to his feet as they pulled out the stool.

Coming into the next round, Heath was fired up, energized by the abuse of his trainer. Now Wesley had the worst of it, and at the end of the round, Daisy watched Sammy scolding

Tate as he swabbed the boxer's cut eye with coagulant.

'This is your fault, Tate,' he was saying. 'Giving him ideas.'

Tate was silent. Daisy seemed to see a lifetime of defeats etched on his face as he sponged Wesley's back and shoulders to cool him off.

At the closing bell, the referee raised Heath's hand, prompting wild celebrations among his entourage. Wesley rested wearily against the turnbuckle and then, after the obligatory embrace with Heath, followed Sammy's white shirt to the dressing room, where Sammy's other fighters, already showered and changed, were waiting to congratulate him.

'Well done, lads,' said Sammy. Four fights, four losses, no knock-outs – for him, at least, it had been a good night's work.

The auditorium began to empty within seconds of the referee's decision. Ron Costello had disappeared early in the evening's boxing, leaving Daisy to watch it alone. As the crowd spilled towards the exit, Daisy looked in vain for him, wondering if she had missed her opportunity.

She found him holding court outside, talking to three people simultaneously, one of them by mobile phone. 'I've got to love you and leave you,' he said. 'I've got the bloke from the telly here. He's not leaving until he tells me why none of my fighters have been getting on the box.' He snapped the phone shut. Before any of his other petitioners could get a word in, his glance fell on Daisy. 'Get what you needed?'

'No, I haven't done the interview yet.'

'You'd better get a move on. It was Heath, wasn't it?'

Daisy nodded.

'You'll have to be quick. I've paid his trainer. They won't hang about.' And with that, the narrow, sweeping beam of his charm and attention moved on, leaving Daisy in darkness.

She moved back inside against the press of people. Now the hall was empty. The ring was already coming down and cleaners moved along the rows of seats bagging rubbish and sweeping up.

A bulb had blown in the corridor and it seemed labyrinthine

in the half-light, snaking away round a distant corner. Daisy edged down it in the gloom and entered Heath's dressing room alone.

Six

Heath was lying face-down on a massage table while his trainer worked his shoulders until his tired muscles were warm and relaxed, like stringy handfuls of pizza dough. Then Heath sat up and submitted to a cursory medical check from the doctor he had kept waiting. Three members of Heath's entourage sat, bored, on a shabby sofa by the far wall.

'And your general health's good?' the doctor concluded.

'Yeah,' said Heath, not bothering to stifle a yawn. He watched the doctor leave, ignored his offered hand and returned his smile with a languid nod, noting his indoor complexion, paunch and cheap shoes, then began to study the shorts that had been laid out for him before the fight: all in iridescent colours, some velvet, some satin, one fringed with rawhide tassels like a cowboy's jacket. The tips of his bandaged hands fingered the different fabrics – an expert tailor, a connoisseur wiping dust off the label of a vintage wine – and he glanced back at the closing door of the dressing room. 'Loser,' he said quietly, shaking his head, but with the finality of a judge passing sentence.

Daisy introduced herself. 'First,' she said, 'let me congratulate you on your victory.' Her voice sounded calm, but her hand shook slightly as she placed the tape recorder between herself and Joel Heath.

Up close, he was shockingly young, barely shaving. His forehead was covered with stipples and scratches from Wesley's gloves. His pale face was still pink and gleaming. He was perspiring slightly. The skin on his torso was as white as ice, and marbled with faint blue veins. Daisy gazed at the perfect, unblemished flesh of his arms and chest. Heath flexed his pectorals self-consciously, alternating them so they seemed to wink at her. He was as healthy as he would ever be, Daisy thought. He was in the full flush of his manhood. There was so much life in him. It seemed unjust.

'Thanks,' he said, without smiling. He could have been hostile, or he could have been shy, it was hard to say. His grey eyes gave nothing away. They were cloudy. Heath was a man imprisoned by his limited intelligence, yet clever enough to feel frustrated by the things he would never master. He had learned to articulate that gap with violence and, now that he was making money, in defiant, profligate spending.

'Two more routine defences and then a shot at the British title – that's what Ron Costello told me – are you looking forward to it?'

Heath looked suspicious. He gave a fidgety, reflexive sniff. 'What's this for?'

'A book,' said Daisy. 'An anatomy of boxing.' At the word 'anatomy', an image rose into her mind of Stuart's cadaver.

'I let the gaffer and my sponsor worry about all that side of things. I just worry about what goes on in the ring. I just fight whoever they put in front of me.'

'You worry before a fight?'

Heath examined his nails. 'I don't worry about nothing.'

Daisy felt uncomfortable. Someone was standing much too close behind her. Along with Heath's trainer, three members of his entourage were watching her conduct the interview with blank, provocative stares.

'Do you have special rituals, are you – I don't know – superstitious? Is there anything particular you like to do before a fight?'

Right now, Daisy would have been happy to hear Heath utter an intelligible and inoffensive sentence, although possibly not the one she was about to hear.

'I like socks.'

'Socks?'

'A lot of fighters nowadays don't bother with the socks because of Tyson, but shoes don't fit right without them.'

The entourage was nodding gravely. One man said, 'Teach on, brother.'

Daisy's list of questions trembled imperceptibly in her hand. 'Heroes,' she said. 'Do you have any?'

'You mean in boxing?'

'In general.'

Heath thought for a second. 'Bruce Lee.'

'Interesting. Why's that?'

There was a flash of something in Heath's eyes: in his life of underachievement, every question was a potential trap. A slow child, but quick with his fists: *you don't look so clever now*. At home with violence, embarrassed by long words. Functionally illiterate. His writing: a hieroglyph on a credit card receipt, or a fan's programme. He searched in his brain for the answer. 'He could make his testicles disappear inside his body,' he said. 'Hardcore, man. All that Buddha shit.'

'Before you got into boxing, you had something of a chequered past.'

'I was young and a bit crazy. I had troubles. Same as everyone. Boxing helped me out of all that. You know, helped me better myself.' The answers were pat and insincere. 'You get me?'

'In your past, you hurt people. What would you say to them now? How would you make amends?'

A memory swam out of Heath's past. A big man looming over him. Punching the screwdriver into his chest. The man staggering back in surprise. The shaft of the screwdriver smeared with dark blood, like oil on a dipstick.

Heath kissed his teeth disparagingly. 'I would say I was hurting too. You don't know the realness of what people like me contend with. You get me? People like you – maybe not you directly, but people like you – want to keep people like me down. Know what I'm saying? When we're living in poverty

42

and that, having nothing, our man-dem suffering, that's okay.
It's only when the problem spills over, that's when there's a
problem. I'd tell 'em not to judge me. Only God can judge me.
And God's given me liberty and a talent. And when I learn
about what my brothers in Palestine are going through, my
brothers in Iraq, I just praise Allah for the gifts he's given me.
I just praise Allah.'

The murmurs of assent from Heath's entourage were louder
now. He nodded and looked round at them, acknowledging
their support.

So that's how you live with yourself, Daisy thought.
Jailhouse religion: a babble of half-digested phrases, and the
exonerating vocation of victimhood.

'It's easy to judge,' said Heath. 'Take you. I could look at
you and say, look at you, you're a godless infidel. You're a disgrace.'

'I'm a disgrace?'

'In some people's eyes.'

'In whose eyes?'

'I'm not saying I'm judging you. But for a woman to dress
like that, wearing make-up and that. It's immodest.' The word
'immodest' stuck grotesquely out of Heath's vocabulary: a
child's foot sloshing around in borrowed adult shoes.

'Who are you to judge *me*?' Daisy couldn't restrain the out-
rage in her voice.

Heath didn't have the strength of character to back down,
to admit he'd gone too far. He knew only escalation. 'I'm saying that to me you look like a whore, and if I was your husband . . .'

A choked cry broke out of Daisy's mouth. She seized the
only thing resembling a weapon she had – the tape recorder –
and swung it at him. The intensity of her reaction astonished
her, but she had telegraphed the blow, and Heath slipped it
easily. Someone grabbed her arm and bundled her out of the
room. There was a peal of laughter as the door slammed
behind her.

43

'Fucking nutcase!'
'Did you see her face?'

That laughter echoed for a long time in Daisy's head. She was choked with her impotent fury. Her eyes stung with hot, angry tears. She no longer wanted to hit Heath, she wanted to murder him slowly, with him conscious of every terrifying second. She wanted electricity to make his eyes start from their sockets and burst and bleed, and him to beg for death. If she could have paid money at that moment to have Heath killed, she felt she would have paid unhesitatingly, without any regret, without even a faint cheep from a troubled conscience. Prison? She would have welcomed it. She relished the thought of the trial, the grief on the face of Heath's mother as they passed around photos of his appalling injuries; as they had of Stuart, of Stuart's beautiful waxy body. Yes, Heath's mother should suffer too. Daisy would refuse to testify, withhold from her victims the satisfaction of understanding why. Prison was nothing. She was in prison now. Better to have real walls around her than dwell in this half-life. And hell? Eternal damnation. She didn't believe in it. But if there was one, Heath would be there too; and she would happily give up heaven to watch him burning.

Occupied with her fantasies of revenge, she was able to block out the sense of something worse: the full stop that stood behind them, the tiny wound that had sucked all meaning out of her existence.

It was raining as Daisy left Valley Hall. The wind freshened her hot, tear-stained cheeks. She held the programme over her head, the pages ruffled in the breeze, and raindrops plopped on to the black and white photos of Costello's boxers. She walked quickly. She wasn't scared: she didn't fear the consequences of anything any more, but the malignancy in her, the hatred she was carrying, made her jumpy.

On an impulse, she went into a pub and ordered a brandy to settle the shaking in her hands. The cool air of the streets was trapped in the folds of her coat and it dispersed, scenting the bar with the smell of rain and gardenias.

At the other side of the bar, drinking with unnerving single-mindedness, sat Tate, the one-eyed trainer who had been so reluctant to let his protégé face Heath. Tate was oblivious to the hubbub in the bar. He finished his drink in a gulp and ordered another, staring past the barman to the rows of inverted bottles and twinkling optics, mesmerized by the bright colours that glistened, by their specious promise of oblivion. The booze burned his mouth and gathered in the pit of his stomach like lava. Tate was grateful for the busy traffic at the bar that allowed him to keep buying his doubles from different bar staff. 'My second,' he said, as he ordered another, smiling broadly, tempted to laugh aloud at his own cunning.

'You deserve it, mate,' said the barman, as he took Tate's money.

'I do,' said Tate, slurring slightly, and unsteady on his stool. 'Have one yourself.' Tate was flying: he felt as free as a skipped stone, stuttering over the surface of a lake. He glanced over the bar and caught sight of Daisy, brooding over her drink. Through the drunken fog in his brain, Tate read the signs in her face of defeat, but coupled with the anger and frustration of someone who wasn't yet inured to loss. Daisy glanced at him, at first hostile, because she could feel his gaze, but then she recognized him by his damaged eye and the melancholy in his face. She softened a little and managed a half-smile.

Tate made his way over towards her and asked with a drunkard's awkward spontaneity: 'You look like you lost something.'

Daisy looked sideways at him without turning on her barstool. 'I broke my tape recorder,' she said.

'How did you do that?' Tate, disinhibited by his drinking, had taken the spare seat beside her.

'It's a long story,' she said. 'Uncooperative interviewee.'

Tate tried to express mock horror with his drunken face, stretching it into a grinning, skeletal 'Yikes!'

'What about you?' she asked. 'What have you lost?'

'Four fights and a St Christopher's,' he said. The saint's name taxed his drunken enunciation. He said it again with effort and straightened himself wearily on the stool.

'Where did you lose it?'

Tate gestured vaguely in the direction of Valley Hall. 'Over there. Present from my mum after the Olympics. Gutting.' He shook his head.

'You were in the Olympics?'

Tate nodded slowly, squinting his bad eye shut. 'Out first round. Lost to a Cuban.'

'Is that how you . . .?' She gestured at the eye with her little finger.

'What? The eye? No. That was *years* later.' The vehemence of his reaction almost took him off his stool. 'You having another? I'm having another.'

'I'm fine,' said Daisy, who had barely touched her drink.

'Barman!' Tate flagged a twenty-pound note at him. 'Hello, sir. A large whisky for me. A large whisky for this young lady.'

'Not for me,' said Daisy. 'I'm fine.'

Tate held his finger to his lips and whispered to her, 'I'll let you into a secret,' and then leaned over and fell off his chair. The crash silenced the bar. Tate didn't get up immediately, but lay there for a moment, looking around him, as if checking whether anyone had noticed.

Two of the barmen helped him to his feet. 'You've had enough, my friend. We're not serving you any more tonight.' Tate shook them off him as they tried to usher him to the door, mustering all the dignity he could. The floor lurched under his feet like the deck of a listing ship. The silence lingered for a few moments after he'd left, then the noise in the bar returned to normal.

Daisy felt suddenly exhausted by the effort of the evening. Her anger had subsided. Without it, she felt weak and empty. Her eyelids drooped. She got up and left; the rain and the cold air revitalized her as she walked back to her car. The click of her heels echoed in the darkness; she heard Heath's voice castigating her. *Immodest*. The hate surged up inside her again.

At the junction by Valley Hall, a police van had pulled on to the pavement. The officers were breaking up a dispute. Out of curiosity, Daisy slowed. There was something incongruous about the policemen there, so clean-cut and sober, all Sunday lunches and village cricket, in the chaos of a Saturday night.

Tate, by now twice as unsteady as when he had been kicked out of the pub, was being cautioned by one of the officers. Tate's face might have looked sullen, but it was really a drunken deadpan, a vacuum of expression. Three youths, also drunk, but more aggrieved and voluble than Tate, were giving their side of the encounter to another police officer.

'. . . started giving it all this.'

'. . . going on about his medal.'

Even the rain seemed to have ganged up on Tate, drenching his shoulders while the policemen seemed virtually dry in their shirtsleeves. 'Where have you been this evening, sir?' one of the officers asked.

Daisy stepped forward. 'Excuse me, officer. He was drinking with me.'

'And who might you be?'

Daisy opened her handbag with a click and took out her old press card. 'Couldn't we do this somewhere where it's not raining? I'm sure there must have been a misunderstanding.'

The policeman studied Daisy's face, looked at Tate, thought of the paperwork and the long evening ahead of them. 'Hop it. All of you.'

Daisy walked Tate away from the scene of the trouble as the youths protested to the policeman. Why did she get involved? Did she spot a fellow loser? Or just hate his antagonists? She certainly had the fearless potential that comes with having nothing to lose. But it wasn't any of those things. It was something else about Tate: that look of noble calamity, Job's look – the man the sky has fallen on, bloodied and staggering, but still holding on to a piece of the heavens.

Seven

The next morning, Tate woke up bewildered in a car he didn't recognize, pinned in by the seat-belt, and so hung over he was sure that his condensed breath on the fogged windows was pure alcohol. The seat had been canted back slightly, but not too much, in case he threw up and choked: a Daisy touch, like the bottle of water above the glove-box. A thumping pain in his head and a white light like a sunburst behind his good eye stood between him and the full recollection of the previous evening, but he knew it had been a night of defeats. He remembered boasting to the girl in the bar about fighting in the Olympics. His scalp crawled with shame at the recollection. How could he have? Sammy said that the cells in the human body replaced themselves every seven years. Tate shared nothing but a name with the promising young boxer who had gone to Moscow.

Someone knocked lightly on the window and Tate fumbled to open it, lowering it five inches with a sickly motion to reveal a white woman in her late fifties wearing a plaid housecoat.

'I wasn't sure whether you were a tea or a coffee person,' the woman said, with all the cheery enthusiasm she would have shown if Tate had been an expected guest, or a distant relation. She showed more, in fact, since she was doing her best to conceal her discomfort with the circumstances of their meeting: the fact that Tate was black, had one eye and was sleeping in her garage.

Tate had had plenty of lost weekends, but the weirdness of this transcended anything he had ever known. Perhaps he was still drunk, or dreaming, or he'd lost his mind, gone psychotic, or even died: there seemed a real possibility that he had reached the end and the afterlife resembled a detached house in Finchley.

'Daisy told me about your medical condition,' said the woman. 'Is it boxing related?'

'No one really knows,' said Tate, who had no idea what she was talking about.

'It's amazing how little they really know about how the human body works,' she said with a sigh.

Tate thought it was best to agree with her.

In her childhood bed, Daisy dreamed of her husband. She was walking down a beach at a freak low tide and so was able to round the base of a cliff to reach a cavern that was usually cut off by water. Stuart was waiting. He sat there calmly in the suit he had worn for their wedding and looked up with mild surprise when he heard her feet on the shingle. 'You've been here all along,' Daisy said. She was struck by the obviousness of her words. The sun was bright. The sea sparkled. Stuart looked beautiful. What could be truer or more simple than this? What misunderstanding had led her to think that he might actually be gone be for ever? She felt flooded with ordinary happiness: there was so much to tell him. It took so little to set everything right again. The relief she felt was extraordinary. And the look on Stuart's face suggested puzzlement that she had ever suffered a minute's anxiety. She felt herself again, at last. She thought: *this is so easy, this is how it's meant to be, life isn't supposed to be difficult.* 'Why don't you come out?' she asked. The sea had risen slightly and a rolled sheet of water unfurled over the floor of the cavern. 'What's the hurry?' said Stuart. Her feet were freezing now, the charm of the dream was dissolving, and she remembered with a pang of disappointment that it had been the last thing he had ever said to her.

Daisy's feet had slipped out of the bedclothes. She instinctively drew them in and rolled on to her side. She'd overslept.

Stuart was dead. Her life had jumped its rails. Nothing was easy. Nothing was the way it was supposed to be.

She was at her mother's house. She suddenly remembered why she'd come: Tate. He'd passed out in the car on the way to the minicab office. Daisy had decided to let him sleep it off in her mother's garage, but he'd been locked in there for – she looked at her watch – over eight hours. He must have thought he'd been taken hostage! She pulled on a dressing gown and rushed down the stairs. The orderliness of her mother's house mocked her panic: this was not a house for rushing, for grief, for the bursting out of violent emotions. Daisy reached the garage door and found it unlocked. She opened it and went into a cooler atmosphere of cement and petrol smells and gardening implements. She padded over the cold floor in her bare feet. The seat was empty. That wasn't good. She glanced around. Her father's old toolbox was gone from the workbench. Had Tate stolen it? Found himself trapped in the garage and used it to break out? She thought how foolish she'd been to bring him here. She rushed back into the carpeted warmth of the house. There were sounds coming from the kitchen. She yanked the door open with the awful premonition of what she would find.

On the table stood a box of Grape Nuts; behind the breakfast bar Daisy's mum Margery clutched a mug of instant coffee; on the kitchen floor, the open toolbox; under the sink, Tate with a wrench, replacing a washer.

'Here she is,' said Margery. 'I'm afraid I've put Tate to work.'

'Good,' said Daisy. 'Morning, Tate.'

Tate pulled his face away from the U-bend to respond with an anxious greeting. He looked relieved to see her.

'What can I get you to eat?' asked Daisy's mum. She looked radiant. It occurred to Daisy that she was too hard on her mother, that maybe she should count on her more, turn up at all hours with strange men, since it seemed to do her good. And for one repellent moment, it crossed Daisy's mind that her mother and Tate had been having sex. Daisy poured some tea and the thought evaporated into a haze of unpleasant sensations.

'I don't have time, mum. I have to be at work today.'

'On a Saturday?'

'Yes. I've just got time to run Tate home.'

'I still don't know why you didn't make up the spare bed. Poor Tate. Sleeping in the garage.'

Daisy's mother waved them off from the driveway. The silence in the car made Daisy blush. She resented feeling awkward.

'Look . . .' said Tate finally, beginning to formulate some kind of apology for events that he couldn't remember.

'You know what?' said Daisy. 'It might just be better if neither of us said anything.'

Daisy dropped him off at a set of traffic lights. As he got out, the lights changed and he barely had time to thank her before she was off, swallowed up by the line of cars. Tate watched her go, then he swung himself over the traffic barrier and headed home.

During her brief pregnancy, Daisy had visualized the foetus, pink and frail like coral or a rare sea animal, drawing energy through her placenta, and through Daisy connected to everything in the outside world. Daisy didn't consider herself particularly spiritual, but this feeling of connectedness seemed important enough for her to try to explain it to Stuart: the sense that she was plugged in to some cosmic engine, the irresistible energy that drove the tides and the seasons, and pushed the magnolia in their garden to put out its early flowers.

Now she had found another source of energy. Two or three times a week, Daisy stood her cassette recorder on the kitchen table and played the tape of her interview with Joel Heath. The act of hating him had taken on a ritual character. *First, let me congratulate you on your victory.*

It seemed to connect her to something equally true and

equally powerful: the profound ugliness of life. She collected and treasured examples of life's hideousness, delighted to find her instinct so often confirmed. *I praise Allah for the gifts he's given me.* She hated the rich, she hated celebrities, she hated the pot-bellied Muslim with his four wives in a people carrier, she hated the blonde bankers' wives in the organic supermarket, deluding themselves that they were saving the planet with wheatgrass juice and yoga. She hated the blighted, ignorant poor, and devoured crime reports for the ample proof they gave her that the world was ruined, like glimpses through a glass-bottomed boat of an inundated civilization: 'beaten to death'; 'left for dead'; 'preyed on pensioners'; 'terrorized the council estate'; 'police and residents were powerless'; 'identified by his fillings'; 'tortured with a crack pipe'. Yes, yes, she thought, that is life: pain, murder, casual, illiterate violence, ruthless cunning, self-seeking. The only rational response was to enrich yourself, lay in stocks of organic rations to your gated, moated homes, cocoon your offspring in tonnes of steel, arm yourself. These were the last days. And this feeling about the world reached its ultimate expression when she watched boxing. Life in its purest form: two half-naked men – what had Costello said? – 'knocking ten bells out of each other' for money.

Once she'd seen the world in this way, it coloured everything. She couldn't hunker down like Imogen and watch cheery sitcoms in a fortified flat. Plague raged outside the window. Everything else was a lie. Even if boxing was hideous, at least it was true. And it *was* hideous – hideous in nothing so much as the way its audience took it all for granted. Of course they did. Of course Stuart was dead. Of course his murderer was unpunished – was celebrated, in fact, for his talent for violence. Of course Ron Costello lived in a mansion in Weybridge with a swimming pool that was bigger than Daisy's flat. What kind of world did you think it was? Daisy's heart was perversely lifted by the sight of misery: feckless beggars her age who'd gone on strike against life, pupating in filthy sleeping bags on the tube;

dirt; graffiti; a vandal called Element who'd etched his mis-spelled name into every window in every carriage on the Central Line. They were obeying the laws of destruction.

Daisy had certain rules about the tape. She never rewound or interrupted it once it had begun to play. On each occasion, she only ever listened it to once. The tape began with her sur-prisingly measured congratulations to Heath on his win and ended with her squawk of impotent rage. *You look like a whore and if I was your husband* . . . Every time, she broke down and cried furious tears, and made a silent inward prayer to whatever god or gods were mismanaging her life that they might permit her some kind of revenge against Joel Heath.

Hate, like love, needs to commune with its object – in a dif-ferent way, of course, since hate is frailer, less real. They are not true opposites. Love can mature from a starry-eyed infat-uation to something more comprehensive, something that includes faults and failings. There's no equivalent, no magnan-imous hatred. Hate is narrow, it thrives by isolating and dehu-manizing its object. Some people find it hard to hate for long. That certainty, that final judgement which hate must rest on is too elusive. But Daisy had a gift for it. Daisy needed to hate that boy, and she had reasons – what must have seemed to her like good reasons. Although the best reason of all was one that she couldn't admit to herself: Heath was keeping her alive. Hating him had become her *raison d'être*. Over time, she had to refresh her memory of Stuart's face with photographs. But always that wound, that tiny injury, remained as vivid in her mind as it had on the day she had first seen it.

When they preserved the bodies of Lenin and Stalin, and the *bomzhi* – the homeless drunks whose corpses they raided for spare parts and on whom they practised procedures before inflicting them on their dead leaders – the Soviet embalmers would drain the fluids from the cadavers and inject the blood vessels and tissue with preservatives. Daisy was a similar case. She had channels for blood and love and lymph. They needed to be filled with something, so she filled them with hate: a hate

53

for Heath that came to encompass the world that had produced him, the world that seemed to value him more than the man he had killed.

Daisy devoured the limited available facts about Joel Heath's life – council estate upbringing, absent father, unmarried mother, no formal qualifications – which even his new religious enthusiasm failed to render less pathetic. And she continued to watch his fights, praying softly to herself: let him suffer as I have suffered.

Heath's ring entrances had grown steadily more elaborate. Nowadays, the arena would darken and a pulsing bank of coloured lights lit him as he danced to the ring and vaulted the top rope. He would land on his toes and wave his gloved hands at the crowd, his grey eyes sometimes passing over Daisy in the crowd without a glimmer of recognition.

In February, he fought a boxer from Brighton called Pete Winter who had an impressively muscular physique: big shoulders that tapered to a tiny waist. But as soon as the fight started, Daisy could see that his movements were raw and clumsy. He held his gloves at the side of his face, where they resembled earmuffs, punched infrequently and tried to evade Heath's hooks with awkward wiggles of his torso.

Daisy was close enough to ringside to see the sprays of sweat that flew off Winter's head when Heath connected with his punches. She could see Heath's tattoos: the hawk inked on the left side of his neck, the bulldog on his right shoulder, and a line of small blocks up the inside of his arm that might have spelled a woman's name: she wondered whose.

Heath had set his feet apart and was throwing powerful shots from a dropped guard that rose at difficult angles for Winter to parry. Nothing that Winter could do was troubling Heath. Winter seemed drained. He tried to hold. Daisy willed her strength and hatred into him. The adrenaline in her system made her hands tremble. She shouted Winter's name and urged him on. The canvas bounced as Heath drove Winter back against the ropes. Winter covered his head and Heath smashed a hook into his ribs. A round later, Winter's corner pulled him out, over the fighter's half-hearted protests.

Daisy left as Heath was being interviewed on the ring apron by a big-jawed television presenter. 'He shouldn't have been in there with me,' Heath was saying. 'Lucky for him, his corner done the right thing. You saw the gulf in class. I was always going to win it. It was written.'

She even followed him once, waiting outside the gym where he trained and tailing his car back to his house in Hackney, where he picked up his girlfriend and headed into the West End. He drove a low-slung blue sports car with bulging silver tyre rims. From behind, its width made his head seem tiny and insectlike.

Daisy lost them in traffic, but saw them again by chance on foot in Bond Street, encountering them so suddenly that she had to duck. The memory she took away was of Heath, his arms dangling carrier bags, pointing at another window display. His gesture and his sated, shopped-out face implied to Daisy that all Heath lacked in life was more and better kinds of what he already had. She was possessed by an urge to turn her car up on to the pavement and pin him against the storefront, crushing his pelvis under the bumper, or breaking his back: not to kill him, but to force on him an ineradicable defeat, the taste of something so bitter that not a thing he could buy on earth would remove it. But in a flash she was past them, and when she came round the block again, they had disappeared into another shop.

Eight

Daisy had dismissed the episode with Tate from her mind, but her act of kindness almost unseamed Tate. He was a sensitive man who had been trying to punch through life like a clenched fist, hardening himself to pain and disappointment, and nothing could have unmanned him more than her unexpected tenderness.

Tate tracked Daisy down at the library. He sent her flowers with a note and took to hanging around there when he wasn't at the gym, or the bus garage where he worked during the day. Daisy thanked him when she saw him the first time, then was coldly polite, and after that ignored him altogether. It wasn't because of snide remarks from Jorge, who had seen the flowers and was capable of putting two and two together. It was her and Heath. It was the feeling that she had no room in her life for friendship, much less love. Sometimes she sensed Tate's gaze resting on her bowed head from where he sat with a book on his lap in the biography section, his long, wiry legs folded into a pair of right angles; and she resented his presence, his sad, longing face like a whipped dog's, and thought it would have been better for both of them if she'd just walked past him that night in October.

Now and again, Tate checked out books: biographies mostly – one about Houdini, another about Alexander Selkirk – a book on Nostradamus, and, too obviously, a self-help book on manifesting your heart's desire that Daisy could barely bring herself to stamp.

Her mother had called several times after Daisy and Tate's

surprise visit. She was clearly intrigued and sniffed around the subject like a bloodhound, eager to nose up the scent of a hidden romance. Daisy stuck to her story: Tate was a colleague. He had a medical condition. She'd been helping out. All these claims were either unverifiable or vaguely true.

Tate sensed her contempt and it gave a desperate edge to his courtship. He was unworthy of her, he felt, his drunkenness in the bar one more stage in a long descent. He thought to himself: *she is my angel*, and wrote mawkish poems about her like an infatuated teenager which he never showed anyone.

Daisy regarded him as a nuisance, but he was hard to avoid.

Tate and Sammy and at least a couple of fighters from their retinue of losers were always present at the boxing shows she still attended. What Costello had said was true. Sammy and Tate's was a losers' gym. That was its purpose, its reputation and its selling point. It was a stable of professionals who turned up at short notice to make up the undercard and pad the records of the truly promising. Even in the ring, before the bell, as the fighters were given their instructions by the referee, Sammy and Tate's boxers were immediately identifiable. Not for them the satin robes and matching trunks, the long monikers, poetic by boxing's impoverished standards of euphony: the Salford Scimitar, the Wandsworth Wizard, the Balham Bomber. Sammy and Tate's fighters tended to have plain shorts, pudgy waists and blurring tattoos. The men they fought had stomachs with muscles like the bars on a xylophone, embroidered gowns and vociferous supporters packing out the venue. As Costello had hinted, in most fights the result was a foregone conclusion. It wasn't staged, like the pantomime contests of televised wrestling, but they were never equal matches. *Fodder, opponents* – within boxing these were the euphemisms for the men that Sammy trained. Managers built their fighters' records by choosing opponents strategically. They didn't risk a difficult match if they could help it – unless the purse was a big one. Which is not to say that there wasn't the occasional upset. Sammy's fighters' chances usually came early on, before the superior conditioning of the favourite began to tell. Sometimes the promoter's fighter was let down by a tendency to bleed which had gone unnoticed in his amateur career. But usually, reliably, Tate and Sammy's fighters lost. And that is why Sammy's number was stored in the mobile phone of every promoter in the country. 'It's a TV sport, isn't it?' Sammy was fond of saying. 'Winners in the red corner, losers in the blue corner. So if we can't get the winners, we might as well train the fucking losers.'

This much was clear to an intelligent outsider like Daisy. It seemed of a piece with the unfairness of life itself, which had first occurred to her all those years ago in Toulouse. Boxing had simply formalized the principles of modern life. But the economics of the sport were such that Sammy's fighters might receive two thousand pounds for a single night's work – more in some cases than the favourites they were matched against. A world obsessed with winning would pay handsomely for its losers.

Tate tried to ingratiate himself with Daisy by giving her free ringside seats to the boxing. She accepted them, and then invited her colleague Simon Black so Tate would understand that she was unavailable.

'Boxing?' Simon Black's pale blue eyes widened behind his rimless glasses.

Daisy picked him up at seven. He was wearing a pair of shapeless corduroy trousers and a blazer. Simon Black had the patrician ability to be inflexibly the same in whatever situation he found himself. Although there was something faintly ridiculous about him, he could be firm and schoolmasterly in a way that intimidated the library's young troublemakers.

Black lived in a mansion block off the Edgware Road. Daisy was curious to peer inside. She had often wondered what dysfunction, or tragedy like hers, or other life like Jorge's, made the library the limit of his ambition.

Black got into the car and brought with him the vague smell of wine and strong cheese. He had had an early supper, he said. For all the veneer of sophistication, his talk of good cheeses, fine wine picked up cheaply from a *cave* he knew in Bordeaux, Daisy guessed his secret was that he lived with his mother. There was something prissy, mummy's boy, about him, from the well-brushed hair to the polished shoes. He grabbed the *A to Z* from the glove box. 'Do you want me to map-read?'

'It's okay,' said Daisy. 'I've done this trip before.'

'I must say,' Black said, 'I'm very surprised.'

'I thought you would have learned not to judge a book by its cover by now,' she said drily.

Black giggled. He slid the book back into the glove compartment and started to retune her radio. In that casual presumption, Daisy thought, was all the difference between him and Tate. There was a sense of entitlement about Simon Black. He reminded her of herself when Stuart was still alive. It seemed to her that Black had an invisible reservoir of love, like a tank of oxygen, that freed him to be prissy if he wanted to, confront troublemakers, smell of camembert. For all his wiry strength, Tate had seemed helpless. She wondered at her audacity in hoping to bring life into the world: a world where if the child was lucky it might find someone who cared for it, and if not, it would struggle like Tate to breathe. But then, the world Daisy had planned to give birth in had been a different world entirely.

Simon Black professed himself very taken with the Hogarthian spectacle of Valley Hall: the muscular male fans from Essex with shaven heads like Regency prize-fighters, their blonde girlfriends with unearthly winter tans, the quaintness of the auditorium itself.

He insisted on buying them both programmes. 'My treat. That T-shirt's rather fun. You know, a lot of common English expressions derive from prize-fighting: double-cross, up to scratch, toe the line.'

Black was like an anthropologist among an uncontacted tribe, filling his notebooks with observations for his research, and anecdotes to entertain the senior common room.

'How on earth did you get interested in this?' he asked her.

Daisy was saved from the inevitable falsehood by the entrance of the first opponent on the undercard. Black's curiosity switched to revulsion as the first punches landed. From where they were sitting, so close to the ropes, the spectacle was ferocious. Everything seemed magnified. The punches sounded louder. They could hear a boxer groan from a sharp blow to the body, see him wince between rounds as his bleeding nostril was stanched with a cotton bud.

'It takes a bit of getting used to,' Daisy said. 'In a minute, you won't notice it.' Black gave a sickly smile. When a spray of blood from a cut eye spattered the ringside seats, Black paled and said, 'I don't think I can take much more of this.'

'Really? Are you sure?'

'I'm just finding it deeply unpleasant. You stay. Sorry, Daisy. I didn't really know what I was letting myself in for.' He looked queasy as he stood up to leave. 'It's just so literal.'

Literal. Daisy felt a dozen mystified glances settle on this strange figure with his dusty vocabulary. He could hardly have been more out of place if he'd worn a periwig and buckled shoes. Had she felt like that once? His squeamishness struck her as quaint and faintly embarrassing. She tried to see the violence as he must have, but she found it hard to recall a time when she had not felt a clinical detachment from it.

He left for the tube station. Any misgivings she might have had about not leaving with him disappeared as soon as Heath's name was announced. She was lost in the bout, her fists clenched as she prayed for Heath's evisceration, but the fight ended in a one-sided points defeat for his opponent.

About a month later, there was a commotion at the library. A woman gasped. Daisy looked up. Tate reeled through the doors, blundered into someone and toppled a carousel of paperbacks, which crashed down, tangling Tate's feet and pulling him to the floor. The library was full of a sudden prickling silence. Daisy's first thought was *he's drunk again*, and she felt a mixture of anger and shame on his behalf. Then someone helped Tate to his feet. He wasn't staggering, but there was a sense of panic about him; something tremulous, like a wounded animal.

'I'm all right,' he said. 'I just need some water for my eye.'

Daisy found a jug in the back room. Tate sat on a chair and laid the nape of his neck on the cold enamel of the sink. His good eye was red and inflamed; Daisy poured a slow trickle of water into it. He blinked and winced as the obstruction was flushed away.

'What happened?' she asked.

'Detached retina.'

'I meant just now.'

'Something got in it. It felt massive. Probably only a speck.' Water clung in beads to Tate's hair. His eyelid flickered reflexively, but his sight was returning.

Daisy poured the rest of the water away. 'What's the vision like out of the bad one?'

'Fuzzy. I see shapes when it's bright. Otherwise nothing.' He towelled off his face. 'Thank you.'

She remembered why she hadn't been afraid of him that night outside Valley Hall, a drunken stranger. Something about Tate had touched her: his innate gentleness. And the next time he offered to buy her a coffee, she accepted.

'Didn't see you at the fight last week,' he said.

'I had other plans,' said Daisy.

'It was a good one.' Tate told her about the bouts she had missed, and chatted about the gym, talking about his boxers with real pride, the up and coming fighters, and the nearly-men whose great chances had slipped through their fingers.

It was surprising, and a bit touching, to hear him talk about his hopes for the fighters he trained. He told her about Saadi, a talented cruiserweight who, after three professional fights, had joined the Hare Krishnas; Alonso, now serving ten years in Wandsworth Prison for armed robbery, who wrote sporadic and badly spelled letters to reassure Tate that he was training hard and looking forward to continuing his career on the outside. And Wesley. Even now, Tate couldn't mention Wesley's name without a look of pain. Wesley had been one of Tate's cherished hopes. Tate had seen the ghost of a gift in the boy which he had wanted to nurture. It was clear to Daisy that the loss to Heath still rankled.

It was hard to dislike Tate, Daisy thought. There was a sweet and disarming melancholy about him; when he talked of the boxers he trained he spoke kindly and with an enthusiasm that occasionally bordered on desperation. And yet – wasn't it delusional for a man who worked at a gym that was known throughout British boxing as Losers Inc. to talk about his hopes for a champion? What need did it answer in Tate to pretend that his boxers were of the same calibre as the men they fought?

Daisy suspected that if Sammy Kimball was the boxers' eccentric uncle, Tate was their elder brother: patient, quiet, interested. What she didn't know was that while Sammy's confidence and bluster and promises of steady money attracted fighters initially, over time they came to appreciate Tate's seriousness; and a few of the more perceptive ones saw in flashes of Tate's movement, his handspeed when he coached them in the ring, the remnants of his unfulfilled gift.

'Is it true you went to the Olympics, Tate?'

'What was your ring name, Tate?'

'I didn't have one.'

'Yes, you did. You must've.'

Tate would close his eyes and lean his head back under the shower-head, let the water wash in runnels down his weary face. 'Smoke. It was Smoke.'

'Smoke? Was it because you loved them biftas? Them doobies?' The boxers giggled, naked except for flip-flops and towels.

'No, melonhead. It was because he was hard to hit, innit?'

But Tate would be drawn no further, and would finish his shower and towel off his lean body without satisfying their curiosity, which only enhanced his prestige in their eyes and added to the sense of mystery about him.

When he led the other boxers in their strengthening exercises, Tate would perform the routines with them, holding the chain of his St Christopher's medal in his mouth as he counted the repetitions aloud to ten, or fifty, or one hundred, and then, at the end, silently add another for himself alone. It could have been a form of penance, or a way of staying ahead of his protégés for ever, always pushing himself harder, doing more; or, if he hadn't been so old and so obviously unable to return to the ring, you might almost have suspected that Tate harboured a desire to fight again as a professional.

Tate's strange concern for his journeymen fighters made Daisy warm towards him. She thought of his tender way with Wesley, like a mother with a child, whispering him words of love and encouragement.

'There's nothing like beating a Ron Costello fighter,' Tate was saying. 'Costello keeps them away from credible opponents as long as possible. He's protecting his investment. The only way to beat them is to find an unknown quantity. I've seen the kid who can beat Joel Heath. Trouble is, Sammy won't look at him.'

Daisy's interest quickened at the mention of Heath. 'Why's that?'

Tate looked at Daisy, her eyes fastened on him with a curious intensity. And that's when he told her about Isaac Plum.

Nine

Isaac Plum was nineteen years old, Tate said, and he lived on a caravan site in Hillingdon with his wife Una and his baby daughter Esme. Every morning he got up at five to run for an hour around the reservoir. Tate had watched him from his car, running with the hood of his tracksuit top over his head in winter, in faded vest and shorts when the weather was warm, in a peaked cap when slanting rain pounded the reservoir and set the water vibrating with its splashes.

By six Isaac would be back at the caravan, by six-thirty off to work filling vending machines on the London Underground. He mingled anonymously with the morning commuters, darting off or on to a tube train at the unlikelier stops – Arnos Grove, Southfields, Upney – carrying a big blue holdall, weighed down with vending packs of chocolate.

Isaac Plum was a genius – whatever the word means. The way a horse's flank ripples to shift a biting fly, or a cat's ear pivots on its scalp when a door shuts somewhere: Isaac had the same unconscious physicality, an instinctive economy of movement that was purely functional but ended up seeming beautiful, and a perception of space that was a cousin of perfect pitch. Tate could see it as he watched the boy run, or shadow-box in the clearing beside the embankment, noting his quick, precise movements, the neatness of his footwork and the torque of his strong waist. And he had tried to interest Sammy in the boy as a prospect. Tate had even written a letter to Isaac, suggesting that he visit their gym.

*

On Friday evenings after training, Sammy would unfurl the projection screen that crossed one of the rafters of his gym and watch old fights. There was a standing invitation for Sammy's fighters to join him at these screenings, but few ever took him up on it.

One evening, Sammy was to be found sitting alone in darkness, watching a grainy video of a dull domestic fight, and was preparing to fast forward to a more satisfying encounter when he heard a knock from below on the door of his office. Sammy peered down into the semi-darkness and saw a slight figure standing with a holdall slung over his shoulder and his fist poised for another knock.

Sammy's big frame obscured the light from the projector and cast a giant shadow on to the gym below him. The boy turned, and Sammy motioned for him to come up.

Isaac climbed the stairs to the gallery; he looked younger than his nineteen years, with his smooth olive skin and cropped black hair. He approached Sammy confidently, one hand outstretched in greeting and one rummaging about in his holdall. Before he had even reached Sammy to shake hands with him, he had pulled out a trophy which he stood on the table by the projector: and then another, and another, wordlessly, until the counter was covered with golden cups of all sizes.

Sammy picked up one of the trophies and read the boy's name out loud. 'Isaac Plum. What happened?' he asked. 'Did you burgle a youth club?'

There was not even an ingratiating chuckle from the boy, who looked at him uncomprehendingly. 'Did you . . .' Sammy began to repeat the joke, before he realized that this obstacle was too great for him to surmount. 'Fucking Tate!'

'He's deaf,' said Tate.

'Deaf?' said Daisy.

'Yeah, deaf and dumb. Sammy reckons he'd never get licensed.'

Daisy had the vivid sensation of a prayer answered.

When Isaac had got back from Sammy's gym, he had been uncharacteristically morose. He cleared away his amateur trophies from every surface – the holdall had only contained a fraction of the ones he possessed – and he packed them away in several cardboard boxes which he stashed in the spare bedroom. Una half-heartedly tried to dissuade him, but was secretly glad to have the space. Only Esme seemed to miss them; she had got used to the way they sparkled when the sun hit them and was fond of snatching at the shafts of light they cast around the caravan.

January came: no snow, but the reservoir began to freeze and Isaac ran with gloves on and a wool hat pulled down over his ears.

Isaac had done well as an amateur, but he had not achieved quite the success that he deserved. Judges felt he was too languid. He wasn't an explosive puncher, and the way he carried his hands low smacked of showboating, as did the unorthodox angles of his punches: the judges couldn't or wouldn't see that he had an innate grace that dared clumsiness.

Paradoxically, Isaac's style was built on *listening*. He once explained to someone that he couldn't *hear* properly with his hands up by his chin in the textbook peek-a-boo guard. He meant that the guard cut down his peripheral vision, blocked the streams of information about his opponent's gait, stance, posture and rhythm that fed his sixth sense, gave him such uncanny powers of anticipation and made him virtually impossible to hit.

And yet, Isaac often lost on points to busier opponents, and it became common knowledge that a workmanlike fighter could edge a decision over him by coming forward all the time and looking more aggressive. There were fights in which Isaac slipped or blocked everything his opponent threw, only to see the referee raise the other fellow's hand at the final bell. He found the results of the contests puzzling, but then amateur boxing is a sometimes puzzling affair. It does tend to reward heart and effort over flair and languid genius.

Isaac had tried to ignore his gift. It felt like a burden at times. He was paradoxically invisible and invincible. He had no great love of boxing as a sport, and his urge to turn professional was prompted by a desire to make money more than anything.

But Isaac was committed to boxing in other ways. He did his running every day whether he was in training or not. He loved it, had the natural athlete's joy in his own body, and he expressed his joy in movement.

Sometimes, at the end of a run, when he had stretched and shadow-boxed in the fresh air, he stood on the bank of the reservoir with a stick and poked at the sheets of forming ice. He could feel the vibrations through the stick as the frozen panes bumped and clunked, but the sounds themselves were as bafflingly elusive to him as the words that Esme had begun to say.

Esme had perfect hearing. Strictly speaking, she took after her mother, who had been deafened after a childhood illness, but Isaac liked to think that Esme being born hearing to deaf parents was a Plummish trait: like the ambition in him not to be contained for ever by the life he had found himself in, to want more than his environment could readily furnish. And while this gave him great hope for his daughter, at times he was filled with despair and self-pity for his unacknowledged power, and no amount of soothing from his wife and daughter could restore him.

Successive disappointments had worn away at him. He was over-sensitive, as genius is apt to be. Una saw his discontent and tried to offer reassurance. *You have us*, she consoled him. But in reminding him of the contents of their little world, she also reminded him of its limits. He felt closed in. His consciousness of his gift nagged at him. There was the anxiety that its vintage would turn to vinegar. And Isaac's talent, so far above the ordinary, threatened to turn corrosive to the same superlative degree.

And then, one morning in March, one week before Isaac

was due to start work as a courier of cigarettes instead of chocolate, he was halted by a woman in her thirties who, to his enormous surprise, began to address him in the hesitant but unmistakable signs of his own language.

Are you Isaac, the boxer? she signed to him.

Isaac put his bag on the ground and gave an astonished nod.

Ten

In spite of the novelty of being addressed in his own language, Isaac was unenthusiastic about Daisy's invitation to return to the gym. He conveyed his disappointment about his previous encounter with Sammy. All the same, Daisy managed to persuade him to meet her and Tate at the deaf club in Shepherd's Bush in a week's time. To her, the boy's deafness was a sign. The neatness of the bargain carried the imprint of divine approval. Some deity of private vengeance had heard her prayer. She would be his words and he her fists.

As they drove along the Uxbridge Road, Tate told her how dismissive Sammy had been of the boy. Sammy hadn't bothered to watch Isaac box, he explained, because he felt it would be impossible to get him licensed. He didn't tell Daisy about the older man's contemptuous replies as Tate had quizzed him over breakfast one day about his reasons for rejecting the boy.

'What?' Tate had asked. 'Too small?'

'No,' said Sammy.

'Too unorthodox?'

'It didn't get that far.' Sammy poked disgustedly at his egg and then called the owner over from the till to show him the runny albumen. The owner whisked the dish from the table with a murmured apology and Sammy called after him, 'You want to watch it, Sandro, they'll take away your Michelin star.'

'Then what?'

'Principally – i.e. the main thing? Too deaf.'

'That's prejudice,' said Tate.

'You what? Prejudice? Oh, sue me, I've violated someone's human rights.'

'He boxed as an amateur. Terrific record.'

'Then why isn't anyone else interested?'

'I dunno. Probably because he's deaf.'

'Of course because he's deaf! How's anyone going to get him a licence?' Sammy shook his head disparagingly. 'Tate – you and your brainwaves.' Sammy's breakfast reappeared from the kitchen and was set down in front of him. 'Here, Sandro: deaf and dumb bloke goes into a library, sees a sign that says "Quiet Please", so he puts a pair of gloves on. Someone sent Stevie Wonder a cheese grater – he says it's the most violent book he ever read.'

Tate brooded in silence. He knew what he had seen in the boy was real. There was something strange and effortful in Tate's stillness: all that thwarted energy. And beside him, Sammy cracked jokes and showed off as if oblivious of Tate's discomfort.

'There's this pool in Roundwood Park, it heals people, right. A blind person goes in – he can see! Bloke with a withered arm goes in – his arm works! Bloke with a wheelchair goes in – two new tyres!'

Sammy noticed Tate's silence and jogged his arm with a big plastic tomato full of ketchup. 'Antioxidants,' he said, as he offered Tate the red orb. 'Mop up free radicals.' For a moment, Tate's good eye flashed at Sammy, but if Sammy noticed Tate's mutinous reaction, he gave no indication of it.

Daisy had been to deaf clubs before, but Tate was surprised to find that the long, shabby room was far from silent. There was shouting, laughter, a group of men by the bar noisily enjoying a football match.

Tate and Daisy sat down at a formica table with Isaac and Una, who was holding Esme. They chatted for a while. Daisy offered to take the baby and Una handed her over. To Daisy, Una looked like a child herself, tiny and pale, with stringy fair hair and a big forehead. It was hard to conceive that a creature so frail could have a dependent.

Una had the relic of a voice and could speak, slowly and faintly, in words that reminded Daisy of a worn inscription or the faded marks of an erased pencil. 'Isaac's already been to see Sammy,' she said. 'He didn't want to know.'

Isaac sat forward on his chair, elbows on his knees, brown eyes flicking thoughtfully from Tate to Daisy to Una, and only a trace of a smile breaking his still countenance when he caught the eye of his daughter, wriggling in Daisy's lap, as dense and precious as a cargo of gold.

Daisy explained that she and Tate were asking Isaac, in confidence, to give them another chance. *We'd like to find out what he's capable of*, she signed.

Isaac shook his head impatiently and signed for a long time. Tate shot Daisy an anxious glance.

'There's been so many disappointments,' said Una. 'He just can't be bothered with it. He's waiting to hear about a job at the airport. If he gets that, it'll be shiftwork. There'll be no time to train.'

Daisy understood his reluctance. They were offering him nothing really: a chance to risk his youth and health.

Over at the bar, there was a handful of muted shouts as someone scored a goal. Hands fluttered and shoes and chairs squeaked on the lino. The men turned excitedly to one another, spelling the scorer's name over and over again with their hands.

Tate cleared his throat. His voice was almost as soft and tentative as Una's. But Daisy was also struck by the change that had come over him and the surprising intensity in his sad face.

'I saw you box in an amateur contest in Repton two years ago. The judges gave it to the other kid. The way you fight was never going to impress them amateur judges. Hands too low. Not busy enough. Too flash. Too loose. But you're the best I've seen in a long while. Really. And I've seen a lot of fighters.'

Daisy translated, quietly impressed by the strength of Tate's conviction. He wasn't hustling the boy, as she imagined Sammy might, nor was he cocky and aggressive as Costello would have been, but his words left no doubt about his belief in the boy.

'I've wanted to talk to you for a while,' said Tate. 'You fight the way I used to fight, but you're better than I was.'

You're a fighter? Isaac signed.

'Was,' said Tate, after Daisy had translated the question.

What weight?

'Same as you – welterweight.'

Isaac looked at Tate with new interest, and then shook his head. His expression changed, as if he couldn't allow himself the risk of another disappointment. *I don't care about boxing*, he signed. He put his right index finger on the side of his windpipe and twisted it as though he were coring an apple.

Tate looked at Daisy for a translation.

'He says it's cruel,' said Daisy.

'Tell Isaac he's right: boxing is a cruel game. And it's full of crooks and shysters.'

Daisy struggled with the vocabulary. 'Crooks and shysters' she could only translate as 'bad people'.

Isaac interrupted by waving his hand at Daisy. When Esme was born, he signed, *I thought it would be good to make some more money. I know I was good as an amateur. So I went round to different promoters. No one was interested. Now I feel like: why should I bother?*

'No one can answer that question for you,' said Tate. 'I've been on this road for ages, it seems like, and sometimes I think I never would have started if I'd known what was waiting for me. I've seen very nearly the worst of it. Fixed fights, crooked promoters. Bad injuries. You're how old? Nineteen? I think of me at nineteen. Thinking I was ready for the world and knowing nothing, and I get scared for myself, for what I was then, and all the dangers I didn't know about it. I can't look you in the eye and promise you it's going to turn out all right. No one can. But there are moments, you must have had them, after a fight, or during a fight, or a run, when you feel like: *this* is what I was put here to do.' Tate's eye searched Isaac's face for a glimmer of comprehension. 'I can't explain it better than that. Now what I think is that that feeling isn't separate from the other nonsense. All that other stuff was the price of it. Was it worth it?' Tate paused for a long time, scrutinizing some inward balance sheet. 'I don't regret it. You have to do what's written on your heart. And if it's written on your heart to be a baggage handler at Heathrow Airport, so be it. But if you're as good as I think you are, maybe it's written on your heart to be a fighter.'

Isaac sighed and glanced away. At the far end of the room, the older deaf men were back in their seats, drinking beer and watching football. A row had broken out over whose turn it was to buy drinks and someone was gesticulating angrily. Elsewhere, toddlers played at the feet of their parents, who were mingling and sharing news under the strip lighting. Isaac was motionless for a while, then he looked at Tate and nodded.

'When can you come to the gym?' asked Tate.

Isaac and Una exchanged glances. 'Th–,' said Isaac in a voice that was as soft and breathy as a low moan. 'Th–'

'Thursday?'

Isaac Plum nodded solemnly.

Eleven

Sammy's gym was in a listed building that had once served as a village hall to the Victorian workers' cottages which lined the spurs of road beside the canal. He leased the upper storeys from the owners, who sold second-hand office furniture on the ground floor. It was striking – of red brick, with high, narrow windows and an anomalous turret that made it resemble a chapel – but still stood well outside the tidemark of gentrification that would have made it attractive to property developers. The gym was on the first floor. The stone stairs continued up to a further mezzanine level that projected over the gym and which housed a rudimentary kitchen. The gym itself was dominated by a single ring, raised off the floor, and fifteen or so heavy bags that hung from the rafters below the mezzanine. At the farther end were doors to Sammy's cramped office and a passageway leading to the showers and a dank weights room in the basement. Sammy had lined the windows with black felt to block out the light for his film screenings; it had the added effect of preventing air flowing into the room, so that on warm days the atmosphere could be stifling.

One morning in early April, Isaac turned up before work to meet Tate and Daisy there. It was raining heavily: bolts of water hissed into the canal.

Wesley arrived soaked soon afterwards: he'd come, as a favour to Tate, to spar with Isaac. There was a new briskness about Tate. After a warm-up, he instructed the fighters to begin sparring. They agreed that Tate would step between them at the end of each round.

Daisy laced Isaac's headguard and gloves. The boy seemed solemn and composed. He straightened his headguard and touched gloves with Wesley as Tate signalled to them to start boxing.

Tate had given Wesley precise instructions. 'Feel him out. See what he's got. Don't open up on him until I tell you.'

Wesley was playing the bum's part, staying back, trying to draw Isaac in, trying to muddle and confuse him. It was what Sammy's fighters were famous for: canny ringcraft, conserving energy, cleverly absorbing and smothering punches, minimizing risks. He shuffled from foot to foot, pulled out of range of Isaac's jab, and then advanced behind a cross-armed defence, leaving limited openings.

To Daisy, Isaac looked disappointingly boyish, his arms dangled loose and low. She wanted him to be brutal and dangerous. She needed to believe he was capable of hurting Heath. Isaac coasted around the ring so lightly that the canvas barely bounced. Then suddenly – flash, flash, flash – Wesley was hit by a series of punches that landed on him with bewildering speed, and as he tried to counter he had the alarming sensation that his opponent had become insubstantial, had slipped through his gloved fingers like a handful of frog-spawn.

'He's making you miss, Wes. Cut the ring down. Back him up with the jab.'

Wesley tried to do as he was instructed, but Isaac was too quick. He disdained Wesley's jab, slipping it easily and turning him on the ropes.

Even Daisy could see that Isaac had phenomenal powers of anticipation, and a range of movement that made Wesley appear leaden.

There was no relief for Wesley in the following rounds. Tate told him to switch stance and box southpaw – leading with his right hand. Unfazed, Isaac did the same, boxing more comfortably from the changed stance; then he switched back and threw a series of left hooks over the top of Wesley's southpaw jab.

Wesley's nose was bleeding. He wiped it with a corner of his T-shirt, staining it red. He was dismissive about the injury. 'It's nothing,' he said. 'There's more blood when I floss my teeth.' Both men were breathing heavily, but Isaac was unmarked. He gave Wesley a one-armed hug, and bowed his head so Daisy could remove the headguard.

Tate pressed twenty pounds into Wesley's hand. 'This is between us,' he said. 'Not a word to Sammy.'

The session confirmed Tate's high opinion of the boy. He was so taken with Isaac that it never occurred to him to query Daisy's interest in him. But Tate's constitution wasn't equipped to digest good fortune. Positive news made him anxious: something in him tripped the gloom switch and he was flooded with a more familiar hopelessness. 'The boxing's not the problem,' he said. 'As usual, it's the politics.'

'Meaning?'

'Getting him a medical certificate. Getting him licensed.'

'Maybe Sammy has some ideas?'

Tate looked at her. 'I'd rather Sammy wasn't involved. Sammy's not right for the boy. Sammy and me want different things.'

Daisy thought she understood. It was the first confirmation of an inkling she had had the first time she had seen the two men in the dressing room together: that it was not an equal partnership, but a kind of tyranny from which Tate was trying to escape.

Tate brooded. 'It's the medical certificate that we need first.'

'There must be a way,' Daisy said. Whatever Tate's urgency about the boy, it paled to nothing beside hers.

'There's a man,' said Tate. 'Costello uses him. I don't know his name, but I can find it. I can't go. It'll get back to Sammy.'

'I'll go,' said Daisy. 'But it means we're partners in this.'

Tate nodded. 'I'll get you the name,' he said.

The man's name was Dr Vanes. He had consulting rooms on

Harley Street. A good address and the appearance of upright-
ness were all he had left to sell.

The receptionist, a fair-haired woman roughly Daisy's age,
handed her a cheaply printed registration card and a plastic
pen and asked her how she would be paying. There was a
£250 consultation fee, she said. No exceptions.

The waiting room was sparsely furnished, like a stage set
that could be struck or abandoned in a moment. Daisy was the
only patient. She pulled a magazine from the pile on the central coffee table. It was five years old – a time capsule from
another era, preoccupied with new discoveries, new fashions,
new diets that had passed away and were already forgotten,
memorialized only in its glossy pages.

Daisy leafed through the magazine, remembering the life
she'd had five years before. And the outmoded fashions, which
now looked so silly and garish, reminded her of the worn-out
optimism of her lost youth and its spirit of innocence – so foolish and naïve, happiness on a precipice, in the aftermath of
Stuart's murder.

'The doctor will see you now,' said the receptionist. She
showed Daisy into the consulting room. From the meaningful
but wordless looks which passed between the woman and the
doctor, Daisy guessed they were husband and wife.

Dr Vanes was in his late forties. He had a rangy, upper-class
physique and a clipped patrician accent to go with it. His hair
had retreated monkishly to the sides of his head. He paused
between sentences as he spoke and creased his face into a
humourless smile. But what struck Daisy most were his hairy
ears and his bulbous, oddly penile nose.

'Have you paid?' was the doctor's first question, punctuated
by that humourless, interrogative grin.

'Yes,' said Daisy.

'Excellent.'

The consulting room had been dressed by the same perfunctory props department which had taken so little care with the
waiting room. It too was bare and brown, furnished with two

77

chairs, a mahogany desk and a vinyl couch for examinations.

'How can I be of help?'

Daisy began to explain: there was a boxer called Isaac Plum –

'Let me just stop you there.' That grin again, this time accompanied by the repeated clicking of his ballpoint pen. 'How did you hear of me?'

'Ron Costello said you might be able to help.'

'You're a friend of Mr Costello's?'

Daisy nodded.

'Has this boxer Plum to your knowledge ever failed a medical?'

'No.'

'A brain scan? An eye exam?'

'I've no idea.'

Vanes made some indecipherable marks on the pad in front of him. 'But he's deaf, you say?' He appeared to think for a moment. 'For some reason which I've never fathomed, boxing's a very emotive issue.' Pause. Grin. 'I played rugby at Guy's. I was never hurt, thank heavens, but I saw some terrible injuries to the back and neck, severe concussions – mainly the chaps in the pack. Now, I can't recall anyone asking for a ban on rugby. Personally, I don't think the government should overly concern itself with how law-abiding people earn their living.' Vanes leant down and opened a large drawer at the base of his desk. He pulled a selection of brain scans from a file folder.

'I'm confident,' he went on, 'that the boy you describe is medically fit for boxing. He needs one of these.' Vanes took a scan and slipped it into a manila envelope. 'A medical opinion that he's fit to box – which I'm happy to provide. And an HIV test. I suggest that he pops along to any GU clinic for that. Or if he wants to go private, it should cost him no more than forty or fifty pounds. Sadly, I don't have the lab facilities for it.'

'But . . .' Daisy began. 'This scan's not his.'

'We can certainly scan him if you like, but it will increase the overall price.' Vanes pulled a calculator towards him. 'And it raises the possibility that he'll fail it. As it is, you're looking at a bill of five thousand pounds.'

'There's obviously been some misunderstanding,' said Daisy. 'I don't want to cut corners. What if he was seriously hurt?'

'Who said anything about cutting corners? I can be a little flexible on the fee. Shall we say four?'

Daisy masked her astonishment at the doctor's brazenness. He grew increasingly desperate.

'Three and a half. Three – that's practically cost. You won't find anyone who's willing to risk it for less.'

'I need to think it over.'

'Two thousand,' he said, grinning abjectly, the tics and habits of decency all gone now.

'I'll get back to you.'

Dr Vanes bowed his head and massaged his eyebrows with the finger and thumb of his left hand. He didn't look up as she left the room.

Daisy went straight to see Tate, her surprise by now turning to fury. 'His medical opinion is for sale! I don't want to do it this way, Tate. It's a scandal. I'm telling you, my old paper would publish this story in a heartbeat.'

Tate grew anxious. 'I hope you didn't say that to him?'

'No, of course not.'

'Who else have you told?'

'No one. Yet.'

Tate took hold of Daisy's arm. It was the first such intimacy between them and she was taken aback. 'Look, you don't understand what you're dealing with. If you talk about this to the wrong people, you'll be in danger. And anyone close to you will be in danger: Isaac, me, your mum, the bloke you work with at the library.'

'Come on, Tate. The world isn't like that.'

'No, not *come on*. Not *come on*, Daisy.' His grip tightened.

'This is how Costello works. This is a different world. This isn't the world you're used to. You must believe me. If not for yourself, then for Isaac and his kid. I've seen things that I wouldn't have believed, except I saw them happen.'

Daisy looked into the kaleidoscope of Tate's bad eye. It seemed to have been sealed over, or burned by something. The film that covered it was like the inside of a sea-shell, and appeared to bear an image of the full moon.

Twelve

While Isaac trained in secret with Tate at the gym, Daisy set about obtaining his licence. She approached the problem conscientiously and thoroughly, as she had approached all the problems in her life. Navigating this new set of difficulties eased some of her private torment. The spectre of Joel Heath seemed to recede a little as she lost herself in the minutiae of the process.

She had decided that she needed a manager's licence herself. Tate was more than happy to initiate her into the mysteries of the craft. Alone in the gym with her, he demonstrated the boxer's arsenal of punches, making the heavy bag judder as he called out the shots. 'Jab. See – it picks the lock. Jab, jab. Then the right cross, the power punch.' He showed how to swab a cut with adrenaline, how to iron out a bump with the cold metal of the Endswell. 'I'd better show you how to wrap his hands while we're about it,' Tate said. He offered her his right hand and told her to loop the bandage over his thumb, interlace it back and forth between his fingers and leave a pad of cloth to protect his knuckles. She worked awkwardly and it took several attempts. Daisy could feel Tate's gloved hand resting on her shoulder.

'How's that?' she asked.

'Great.'

The two of them fell silent as though in the presence of a profound intimacy. Tate opened his mouth to say something, but Daisy cut him off. 'That's all there is to it, then.' And she let him unwind the bandage himself.

*

Not long after she had sent off her application, the Board of Control invited her for an interview. Six interchangeable middle-aged men sat around a meeting table. They quizzed her about her motives for entering the sport. She told them she had been fascinated by boxing since childhood and was at a time in her life when she was looking for new challenges.

The technical questions were easy after Tate's coaching. She detected hostility from only one of the board members. He kept trying to trip her up, as if he wanted to prove that her knowledge was bookish and irrelevant.

'Let's say the fight's over. The promoter's not shown up. Neither has the coach. What's your first priority?'

'I take him to the doctor for the medical check.' Daisy paused. 'Then I'd make sure he gets paid.'

A man nodded approvingly. 'We'll let you know of our decision.'

Daisy received her licence. But the news was mixed: Isaac's application to box had been refused on medical grounds. It seemed the board were concerned about his deafness after all. Daisy lodged an appeal immediately, but she could tell the disappointment had affected Isaac and Tate. To prevent them getting cast down, she insisted that the training schedule continue as it had before the rejection. The three of them would continue to meet at Sammy's gym three times a week in the early mornings. An appeal date was set.

For a moment, it seemed to Daisy that the bad news about Isaac's licence would lead to recrimination and the break-up of their little conspiracy, but it appeared, on the contrary, to have brought them closer. In the weeks leading up to Isaac's appeal, Daisy's skills as a translator were largely redundant while Tate and Isaac were at work together. The two of them had developed a sufficient non-verbal rapport to communicate without Daisy's help.

She would linger on the ring apron, hanging on to the top rope, and watch them using the pads to develop Isaac's technique.

The understanding between the two men had grown instinctive. Tate used simple mimes to build an increasingly elaborate sequence of movements: so the straight right would be followed by a roll to the left, Isaac's head would bob down and up, and then his whole body would twist as he returned a cocked left hook into the pad with a boom! that would make the empty gym echo; then a pair of them, then a pivot step to the right, a hook to the body, two uppercuts, two straight punches. Isaac grasped each link with minimal prompting, responding to the movement of the pads, or the dip of Tate's shoulders, so quickly that it was sometimes hard for Daisy to tell which of them was initiating the action. The two men had the same lightness of movement, the same compact balance, although there was something frail-looking about Isaac's arms and legs. Tate looked solider. His once navy T-shirt had faded to grey from repeated washes and it was soaked with sweat. His tracksuit pants were rolled into a cuff at his knee, and as he bounced on his toes, a muscle on his calf bulged, as hard and round as a tennis ball. The first time Daisy noticed it she felt a flicker of something inside her – the silver flash of a fish as it breaks the surface of murky water and dives deeper, out of sight. Tate was focused and coiled, dripping sweat on the canvas as he came back with stinging blows if he felt Isaac's guard was too open. He showed Isaac how to deliver more power with his punches, using the rotation of his waist and shoulders, how to use the lines of power that crossed the axis of his body from the balls of each foot to the opposite hand. Now, when Isaac hit the heavy bag the rafters shook. Sometimes, they would spar lightly, with body shots only, and Tate would try to impart the subtle tricks of infighting, how to clinch, how to throw your opponent off balance, how to break away from an opponent who was determined to smother your style. Daisy watched, fascinated, mesmerized by Isaac's athleticism and Tate's energy.

Tate was a man transformed, filled with an unfamiliar vitality, waking each morning with a sense of hopefulness and purpose. At work every day he looked forward to his sessions with Isaac, and even in this short space of time he could feel the boy flourish under his tutelage. It was astonishing to watch the boy's style grow and change, but more than that, it liberated something in Tate to catch in Isaac unsuspected echoes of his younger self.

After training, Tate would lock the gym and the three of them would go to work. Tate and Daisy's routes coincided for part of the journey and sometimes they would travel together.

'What will you do if he doesn't get the licence?' Tate asked her one day when they had said goodbye to Isaac.

Daisy shrugged. 'My life will go on,' she said. She was afraid to tell him how much she had invested in the boy's success and preferred to risk sounding indifferent, but her remark must have struck Tate as cold-blooded. He replied with unusual sharpness:

'Because it's fifty-fifty at best for him, isn't it?'

'I don't understand,' she said. 'You were as keen for this as I was. You knew the risks. We didn't make him any promises.'

'But you can't just play with people, Daisy,' he said, with an unguarded flash of anger.

Daisy was puzzled by his reaction, but it suited her to let Tate think that her interest in the boy was a whim, a middle-class girl's hobby, and she didn't contradict him as strongly as she might have. A month later, she travelled to Cardiff for a special meeting of the Board of Control.

'Isaac Plum is the reason I entered this sport,' Daisy told them. 'I believe he is an exceptional talent.'

'We have some misgivings about licensing him,' said one of the board members.

'In recent years, various things have shown the sport in a bad light,' said the man who had tried to trip Daisy up at the previous interview.

'Aside from his deafness,' said Daisy, 'Isaac is fit and well. I don't think anything could show the sport in a worse light than your refusal to license him based on no more than a disability. What's more, there's precedent for this.' Daisy took a folder out of her bag. 'There have been deaf boxers since the days of the prize ring. I've looked into this very carefully. There was a man named Eugene Hairston. Another called James Burke.'

'We're not talking about prize-fighting,' said the man. 'We're talking about boxing in the modern era.'

'In the modern era,' said Daisy, 'there was Mario d'Agata. You've surely heard of him? An Italian. He was world champion at bantamweight in the 1950s.'

'There are technical issues. How will he know when the round's over, if he can't hear the bell?'

'The low-tech solution is that the referee steps between them,' said Daisy. 'When d'Agata fought, they had flashing lights that signalled the end of the round. With the technology we have available now, these are not even obstacles.' She pushed her dossier across the table. 'Let me leave this with you. I have to say that if Isaac's licence is not granted this time, we'll be considering a legal challenge on the grounds of discrimination.'

The board voted by five to one to let the boy box.

Daisy was at home when she heard. She turned up at Tate's doorstep, longing to break the good news to someone. Tate lived in a little workman's cottage just off the Harrow Road that had belonged to his mum, Evangeline. He was taken aback to see Daisy and self-conscious about the state of his house: the neglected odd jobs, the wooden bracing supporting the Victorian brickwork of his front porch, the broken wheelbarrow with its cargo of rainwater that stood in his tiny patch of front garden.

'He's got it!' Daisy said and, transported with her delight, she enveloped him in a hug which he returned half-heartedly. It wasn't that he didn't want to hold her, but the opposite. She sensed his unease and detached herself, recollecting herself and feeling embarrassed at her behaviour. 'I'm going to go and tell him.'

'Okay.' There was a flicker of sadness in Tate, that all her excitement was for the sake of the boy.

'Don't you want to come?'

'I've got a few things to do here.' Tate retreated into the house.

Daisy must have known in some part of herself the reason for Tate's disappointment, but she chose to ignore it. Despite not thinking herself beautiful, she wasn't blind to her effect on him, but her relationship with Joel Heath, her perverse memorial to her dead husband, was all-consuming. She couldn't open her life to anyone else.

Isaac was sitting down for supper when she arrived to tell him. He stood up in delight when he saw her, all eyes and attentiveness, like a fox poised to spring; his stillness as perfect as his movement in the ring.

Tate missed the next training session. Without him, they had no keys to the gym. Isaac couldn't even get changed to go running. Tate turned up for the next session full of apologies, explaining that he had had gastric flu. His eyes were bloodshot.

'Are you all right, Tate?' Daisy asked.

'Yeah. Bit dehydrated.' His hands shook as he pulled on the mitts; his skin seemed to give off a vapour of neat alcohol. It made Daisy uneasy, but she thought it best not to mention it.

The arrival of the licence marked the end of the phoney war. Daisy's focus narrowed again; she was all business. Deliberate or not, her manner wounded Tate. There had been that closeness between them when he had coached her for her manager's licence. Now he felt frozen out.

Tate turned up at the library and borrowed a book about the Sicilian mafia, then asked Daisy out for coffee. He found it difficult to meet her glance, talked abstractedly about the boy, potential first fights, possible promoters, and all the time Daisy felt the presence of some unexpressed revelation on Tate's part which remained unsaid, which caused a knot in her stomach; a secret all the more unwelcome because it reminded her of her own.

Someone else was keeping a secret too. Sammy Kimball was a creature of habit, he loved routine and regularity. He had eaten breakfast at the same café virtually every morning of his adult life, and nothing irked him more than departures from the norm: 'No *mustard*? What, all out of it at the cash and carry? Call this a restaurant? I'll start bringing my own condiments.' But even Sammy occasionally deviated from his traditions. One morning, he had arrived at the gym early to catch up on paperwork. The hasp on the double doors was missing its padlock. This boded very badly. Once before, Tate had failed to lock up properly and yahoos had entered the building at night. They stole nothing, but cut down two heavy bags, defaced some of the posters with badly drawn moustaches and ejaculating penises, and were foolish enough to tag the toilet walls with graffiti. Some of Sammy's boys had recognized the signatures and paid the perpetrators an equally unexpected visit.

Sammy armed himself with a broom handle from the cupboard in the stairwell and crept up towards the gym. As he approached he could hear the familiar sounds of a boxer at work: the bounce of feet on the canvas, the staccato shots of gloves on pads, but no music, strangely, and none of the urgent, vaguely sexual shouts that punctuate a boxer's movement during training: 'Sharp! Now do it like you mean it. Come on, baby, let it flow.'

From the entrance of the gym, a forest of heavy bags obscured Sammy's view. He didn't enter, but crept up the final flight of stairs to the gallery, treading lightly, like a burglar, and balancing with the broom handle.

At the top of the steps, Sammy peered down over the edge of the gallery into the ring. The round-clock buzzed. Tate dropped his hands by his sides and rolled his shoulders to ease the tension in his upper body. Sammy recognized the deaf boy,

87

who went to the ropes, where Daisy towelled his face and put the water bottle to his lips. On the bell, they began again, moving through a drill of moves and combinations with spellbinding speed and variety. When Sammy had got over his initial displeasure at having been deceived, he was overcome with a sense of wonder. Sammy was a cynic, which is to say a thwarted idealist. The boy stirred in him long-forgotten youthful dreams. In his long but inglorious career as a serial loser, he had faced genuine talent often enough to recognize it when he saw it. The boy had everything. David seeing Bathsheba's dripping hair and naked body in the moonlight didn't covet her more than Sammy coveted Isaac Plum at that moment. And Sammy's approach was just as devious.

He began by cadging information from his most loyal boxers about Tate and Tate's new female friend. Inevitably, the longer the conspiracy had continued, the less vigilant they had become about protecting it. Someone had seen them together with Isaac. Someone else knew Daisy worked at the library. When Sammy had pieced together all the intelligence, he moved decisively.

Sammy paid a visit to Daisy at work. He snooped around the shelves until the line at the desk had dwindled to nothing, and then he approached her.

Daisy hadn't recognized him at first. He was taller and more muscular than she remembered, his boxer's physique still broad and sturdy decades after he had last fought for money, and he had on a brown fedora which concealed the bald dome of that spectrally pale head.

She greeted him coolly; he asked if they might have a word in private. Simon Black was happy to mind the desk while they went into the lobby to talk. Outside, rain was lashing the pavement. From time to time, the heavy front door groaned open and in came a passer-by seeking sanctuary from the downpour.

Sammy fingered the brim of his hat and smoothed a few

damp hairs on to his skull. There was something so skeletal about his pale, gaunt head. Daisy thought that with a scythe and a cowl, Sammy could have played Death in an allegory.

'It's about Tate,' he said.

'What about him?'

'The pressure.'

'The pressure?'

Sammy merely nodded as though Daisy would know exactly which pressure he was referring to. 'First off,' his voice shrank to a whisper, 'he doesn't know I'm here. I've come to you in confidence because I'm worried about him.' Sammy raised his eyes from his hat to meet Daisy's gaze. 'You know about the drinking?'

Daisy shifted uneasily on her feet and crossed her arms defensively. 'What about it?'

That was good, Sammy thought. That was better than good. She knew Tate drank. The rest would be much simpler. Sammy's voice took on a plaintive tone. 'I'd hate to see him go under. This is hard for him. Tate can't take any kind of pressure. He could have been a champion. He had the talent – very gifted – but he never had the mental toughness. Me, I was the opposite. He told me all about you, and the boy, and your plans for him.' Sammy watched her intently, reading her face for clues. 'Turning him pro, getting him fights. But Tate's having trouble coping. I could see it in him. Years I've known him. He can't hide nothing from me. "What's the matter?" I go. He's "I can't handle it, Sammy mate. I've bitten off more than I can chew." He wants me to help – take over really. But he was a bit afraid how it would look to you. He's very proud. But he's this close' – he measured out a millimetre with his finger and thumb – 'This close to drinking again.'

Daisy felt a surge of concern for Tate. She thought of him, rumpled and stinking of drink, pushing his trembling hands into the focus mitts. 'What can we do to help him?' she said.

That evening, Sammy approached Tate while he was doing

padwork in the ring with one of the pros. 'Tate mate, I want to have a word with you.' Sammy didn't like to signal the nature of his business too well in advance. He preferred to keep people guessing.

'What is it?' asked Tate, experiencing precisely that little surge of paranoia that Sammy's manner was designed to produce.

'Meet me upstairs after.'

Tate came straight up after his shower. Sammy was seated and waiting. Tate tried to lighten the atmosphere with some banter, but Sammy moved swiftly to the matter in hand. 'What's the main lesson I've tried to teach you over the years?' he began.

'The *main* lesson? I don't know . . .'

Sammy passed Tate a cup of tea. 'Well, I hope I've taught you something.'

'Oh yeah, of course you have . . .' said Tate. He heaped four spoonfuls of sugar into his mug. If pushed further, which of Sammy's contradictory platitudes should he repeat? Something about giving 110 per cent all the time, or the importance of not taking things too seriously at the end of the day? Something about the need to work together as a team, or the indispensability of a strong leader? Tate mulled: no, he would say something about laughter being the best medicine.

'You know what I'm going to say, don't you?'

'Yeah,' lied Tate.

'Never,' Sammy announced with an admonitory wag of his finger, 'never be afraid to make a mistake.'

'That's right,' said Tate, as though this very maxim had been about to leap from his lips.

'You know me too well, Tate mate. You know me too well.' Sammy shook his head and looked fondly at his one-eyed sidekick, who was clearly uncomfortable and clearly lying. 'And I bet you know why I'm saying this, and all.'

Twist or stick? thought Tate. *Stick.* 'No, Sammy mate, I don't.'

'The boy, the deaf and dumb kid Plum. I made a judgement about him which, with twenty-twenty hindsight, I see may have been . . . not wrong . . .' Sammy groped for the correct formulation. 'Not wrong . . . but not right either.'

Tate suddenly had a bad feeling about where this was heading.

'So, there I am a few days ago. Popped in to the gym a bit early because Sandro's was closed. Found the door of the hall unlocked. That's not good, I'm thinking – remembering the time those kids got in and messed the place up. So I come in quietly. Right up here, more or less where you're sitting now, and I look down. And what do I see? You and Plum on pads. And what a pretty little mover. He reminds me of someone. A boxer I once knew called Smoke.'

'He's got quick hands,' said Tate.

'And good feet. Good everything. Might be a bit chinny, for all we know, but we'll never find out until we match him.' Sammy reached into a briefcase at his feet and unskinned a whisky bottle from a crackling brown-paper bag. 'So here's the thing – I've changed my mind. I want the boy back under me. I want him to be given another chance.'

'You do?' Tate looked down at his big scarred hands, but his good eye flicked nervously in the direction of the amber bottle.

'Yeah, I do,' said Sammy, and he nodded. There was a rasp as he unpicked the seal of the bottle and then span the cap off in a single motion with the flat of his hand. 'Fancy a drink?'

Tate licked his dry lips and said nothing.

'Have we got any ice?' Sammy asked.

'In the fridge,' said Tate in a weak voice.

'Movement like that,' said Sammy, 'you've either got it or you don't. And he's got it.' Sammy scraped a gravelly handful of ice out of the freezer and put it in his glass, then reached into the ice box and pulled out a banana. It was frozen hard. He held it up, a yellow boomerang, his brow furrowed in interrogation.

'Smoovies,' explained Tate anxiously. 'In a blender, with

91

fruit and milk. Some of the fighters have them after training.'

Sammy shook his head. 'Very starchy. You want to get them on eggs and tinned fish. Eggs: *that*'s muscle-building food. Two kinds of protein – the yellow and the white.' He closed the fridge door. 'So that woman who was in here with you, the librarian . . .'

'Daisy?'

'Yeah, Daisy, yeah. I've had a word with her and she's up for it.'

'Up for it?'

'Helping us out. Because she speaks deaf and dumb.'

'You have? When?'

'Yesterday.'

'I don't know,' said Tate. 'I was happy training him myself.'

'But, Smoke, he needs the logistics. And I'm happy to provide. It's about teamwork.'

'I'm not sure.'

Darkness was closing in around Tate. Sammy had Daisy. And whoever had Daisy had Isaac, that was the size of it. His rapport with the boy extended as far as the ring ropes, but not beyond. Outside the ropes, because she was a woman, or because she spoke his language, or because something about her simply inspired Isaac's trust, Daisy had become the boy's chief ally.

Back here again, thought Tate. He realized with a pang how much he had enjoyed his conspiracy with Daisy. And now it was gone. Sammy's involvement would change everything. Tate was in danger. He hadn't realized how much he had invested in the boy. It was a reckless middle-aged love: not a second chance to redeem the vanished talent of his youth, but his last hope, and with it gone, he would be left with nothing.

'You sure you won't?' Sammy shook his tumbler and the ice rang against the sides like muted wind-chimes.

Tate was silent, paralysed by a titanic inward struggle. He blinked, and the good eye seemed to water slightly. 'Maybe just the one,' he said.

Sammy poured him two fingers of whisky and they clinked glasses.

'To Isaac Plum.' Tate said nothing.

Sammy swallowed and smacked his lips. Then he stood up and grabbed his coat. 'Blimey, I'm supposed to be having a drink with one of Costello's new matchmakers. Forgot the time. Do you mind locking up?'

Tate was motionless.

'Later, Tate.'

Thirteen

Tate vanished. One minute he was there, the next he had melted away like a summer hailstone, leaving no trace. The first Daisy knew of it was when she came to Isaac's first training session with Sammy. It was her first evening in the gym; her first time with more than the three of them present. The place was as full as it ever got. There were fights coming up and Sammy's roster of losers was grateful to be busy.

The gym was transformed by the presence of the toiling boxers. Their exertions filled the poorly ventilated room with a warm, almost agricultural fug of sweat and unwashed wraps. The fighters walloped the heavy bags for the three minutes marked in red on the round-clock and then rested for one. Some skipped, or shadow-boxed, or hit the speed-bag, or worked with Sammy on the pads. Daisy noticed that the contrast between Sammy and Tate extended to their demeanour in the ring: Sammy moved unhurriedly as he called the shots, the pads loose on his hands, where Tate had been full of a furious intensity, the focused heat of the sun through a magnifying glass.

Daisy waited in the damp and cavernous gym, looking at the photographs that decked the walls, pausing before the one of Tate in satin shorts, with two healthy eyes and a look of aggressive confidence that seemed alien to the melancholy cast of his face.

Isaac emerged from the changing room during the one-minute break into a mill of boxers. They ignored him, too busy sweating, joking, refreshing themselves with gouts of water, hawking into the gruesome spittoon.

94

Where's Tate? Isaac asked, hampered in his signing by his gloves. Daisy had no idea. She had already asked Sammy, who'd simply shrugged. No one seemed to know.

Sammy brought the two of them up into the ring. Daisy clambered through the ropes to join Isaac in the ring centre and was surprised by the spring in the canvas. 'Fuck the skipping, fuck the exercises, that's all bollocks,' Sammy began. 'Anyone can do that. He's got to learn to avoid being hit. The guy's only going to throw two punches, a left hand or a right hand. And if you know how to slip the right hand and block the left hand, you're going to live a long time.' He almost added 'Don't worry about winning,' which was the usual coda to this speech, but stopped himself. 'I don't want to kill you in the gym. I want to keep you fresh. You only need to train three times a week as long as you run. You can have a new yacht, but if there's no wind an old rowing boat will overtake it.'

Then they began their padwork. Sammy had nothing like Tate's understanding with the boy, but Isaac was too good not to look good when Sammy gave him space to express himself. The hubbub in the gym stilled as boxers stopped what they were doing to peer at Sammy's new prospect. What was he doing here? He looked too classy for Losers Inc. Tate had added power and a ferocity of intention to Isaac's other gifts. He was quite obviously a prodigy. The boxers shrugged at one another. Maybe a bleeder?

They tried to talk to him in the showers afterwards, but he merely smiled and pointed at his ears; they quizzed Daisy instead. She tried to play down her own excitement, but she found their enthusiasm generous and heartening.

Daisy left that first training session optimistic. It was a week before it dawned on them all that Tate's absence was more than temporary.

Tate had gone missing before, of course: his ten years with Sammy had been punctuated with disappearances, but this departure had a finality about it.

Daisy was concerned enough to ring Tate's numbers, go

round to his house and even quiz the boxers who knew him best, but no one had any idea. They tried to be helpful, but the few details that emerged were contradictory and only deepened the mystery. He'd been seen at a fight in Nottingham. Someone had caught a glimpse of him in the audience of a televised fight, or a football game. It was futile.

Sammy had his own theory about Tate's disappearance, which he was happy to share with Daisy. 'I was afraid of this,' he said. 'It's the *Leaving Las Vegas* scenario. I always worried this would happen.'

Daisy had seen the film. She thought it unlikely but probably not impossible that Tate had filled a shopping trolley with hard liquor and gone off to drink himself to death in a Las Vegas motel room. She surprised herself by missing him. He was infinitely preferable to Sammy.

Sammy told the same bad jokes again and again without a jot of shame. 'Boxing's a great game,' he was fond of saying. 'I've got friends all over the world. None here, but I've got friends all over the world.'

Daisy quickly grew tired of it and wished he would shut up, but the boxers were like children: they enjoyed the repetition, and took turns punching the numbers on Sammy's juke-box of monologues:

'Sammy, tell the one about Stevie Wonder.'

'What was your name when you was fighting in Denmark, Sammy?'

Over the course of his long career, Sammy had fought under names and at weights that even he could not remember. He had lost on a Saturday in Marseilles and then fought again the following Wednesday in Bethnal Green. He had fought on undercards across the UK, in Ireland, West Germany, Italy, Spain and Belgium, learning his loser's craft along the way: how to fire up the crowd so that they hissed and booed him like a pantomime villain; how to conciliate them afterwards (the defeat alone usually accomplished that); how to survive round after round with fitter and more committed opponents;

how to rise gamely from the canvas, pleading with the referee to let the fight continue, while intimating with a disoriented look, or a wobbly leg, that he should wave it over; and how to get paid.

And yet for all his bravado, all his jokes, and his self-conscious role as a lovable eccentric, training Isaac Plum seemed to bring out an unexpected seam of diffidence in Sammy. Though he projected an aura of self-assurance and seemed to share Daisy's high ambitions for the boy, he hesitated uncharacteristically before committing Isaac to his first professional fight, and speechified more and more. Words were Sammy's defence. As a skunk sprays foul musk from the glands in its behind, so Sammy sprayed a disabling fog of words, through which Daisy looked in vain for the man himself. He never stopped talking, yet the more he said, the less she felt she knew about him. And she began to wonder if Sammy was up to the task.

A nasty episode at the start of the season brought it home to her. Jonah Kingston was one of Sammy's regular losers. His girlfriend had had a baby and, in need of extra money, he'd taken a fight at middleweight – a stone below his usual fighting weight. It was unclear how he had taken it all off. Daisy had overheard whispered consultations between Jonah and Sammy in which the words 'ketosis' and 'cut out your carbs' had figured. Jonah seemed a little lethargic in training, but the weight had melted off him. After the weigh-in, he sucked up pints of chicken noodle soup that he had made from a packet – another Sammy tip – and complained of a ringing in his ears.

Daisy and Isaac were at ringside. Jonah's body had never looked more impressive. There was not a trace of fat, and his skin seemed shrink-wrapped round his formidable ebony musculature. But he struggled from the opening bell. His thirsty body had refused to release perspiration for the first two rounds. Jonah's opponent, a competent fighter from Telford, found himself in awe of Jonah's physique and his drained, sullen eyes; but he grew in confidence as the fight wore on. Jonah appeared to have been sculpted out of bronze, but he also moved around the ring like an equestrian statue. His limbs were ponderous and stiff, his movements predictable. Sammy howled at him from the corner, but he had nothing: no snap, no vigour. Jonah's opponent hit him at will, and the crowd booed his reluctance to come out of clinches.

The referee stopped the fight after a barrage of unanswered punches at the end of the fourth round, stepping between the two boxers. Jonah rested his weary head on the referee's shoulder, his neck bent over like a flower wilting on its stalk. Drips of blood from Jonah's cut mouth formed a red shamrock on the referee's white shirtfront. Daisy and Isaac went with him to the hospital.

Sammy turned up an hour later. He found the wounded boxer in a corridor, lying on the stretcher the St John's Ambulance men had used to carry him. Jonah's girlfriend Yolanda stood beside him. Daisy had unwound the tape from his knuckles and cut off the damp bandages. Yolanda had scrunched and balled a dressing gown to make a pillow for his battered head. The tassels on his golden boots hung limply down, a bag of saline solution sprouted from his arm.

Yolanda folded her fingers into Jonah's bruised hand. He opened his eyes: they flashed whitely in the dim corridor. Yolanda tightened her grip on his fingers. Jonah mumbled something. Sammy strained forward to hear: the boxer's fractured jaw had been anaesthetized and wired shut and he mangled his consonants like a poor ventriloquist.

'You chold me to hitch him with gogyshotsh,' said Jonah in a mournful whisper.

'No, I didn't actually, Jonah mate,' said Sammy, correcting his hurt fighter with pedantic patience. 'What I *actually* said was: work him to the body, but watch out for the big right hand looping down over the top.' Sammy patted Jonah's head and moved around to the other side of the stretcher. 'Never mind. Live and learn. You'll blow him away next time. He doesn't have the power to live with an in-form Jonah Kingston.'

'There ain't going to be no next time. I'm finisched with thish schit!' Jonah's ferocious, spitting whisper lifted him momentarily off the trolley.

'He did everything you told him, Mr Kimball. Now look at him,' said Yolanda. 'My beautiful baby.' She put her tear-stained face in her hands.

'Hasty words, my son. It's defeats what test your mettle. It's nights like this what make a man.'

The squeak of shoes on the hospital lino cut short Sammy's peroration and announced the appearance of the doctor.

'Your temperature's stabilized,' he said. 'You were terribly dehydrated. Tell me something, Jonah – did you have difficulty making the weight?'

Jonah shook his head. Sammy grew indignant. 'You're impugning my professionalism. I would never, ever take risks with the life of one of my fighters.'

After Jonah's defeat, there were a couple of other bad knock-outs, which carried a thirty-day suspension, and there was some muttering in the showers. The consensus was that Sammy had grown reckless in Tate's absence. Tate himself had become slightly mythologized. His deeds and dissipations grew in the retelling: he'd once sparred with Sugar Ray Leonard and knocked him out; he'd boxed drunk in the Moscow Olympics; a scientist at NASA had wanted to study the secret of his quick hands.

For Daisy, the speculation about Tate and the misgivings about Sammy were equally irrelevant. Sammy and Isaac were all she had and she was committed to them.

In the ring, there appeared to be a kind of unspoken contract between the boxers. The violence was controlled. Very occasionally tempers frayed in sparring, someone would get a nosebleed or a cracked rib, but Daisy was surprised most of all by how peaceable the boxers were, spent and gentle after exorcising their violence in the ring.

Most evenings, after training, the boxers would strip off

their shirts to weigh themselves, lining up to use the scales that were kept in Sammy's office. She was struck by their preoccupation with their weight. Most of them struggled to lose it, whereas Isaac had difficulty keeping it on. Their favoured method of weight loss was long, slow runs by the greasy canal on the other side of the road from the gym, which had the added virtue in Sammy's eyes of 'building good wind'.

Knowing that they used the canal towpath gave Daisy the confidence to walk there. One frosty morning, she used it as a short-cut and was rewarded with the sight of six geese in flight, the flap of their wings audible, snapping like sails as they laboured to bear their bulbous bodies aloft.

Daisy's investment in the future – even one as tenuous and distant as a fight with Joel Heath – seemed to be a recipe for improved mental health. She looked so well that her friend Imo wondered if she was seeing someone. The truth was that, at first, all the pleasures of her association with Isaac Plum – liking him, her affection for his wife and child, the shape the training sessions gave her week – had been peripheral. At her core, she was possessed by an obsessive determination to see Isaac fight Joel Heath. She wanted Isaac at his physical peak to batter Heath to within an inch of his life. She fantasized about seeing Heath on the trolley with his jaw wired. Sammy talked of the skulduggery that went on in the ring. 'I've seen all sorts,' he'd say. 'Loaded gloves. Padding ripped out. Nothing but bandages and a little leather between the knuckles and a man's face. Not a pretty sight.' Daisy imagined Heath's face ballooning with blood and fluid.

Now, with Tate gone, Daisy was involved in every aspect of Isaac's training, recording his weight, translating for him, giving him lifts, wiping his face between rounds, patting his arm three times to let him know the bell had rung, squirting water on to his head or into his mouth, inserting his gumshield, holding out the waistband of his shorts and fanning in air to cool him down on the hottest days, when the heat sat like a lead weight on the poorly ventilated gym.

Alongside the other fighters queuing for the scales, Isaac seemed slight and vulnerable, his limbs wiry and thin, the muscles of his chest faint squares, his nipples tiny and pink.

As Daisy watched him day after day, sparring impressively with Sammy's other fighters, from the most murderous heavyweights to the cutest and slickest bantams, more and more she realized she was growing to love him. And oddly, the more she loved him, the more she imagined him losing, and losing badly, to Heath. She pictured how she would cradle his injured head, smooth out the bumps on his brow, while Sammy gave final desperate instructions. Isaac losing: she would know just what to do. That was the source of the tremendous liberation she felt. Isaac's losing would be a recapitulation of Stuart's murder. And she would do what she should have done then: she would kill Heath herself.

Fourteen

Did boxing coarsen Daisy, being around all that blood and ugliness, dwelling in that violent world? If anything, what drove her was the realization that boxing wasn't violent *enough*. The idea of killing Heath was linked to Daisy's sense that mere victory would be inadequate.

In prison, they talk about the 'switch'. The word belongs to the felon's insecure world of few resources where the ultimate authority rests on one person's capacity to inflict harm on another. 'I switched on him,' they'll say with pride. It means: I turned on him, hardened my heart, showed him he could expect no mercy. In their world, forgiveness and compromise are signs of weakness. But the idea also acknowledges that no one but a psychopath can remain switched all the time.

You switch on someone if they fail to honour a debt, if they try to cheat you, affront your dignity, question your judgement, or step on your toe. Whole nations can switch too. Then it's one people, or one gang or tribe, against another. But its essence, the switch itself, is that binary moment when one person represents all that is good, and his opponent all that is bad. It's a survival mechanism, a hold-over from more primitive times. Normally, humans can tolerate ambivalence about each other, recognize that nobody is either perfectly good or bad. But when the switch occurs, we begin to talk of good and evil, the battle lines are drawn, and we long to wade through our enemies' blood. And maybe ambivalence is a luxury of relatively affluent times, when there is enough to go round. When there isn't, when there wasn't, someone got barred from the

water hole, someone was left in the desert to starve, or someone was killed and eaten.

Boxers know about the switch. Those punch-ups at the
weigh-in, those ponderous and implausible wars of words
before the fight that so many people think are a ploy to gener-
ate ticket sales, they serve another function. The fighter is
preparing himself to hate. There is not enough to go round in
a boxing ring: the game is designed to produce one winner. A
draw is the least satisfactory result. And when people throw
themselves behind a boxer, or a team, or an army, they want to
experience that atavistic thrill where the world – this complex,
sublunary mess of blurred lines, half-truths and provisional
judgements – gets simplified down to black and white, good
and evil, us and them. For the truth is that binary thinking
holds enormous power.

'You've come about another boxer?' said Dr Vanes as he
escorted her from the waiting room without a trace of surprise
on his saturnine face. He looked unslept and slightly thinner.
'It was Plum, was it not? The deaf chap.'

'Good memory,' said Daisy.

'Medical training,' said Dr Vanes sadly. 'It's all rote learning
– or was in my day. Develops the memory muscles.'

There was something pitiful about the man, trapped in his
office like an insect in a glass jar, with the illusion of light and
space around him, but in fact cut off from life and dying.

He doodled on his pad. 'How can I help?'

'A friend of mine. Her life's in danger.'

'Has she been to her GP?'

'It's not a health issue.'

'No?'

'She needs a gun.'

Dr Vanes got up, went to the door, opened it, looked out,
came back to his desk and sat down. His expression hadn't so
much as flickered. 'That's outside my area of expertise, I'm
afraid.'

'I thought that, as a consultant, you might be able to refer me on to a specialist,' said Daisy. Dr Vanes's eyes held hers for a second.

'I'm sorry. I can't help you. Your friend will have to go elsewhere.'

'Thank you for your time,' said Daisy. She stood up.

Vanes drew his notepad across the desk towards him. The slips of paper were headed with the logo of a pharmaceutical company that had long since renamed itself. 'I'll write you out the usual prescription.' He smiled at her.

Outside, heart hammering, Daisy opened the folded paper. Beneath the logo Vanes had written '£5,000'.

Daisy returned the following day.

This time she was taken straight through to the consulting room by the doctor's sullen assistant. Daisy glanced into the waiting room on the way in and glimpsed a middle-aged man, Italian in appearance, wearing a tracksuit and a woollen cap, with his feet up on the magazines. He caught her eye and looked away immediately. The specialist, she thought.

Vanes was waiting by his desk. On top of it stood a Fortnum and Mason's carrier bag. Vanes was very twitchy. Daisy pulled out a jiffy bag of notes and handed it to him. 'I could only come up with four,' she said.

'Ah.' Vanes grinned and bared his teeth. 'That might queer things. Wait here please.' He left the room. Daisy knew he was checking with the specialist, persuading him to take a lower fee. She also knew she was being overcharged. But she didn't care.

She moved closer and peered into the bag. The plastic was pinched and dusty. Charity shop, she thought. It was filled with cheap second-hand clothes, scarves and blouses, balled up clumsily as camouflage, stuffed in there by a man. She reached in. Her hand closed on something so cold that it made her gasp. The door opened and she stepped back with a start.

'That's okay,' said Vanes. He was as tense as she was.

'Does it have . . .?' She wanted to say *ammunition*, but it seemed to go against the implicit decorum of their exchange.

'I'm assured that you have anything you need. I can't vouch for it personally, of course. It's very much *caveat emptor*, I'm afraid.'

'Is that Latin for "no honour among thieves"?' said Daisy.

Vanes held the door for her. '"Let the buyer beware".'

On the way out, Daisy glanced again at the waiting room and saw it was empty.

At home, she unpacked the carrier bag on the kitchen table. The gun was sleek and silver, wrapped in a black scarf. Also in the bag was a full box of forty bullets: heavy .38 calibre shells.

A week later, she took the train to West Humble and went walking in the thick woods of the North Downs. She had the gun and a packed lunch in her backpack. When she was sure she was alone, she took her bottled water from the pack and set it against a tree as a target. Then, from ten feet away, she fired a single shot. The gun bucked against her hand. Its report rang through the woods. She went shakily to examine her marksmanship: the shot had missed the target by more than a foot and lodged itself in the bark, too deep for her to prise it out, but too deep as well for anyone to notice.

For her second shot, she stepped much closer to the tree. This time she could feel the heat of the muzzle flash bouncing back off the target. The bullet went cleanly through the bottle. She wrapped up the gun and put it back into her bag. She would have to get as close as possible when the opportunity presented itself.

Stuart had loved this place. They had cycled the stumpy downhill tracks together on rented bikes, amazed at so much peace, such greenness, so much silence, so near the capital.

Daisy hiked to Polesden Lacey and wandered its vast gardens, then decided to go inside.

'I need to check your bag, madam,' said the National Trust warden.

'Why's that?'

'No flash photography.'

'I haven't got a camera.'

'Any bombs?'

Daisy smiled and shook her head.

The warden waved her through into the panelled hush and eighteenth-century furniture. 'I believe you, madam. You've got an honest face.'

Fifteen

Six weeks after Jonah Kingston gave up boxing for good, Sammy took Daisy aside and told her he had picked an opponent for Isaac's first fight. He had agonized over it: Sammy had no matchmaker to help him scout for opposition. In fact, the most obvious place to find a body for building the boy's record would have been Losers Inc. itself. But though fights between stablemates were not unknown, a match-up between two of Sammy's notorious underachievers was not a mouthwatering prospect for a promoter. 'More people would pay to watch me argue with my missus, Sammy. You've got to be winding me up.'

Still, Sammy was owed favours and he kept getting offered fights for Isaac – just not the ones he wanted. In the end, he'd had to agree to a more ambitious and potentially troublesome first fight than is either usual or wise. The man's name was Tyrone Senior. He had had fourteen professional fights and seven wins in a career interrupted by a lot of 'time away': i.e. spells in prison for crimes committed to get the money he never seemed to make boxing. Senior was dropping down a weight division to take the fight.

About a week before the fight, Imogen came round to Daisy's uninvited. They drank wine together and rediscovered some of their old intimacy.

Daisy filled Imo's glass and then her own. 'Help me choose music for his ring-walk.'

'Really?'

Daisy went into the airing cupboard for the boxes of Stuart's old LPs. She clicked the light on with a string.

'I thought you said he was deaf.'

'Yes – but it lifts the crowd. And he told me that if it's loud enough he can feel the vibrations.' Daisy's voice was half-muffled by bulky winter coats and boxes. She emerged, dragging a carton of records, and went back inside.

Imo leafed through the records in one of the boxes. 'How about this? *Classic Adverts*.'

There was a snort of derision from the airing cupboard.

'Seriously, Daze. Remember the Old Spice ad? *Carmina Burana*? It makes me think of *Excalibur* and all those knights with apple blossom falling on them.' Imo put it back in the box. 'Well, I don't know why you asked my opinion. I thought House of Pain was a patisserie. Oh, remember this!' She put on a record from their student days and began to dance. For a moment, the music punched a hole in the present and the past came swarming through the breach: the hopes of Daisy's youth, but desiccated, like dried flowers in an album. Daisy's eyes welled up. Imo mistook her quiet rage for sadness and put a consoling arm around her.

'"Kiss"? What's it got to do with fighting? It sounds soppy to me,' was Sammy's response to the chosen music.

'Take my word for it, Sammy. It works.'

Sammy had a library full of fight tapes in a cupboard up on the landing. A week before the fight, Daisy rooted through them to see if they included footage of Senior's previous fights. There were hundreds of cassettes, the books that comprised Sammy's library – *The Pritikin Diet, Fit For Life, Eat Right for your Blood Type*, half a dozen boxing biographies and a couple of books on neurolinguistic programming – and even cans of film stacked on the shelves like piles of outsized nickels. On the lowest shelf were six or seven tapes with Tate's name on their spines. Daisy took them to watch at home, telling herself that they would be educational.

She was spellbound by what she saw. She had watched enough bouts by now to recognize the peculiar physical gifts of a talented fighter; and even though part of her rebelled when fans of boxing tried to dignify their lust for blood with allusions to the Tao, to jazz, to ballet and the like, she could see that in the young Tate, just as in Isaac Plum, there was something marvellous – craft and instinct, the grace and economy of his movement, the flow of his lean young body and the flash of his hands. And beside the drama of the physical contest, there was always the spectacle of Tate's internal conflict, the tragedy of Tate against himself, Tate the nearly man, Tate the gifted choker, always almost winning, always losing.

There was a brace of fights on the final tape in which Tate looked sluggish, where his trainer cajoled him between rounds to no discernible effect, and the mystified commentators murmured that something wasn't right with Tate, that he'd taken the fights at short notice, that he seemed underprepared. To Daisy there was no mystery at all: Tate was hung over, his strength gone, his balance shot to pieces, and all his dishonoured gifts in terrible decline.

In the final fight on the tape, Tate, dispirited and unfit, was relying on his vanishing reflexes to outbox a tough slugger called Geoff Sugar. Daisy watched as it descended into a gruesome war. For the first round, Tate was able to keep out of range, until, coming out of a clinch, Sugar cracked him with a shot to the liver that made his legs wobble. The pain of the blow must have energized Tate. There was a brief efflorescence: something – anger, fear, hurt pride – ignited his powers again. He boxed brilliantly for the following three rounds, but Sugar was still catching him, and whenever he did, Tate was shaken. He looked panicked, his face horribly marked. There was confusion in his corner. By round seven, his left eye was completely shut. Clearly in pain and disorientated, Tate was no longer able to make Sugar miss, but hung on futilely, absorbing a stream of punches to the head that brought the crowd to their feet. The referee waved the fight over. There was the obligatory hug between the combatants that somehow never failed to be moving, and Sugar went to commiserate with Tate's corner.

Daisy switched the tape off. She wondered how she would manage if Isaac ever returned to the corner with a face marked up like Tate's, bloody and cut. Could she balance the claims of his well-being against the need for victory? Did she have the stomach for it? The possibility, which she had never dwelled upon, that Isaac might damage or lose his sight began to haunt her. How would he live then? And what did it mean that she cared so deeply watching Tate get beaten, a victim of his own courage? The tenderness she felt for Tate's wounded body stirred up thoughts in Daisy that were almost unthinkable.

Isaac and Daisy watched the tapes of Tyrone Senior in Isaac's caravan. Una cooked, filling the cramped space with the smell of frying sausages. And then, after supper, she came to sit on her husband's knee as the video started up.

There was dead space before the pictures rolled. Isaac turned mischievously to Una: *dirty film*, he signed. She cuffed him affectionately on the head. *See?* he signed to Daisy, *they all want to beat me up.*

Isaac was happier and more relaxed than Daisy had ever seen him. Not even the spectacle of Tyrone Senior, squat and densely put-together, brutalizing two opponents in a row, was able to faze him. Partly, she supposed, it was his being around his family: Esme gurgling contentedly from her cot, Una's love radiating throughout the tiny home along with the intrusive smell of her cooking. Isaac looked like a man whose life had begun at last.

Una excused herself half-way through the first fight and went to check on her daughter. She didn't come back. *Tired*, Isaac signed. Daisy wondered. What must it be like for her to watch a man who would shortly be trying to knock her husband unconscious?

Isaac seemed almost reluctant to let the evening end. He walked Daisy out to her car. She asked him what he thought of the tapes. Isaac shrugged. *He's a big puncher*, he said, *but I'll fight my fight.*

In the fresh night air, with lights gleaming from windows across the site, the place looked like a village, quaint and tranquil. Daisy and he stood for a moment on the steps of the caravan. Isaac turned to her with a smile. *I hate it*, he said. *Seventeen years. Enough*. He looked out over the field. 'Nuff!' he said for emphasis, and shook his head. The word hung, sharp and loud in the cold air, like a bark.

Tyrone Senior made his entrance first, to a piece of belligerent rap music. Isaac, Daisy and Sammy waited for their cue from the whip. Isaac had on white boots and shorts and a satin cape that Una had made and which she had embellished with an embroidery of Esme's name. Sammy had tried to discourage him from wearing it on the grounds that it was too effeminate, but Isaac was unbudgeable. This stubbornness was a new trait in him, and Sammy didn't like it; but there was worse to come.

A mystified silence settled on the half-empty auditorium as Prince's falsetto voice squealed 'Kiss!' over the public address system. Sammy gave Daisy a disgusted look. 'You said the music worked,' he said.

'It does,' Daisy insisted feebly. Her cheeks burned as she followed Sammy and Isaac out to the blue corner, mentally cursing Imo, glad that at least Isaac couldn't hear it. 'It's got no bass on it,' she explained.

'That's right,' said Sammy, as he stepped through the ropes. 'It's the bleeding DJ's fault.'

A small contingent of drunken fans were singing along in reedy, castrated voices.

'Fight's not even started yet and you've made the boy a laughing stock,' Sammy bickered. 'Honestly. What's wrong with "Eye of the Tiger"?' He plonked the bucket down as Daisy followed Isaac into the ring centre to translate the referee's instructions.

She had hardly slept the night before, haunted by the recollection of Tate's and Jonah's injuries. Isaac seemed preternaturally relaxed, winking at Daisy as she left the ring with the satin cape at the command of seconds out. She loved the boy for his being so businesslike, for the aura of calm around him.

At the bell, the ring-lights flashed for Isaac, and he and his opponent touched gloves in a show of sportsmanship. Senior was the first to throw serious punches. Isaac, as he often did in sparring, was happy to sit back in his relaxed guard – that American stance with the dropped lead hand that had turned amateur judges against him – as if he first wanted to sample his opponents' offerings, build up a mental image of their strengths and weaknesses, before he went on the offensive. He began scoring with his jab from the middle of the round, but still boxed cautiously, as though with a touch of nervousness. The first round ended with honours even.

Between rounds, Ron Costello pushed his face through the ropes as Daisy was holding the water bottle to Isaac's lips. 'Thought you were supposed to be writing a book,' he said.

'I found something I like more,' she said.

'Tell him to pick it up a bit,' said Costello. 'I don't care if he thinks he's Baryshnikov, the crowd haven't come to watch an eff-ing dancer. They came for six rounds of smash-mouth boxing.'

Meanwhile, Sammy was giving Isaac minute and detailed instructions that Daisy was unable to translate. 'Back him against the turnbuckle, pivot half a foot, slip under his guard, and then let go the uppercut to the body . . .'

Daisy was trying her best, but seemed only to be confusing Isaac. Fortunately, Isaac was growing into the fight. He had a slight reach advantage and was using it to skewer Senior with the jab, frustrating him to the point where Senior would jump in in desperation, hoping to fight inside, only to find that Isaac had floated out of range behind a barrage of punches.

The fight was scheduled for six rounds. In the end, it lasted five. Senior's corner were on the verge of throwing in the towel after four; it was Senior himself who insisted on coming out for one final and fruitless round, deceived by the softness of Isaac's style into thinking that if he could only catch him, he could stop him.

He never caught him. Daisy and Isaac were the last to see the towel as it sailed into the ring and crumpled like an enormous wounded bird.

Afterwards, Sammy was expansive, posing for photographs with his arm around the boy, holding forth about his fighter's talent, his face shining with gratified pride: 'He's the real deal, a deaf wonderkid, more elusive than Lord Lucan.'

But at the moment of his victory, Isaac had leaped in the air and turned to hug Daisy. And for a long time after, she remembered the feel of him, his damp, hard body and the curious deadness of his ear against hers.

Sixteen

Isaac's second contest was at Valley Hall. It was another stoppage. At the end of the fight, coins rained from the crowd into the ring. Daisy instinctively used her body to shield Isaac from the missiles.

'Nobbins,' said Sammy. Daisy thought it was some private expletive, then Sammy explained that the coins were a tradition, an aficionado's reward for a good performance.

Four more fights, four victories, three of them by stoppage. Isaac never ended these contests with a single concussive shot, but by attrition, wearing the opponent down with his speed and range of movement. There was something oddly gentle, almost feline, about the way Isaac disposed of his opponents. Only the fourth fight went the distance, but even there Isaac comprehensively outboxed the other fighter, a man named Michael Slattery. The contest was fought over six rounds and there was little doubt that, if it had been scheduled for ten, Isaac would have stopped Slattery too. Even the Prince song was working for Isaac's ring-walk.

'I thought my boy was good until I saw your boy,' said Slattery's trainer, as he and Daisy followed their fighters back to the dressing room. Sammy was still at ringside, schmoozing promoters, bragging about Isaac like a child with a loose tooth.

'Your boy fought well,' said Daisy. 'You should be proud of him.'

'Well?' Slattery's trainer was a black man in his sixties called Cleon, but known universally as Loverboy. Loverboy had long greying dreadlocks. There was bemusement as well as bitterness in his voice. '*Well?* He couldn't lay a glove on your boy, and they don't give no points for artistic expression.' *Expreshaan.*

'No,' said Daisy, 'but it might be a better sport if they did.'

'Where you find him?' asked Loverboy. 'Because I know Sammy didn't teach him to fight like that. The boy a duppy. He can't be hit.'

Daisy halted at the door of the dressing room. This was as far as she went. She was in and out of the changing room at Sammy's without embarrassment – much to the curiosity of Imogen, who asked, 'What are their willies like?' – but some of the older trainers were superstitious and even hostile about her presence at fights, so while she insisted on being with Isaac before the bout, she would leave him to shower and change afterwards. Don't worry, he told her, after a particularly frosty encounter with a prudish old Scot, soon he would have a changing room to himself. *Famous*, he signed, and mimed reclining in surroundings of spacious opulence. In fact, the best that could be said of any of the changing rooms was that they were ordinary, while some were positively mediaeval. The facilities at Sammy's were a case in point: a water supply that alternated between freezing and the correct temperature for blanching vegetables, mildew on the walls, long-abandoned underpants on the pegs, and a nameless goo at the margin of the showers that every boxer brought flip-flops to negotiate. Every gym in the world was the same, Isaac told her. And yet, the boxers themselves were fastidious about clean clothes and applied deodorant with the zeal of crop-dusters. As for the willies, she explained to Imo, she was taken aback by their sheer variety: a vast collection of frail and faintly ludicrous aquatic vegetables – long thin ones, short fat ones, pink ones, yellowish ones, brown ones, circumcised ones that resembled bald men in roll-neck jumpers, and, it had to be admitted, one or two that were simply enormous, and which became a running joke between her and Imogen, who would allow a dreamy look to come into her eyes as she shook her head and murmured, '*Too* big.'

'I didn't find him,' said Daisy. 'Sammy's partner Tate found him.'

'Tate?' There was incredulity in the trainer's voice.

'Do you know him?'

Loverboy looked slightly offended. 'I trained him. I knew him from time. I was in his corner when his retina detach. He never mention me?'

'Now I think of it, he did say something about you.'

'Really?' Loverboy was obviously gratified by Daisy's lie. 'Smoke. He was a cute fighter. He fought a lot like your boy. Real slick, technical fighter. How is he?'

'He's been away for a while.'

Loverboy nodded. It didn't surprise him. 'You know, between us, and don't think this is hard feelings talking, Sammy's the wrong trainer for the boy.'

'He's got a lot of experience.'

'Experience.' Loverboy kissed his teeth derisively. 'He's got the wrong experience. Every man have a level. This boy's way beyond Sammy's level. You watch and see.'

Just then, Sammy appeared in the corridor. The smile on his face grew tight and hard as he caught sight of Loverboy.

'Loverboy Edwards,' he said, less a greeting than an acknowledgment of the man's unwelcome presence. 'Still telling lies about me?'

'Sammy,' said Loverboy, echoing his unenthusiastic tone. 'Sorry there's not time to stay and reminisce about old times.' He nodded farewell at Daisy before disappearing into the dressing room.

'Yeah, whatever. Nice to have you out of retirement,' said Sammy. He turned to Daisy once Loverboy was out of earshot. 'Loopy. Too much of the wacky baccy. He grows it on an allotment somewhere.' He made a sour face as he pulled on an imaginary cigarette. 'Used to be a good trainer years ago.'

*

Half a dozen victories on his current form, and Isaac's case for fighting for the title would be unanswerable. And as he rose through the rankings, Heath was dropping. After unsuccessfully fighting for the Commonwealth Championship, Joel Heath had lost one and then drawn his next fight. If Daisy could steer Isaac to the British title, she could dictate the terms of the fight with Joel Heath.

It was Sammy that Daisy wasn't sure if she could trust. He had fallen in love with Isaac. After a lifetime of training the sport's also-rans, he had a potential champion on his hands. 'I was due one,' he said. 'It had to happen one day.'

Every now and again, mysterious men in suits turned up at the gym to watch the boy train.

'I think we should talk to Costello about promoting the boy,' said Sammy.

'I want to stay independent for the time being,' said Daisy. 'He doesn't need Costello. There's all sorts of horror stories about Costello.'

'Costello could get him a pop at the title.'

But Daisy dug her heels in. All her power derived from her relationship with the boy. If Costello got hold of him, she would no longer be able to direct his career. Sammy knew that he couldn't prevail on her. Daisy had won the boy's trust. No one else had the patience or the imagination to learn his language.

Sammy had a number of suggestions for Isaac's next opponent. Daisy had heard of none of them, so Sammy suggested she stay late and watch some videos of them fighting.

They sat in the gallery at the rear of the gym on a burst sofa whose stuffing resembled nesting material and tended to cling to woollen clothes. Sammy insisted on fetching an old duvet cover from somewhere and draping it over the seat. He seemed oddly agitated. It occurred to Daisy that this was the first time they had ever been alone together.

Sammy adjusted the settings on the giant screen, wielding the remote control like a conductor's baton. 'I'm forgetting my manners,' he said. 'Something to drink?'

Daisy demurred. There was something creepy about this new, solicitous Sammy. She felt a tingle at the base of her neck and suppressed a shiver.

'I can't tempt you to a drop of the hard-core stuff?' Sammy pulled a bottle of whisky out of a paper bag. About half a cup of whisky sloshed in the bottle as he shook it.

'The hard-core stuff?' Daisy took the bottle from his hands. Sammy hovered expectantly. 'I'll get you some ice.'

'It's okay, Sammy. I'm fine.' She handed the bottle back. 'I'm not a whisky drinker.'

Sammy shrugged. 'You never know. You might enjoy a nude erection.'

Daisy looked at him. 'What did you say?'

'A new direction.' Sammy stood the bottle on the floor and started the video. 'Seconds out,' he said.

There was no preamble. The video began abruptly with the clash of two fleshy bodies. It was a couple of seconds at least before Daisy realized that she wasn't watching boxing at all.

'Must have sent this by mistake,' Sammy whispered.

Daisy looked at him. His cunning face was a mask of curiosity and innocence, too clever to look overtly aroused. 'Turn it off, Sammy,' she said. Then she screamed at him, 'Turn it off!' Sammy found the power switch and the images stopped.

'What?' he said, rattled by the intensity of her reaction. 'I didn't know it was a grumbleflick, honest. I would never . . .'

'I'm going to give you the benefit of the doubt this time, but if you ever pull a stunt like this again, I'll fucking kill you.' There was affectless calm in her voice. They were both silent for a moment as they each took in her words with surprise. They both realized she meant it.

'It was a mistake.' Sammy was simpering now. 'We need to talk tactics. I'll find another tape of the lad.' He took a key from his pocket and opened the built-in cupboard by the door. 'See? There's bound to be one of him here.'

Sammy, humming to himself, scanned the shelves, trying to muster a nonchalance he didn't feel.

Daisy was half-way down the stairs. 'I'm too tired, Sammy. Long day and early start tomorrow.'

'Suit yourself.'

When she reached the street she looked back, gazing at Sammy's silhouette in the window as he continued to rummage in the cupboard.

Imo came straight over after Daisy's phone call. She insisted on hearing the story again. She seemed more upset than Daisy. 'What does he look like?'

Daisy gave an accurate physical description of Sammy.

'Oh gross! Do you think he was trying to put the moves on you?'

'Actually, no – I think he was trying to intimidate me. I think he wanted me to run out of the room screaming.'

'. . . but to spring it on you like that. What did he think? That you'd be so overcome with desire you'd beg him for a shag? How did you get involved with these people?'

Daisy said nothing. She knew what Sammy wanted: the boy. He had underestimated her, but his intention was obvious. The boy was like gold to him. For all these years, Sammy had never dared dream of a talent like Isaac's. He wanted the boy for himself. He coveted his talents, the reflected glory that comes with training an authentic champion. He didn't want to share him with Daisy. He was scheming to get rid of her. This was his first clumsy move. She needed to protect herself.

'Are you sure you're all right?' said Imo.

'I'm fine.'

'What if he does it again?'

Daisy thought of the gun in her sock-drawer. 'He won't.'

From then on, Daisy grew more guarded with Sammy, while he grew more clownish and effusive. Nothing about Sammy was as funny as it seemed. He relied on being underestimated; it was cover for his monkeyshines. Daisy debated with herself, wondering what to do. She was still wrestling with this dilemma when she and Sammy and Isaac were over-taken by a more immediate crisis, for after one more victory, on his seventh professional outing, Isaac lost.

Seventeen

Isaac had come down with food poisoning a week before the fight. For thirty-six hours he had the runs, couldn't keep food or fluids down and was unable to train.

Daisy told Sammy to cancel the fight, at whatever cost; but while Sammy agreed in principle, he procrastinated until the morning of the fight, when Isaac got out of bed, pronounced himself fit and insisted on going through with it.

It was pure fighter's bravado. Isaac had slept poorly, was dehydrated and well under his usual weight, but everyone, including Isaac himself, had been seduced by the myth of his invincibility. That myth was shattered at Alexandra Palace in the sixth of the scheduled eight rounds, though not without a whiff of controversy.

At the close of the fifth, trailing well behind on points, the useful Dexter Ojemba threw a deliberate low punch that struck Isaac flush on his protective cup. Isaac turned to the referee to complain, dropping his hands as he did so, and was immediately caught on the jaw with a right hook that deposited him on the seat of his pants. That time the bell and lights saved him from further punishment. He flopped breathless on to the stool. Daisy asked if he was all right. He nodded at her, but his eyes seemed cloudy and unfocused. Instead of giving Isaac instructions, Sammy was wrangling with the referee, shouting at him to dock at least a point from Ojemba's score-card for the low blow. The referee ignored him. There was a buzz in the crowd now, as the audience scented an upset.

Isaac's head still wasn't clear when he went out for the next round. His body tingled along one side from the force of Ojemba's hook and he had no feeling at all in his right foot. He hoped to keep Ojemba at a distance with his jab while he collected himself, but his opponent had other ideas. Ojemba leaped inside on the bell, leading with his lowered head and driving Isaac against the ropes. The boy suddenly looked frail, his pale limbs skinny and vulnerable. There were boos from the crowd and Sammy was incandescent: 'Referee! He's butting him, ref! What is he, a billy-goat?' Isaac tried to break the clinch. Ojemba freed his left hand and used it to punch Isaac in the balls. Aching from the blow, Isaac again turned to the referee to intercede. This time, Ojemba's right hook put him unconscious to the canvas.

It was a bad knockout. Isaac lay completely still for several seconds and the paramedics entered the ring. Something inside Daisy went icy cold. Isaac came to and was helped to his corner on the groggy legs of a drunkard, unresponsive to any of Daisy's gesticulations. Sammy fussed and protested. 'It's a bloody disgrace!' As Isaac's condition improved, he grew more and more indignant, vowing to appeal against the outcome. Daisy was more concerned for Isaac.

The fight doctor checked Isaac again in the dressing room, dilating his pupils with a tiny flashlight.

'You'd better check his knackers and all while you're at it,' fumed Sammy. 'What's that ref thinking? I tell you something: it's a good thing he's already had kids, because I don't think his tackle will be functioning normally after the beating they got tonight. Losing's one thing. But this – it's a travesty.'

The doctor clicked off his torch. 'You're out for thirty days, I'm afraid. Bad knockout. No headshots in sparring, Sammy.'

'I don't need you to tell me how to do my job,' was Sammy's indignant response. 'If you want to teach someone their job, have a word with the effing referee.'

Daisy went outside. The defeat had shaken her. The image of Isaac's unconscious face had stirred up darker memories.

She stood on the steps of Alexandra Palace. It was as though the punch that had knocked out Isaac had snapped Daisy into a sharper awareness of her own predicament. *What have I become?* she thought. What could matter more than Isaac's well-being? Three days earlier had been the anniversary of her wedding. It was autumn again. Sycamore leaves as big as dinner plates rattled in the wind. She had been fooling herself, fleeing from the ghastly futility of her own life into a fantasy of revenge. Daisy Adams, Daisy Polidoro, whatever she called herself, it couldn't hide the truth that she'd been dead for years and this sorry afterlife was no consolation for anything. Something the size and shape of a fighter's glove choked her heart. But amid the anger and bewilderment was a sense of liberation. For the first time she could remember, she realized she loved something more than she hated Joel Heath.

'What happened to the boy?' The voice belonged to Loverboy Edwards. His dreadlocks strained like a coiled octopus inside his multicoloured woollen bonnet. He was wearing a green tracksuit which he had customized with some heraldry of his own devising. Fabric letters on the back of his jacket spelled out 'The Scientist' above coloured patches cut to represent a boxing glove being souped up with a screwdriver and a can of Three-in-One oil.

Daisy was hostile, resentful of his intrusion. 'He shouldn't have been fighting,' she said. 'He had food poisoning.'

'*Raas.* He looked tight, even before he got knocked down. It's not food poisoning. It's Sammy poisoning. He should never have lost to that boy.'

'Thanks for the words of comfort,' said Daisy.

'Why should you feel better? He boxed like an amateur – looking to the referee to get him out of trouble. People will catch him like that. They're going to see what happened tonight. They're going to know they can't win in a clean fight, so they'll hit on the break, in the clinch, butt, throw elbows, bite, punch his testicles. The boy needs to be able to fight ugly, out of his comfort zone. He's got to use his dark side. But by the looks of you, now he's lost you don't care what happens to him.'

'You couldn't be more wrong. I do care about what happens to him. Whether he boxes or not, I'll be there for him.' Daisy resented the old man's hectoring tone. She couldn't resist a dig. 'And I tell you something else – when he walks away from this sport, he'll be able to see out of both his eyes.'

Loverboy drew his head back slightly, and looked at her in surprise, as though Daisy had tried to poke him with something. 'You don't know what you're talking about.'

'No? Well, you certainly helped Tate get in touch with his dark side – it must be everything he sees out of his left eye.'

'Stupidness.' Loverboy shook his head angrily.

'You've got a nerve lecturing me. I watched the fight. You sent Tate out, round after round, in a fight he couldn't win.'

'You'd have done the same.'

'No.'

'Tate was outpunching him five to one. Tate could have licked him any day of the week.'

'We must be talking about a different fight. I'm talking about the one where it looks like Tate has gone through a windscreen.'

Loverboy took a sharp breath, as though he'd been winded. 'There were reasons for that.'

'I though the fighter's safety was paramount.'

'I told you there were reasons.'

'Well, you should take another look at the tape. You should look at Tate's eye – in fact, you should look at Tate, because I don't think there are ever good enough reasons for *that*.'

Loverboy suddenly looked deflated. She thought he was about to burst into tears. He seemed so crestfallen that she began to apologize, excusing herself because of her upset and the manner of Isaac's defeat.

The old man shook his head. 'We couldn't believe what was happening. Each round Tate came back to the corner still just nicking it on points but each time he looked worse. "Every time he hit me, boss, it hurt like hell. He don't look like much, but he can bang!" I'm telling him, "Use your science! Stand off and box the man." Every round, same thing.' Loverboy shivered; his tracksuit was thin and silky and a chilly wind was blowing across the city. 'I couldn't believe Tate lost. When the fight stopped, I go and shake the boy's hand. I grabbed his glove like this.' He closed his hand like a pincer on an imaginary glove. 'My fingers went straight through to his knuckle. You understand? No padding in the glove – that's why Tate's face looked how it did. I'm gripping it tight, calling to the referee, but it's all slippy with sweat and vaseline, and Sugar just twisted it away, like this, still smiling at me, back to his corner and they cut them off. I'm still fussing to the referee, so he goes over to them and they showed him a different pair of gloves they'd just dropped in the bucket. But the laces were fresh, the inside didn't even smell of sweat. The ref's not interested. "Bring it up with the Board." What could I do? Sugar was fighting for Costello. Tate said to leave it: "I'll win the rematch, boss." I'll win the rematch, boss. But the eye, you see. The eye was ruined.'

'What happened to Sugar?'

'Dead,' said Loverboy.

'Well, who wrapped his hands that night? Who was in his corner?'

Loverboy held her gaze without speaking.

'But who was it?' she persisted.

'Kimball,' he said, as though he couldn't bring himself to utter Sammy's Christian name.

Eighteen

Daisy had wanted to appeal against the result of the Ojemba fight. Her indignation was shared by some in the audience, but others felt the outcome reflected Isaac's inexperience.

Defend yourself at all times. The phrase was part of the referee's instructions. Daisy had translated it half a dozen times without giving thought to what it meant in practice. Her mind was always on other things: the physical closeness of Isaac's opponent, self-consciousness about being up on stage, anxiety about the outcome, and, overwhelmingly, the sense of anticipation in the crowd, the feeling of salivation, that the auditorium was in some way an enormous stomach, hungry for bones and blood.

Always defend yourself was how she translated it. She would form the signs reflexively, knowing that Isaac wasn't really paying attention. It was a ritual, like grace, like the mumbled words of the prayer which she muttered as she dipped under the rope leaving Isaac to face his opponent. The ring, she felt, was sacred space, holy in some way to one of the forgotten religions of mens' hearts, whose god or gods demanded blood sacrifice. Whereas Isaac had been naïve, Ojemba's opportunism had been in keeping with the spirit of the ring's presiding deity.

Still, Daisy reproached herself bitterly for the defeat and the knockout. She had failed to protect him, been too ready to listen to Sammy, too wrapped up in her own plans to see how vulnerable Isaac was to a millisecond's inattention.

Meanwhile, Sammy was full of the usual boosterish talk –

defeats that test your mettle, you'll come back a better fighter, this could be the making of you, the others will stop ducking you now.

The loss served to crystallize all Daisy's doubts about Sammy: the porn movie, Jonah's horrendous stoppage, the lack of imagination in training. At best, he was guilty of an oversight, of being blasé; and at worst, if Loverboy was right, he had conspired to blind someone.

Daisy had to steal the tape again to confirm the truth of what Loverboy had told her. She watched it through to the end this time, winding and rewinding the crucial parts to authenticate the old man's story. She even screened it for Imo, without telling her why, hoping her innocence and fresh eyes might latch on to a detail that had passed her by. The critical sequence of events was this: the fight concluded, Loverboy shook Sugar's left hand; Sugar, expecting no more than a perfunctory handshake, had already turned towards the other cornerman, but Loverboy would not let go – the surprise on his face changed quickly to a look of agitation. The camera cut across to the other side of the ring, where Tate was congratulating someone in Sugar's corner. Back now to Loverboy, who had been prised away from Sugar's glove, but was clearly angry. Then a press of bodies swept into the ring for the formal announcement of victory, and Loverboy disappeared from sight. Sugar gave his post-fight interview alone at ringside, the sweat on his face gleaming from the harsh television lights. He paid tribute to Tate, looked forward to his next fight, thanked his promoter Ron Costello, his trainer Carl Vent, and his cornerman Sammy Kimball. It was circumstantial evidence that Loverboy was telling the truth, but it was hardly definitive. And Imo wasn't much help.

'He just looks like he's angry that his man lost,' was Imo's reading of the freeze-framed image of Loverboy's furious stare. 'That's what men look like when they lose.'

'But look – watch his hand go in,' said Daisy, as she

rewound. 'He's reacting to the handshake. It's like there's something wrong with the glove.'

'Like what? You think there's a spanner in it? Like in cartoons? Do they really do that?'

'In all the other fights, even when he was hit a lot, Tate never bruised like that. He was like Ali . . .'

'Who's Ally?'

'Muhammad Ali. The Greatest? Floats like a . . .'

'Yeah, okay – I just didn't hear you.'

'He didn't mark easily.'

'Yeah?' said Imo, who found it hard to summon enthusiasm for this ancient injustice and was leafing surreptitiously through a copy of *Hello!* magazine.

Before she confronted Sammy, Daisy wanted to make her misgivings clear to Isaac. Whatever she did next would have repercussions on his and Una's life. She drove over to Hillingdon one Sunday afternoon.

Isaac was stretched out on a sofa in his tracksuit watching horse racing with the sound off. He bet small sums, but even if he hadn't, he would still have enjoyed the spectacle. He would sometimes own up to an ambition to be a jockey. As a thoroughbred himself, he had a secret kinship with the horses.

Daisy explained to him why she had come: she was beginning to have grave doubts about Sammy's competence as a trainer. The recent loss made it impossible for her to ignore them any longer. She didn't want to work with him any more. But she was willing to set her doubts aside if Isaac wanted to carry on working with Sammy.

Isaac said he had been disappointed when Tate left. He felt that Tate had had a lot to teach him. He didn't blame him for the Ojemba fight, but he didn't think Sammy was showing him anything new in training. It was always the same old story. 'Same old story' – he actually said the words, mumbling them as though through a mouthful of marbles. But, he pointed out, Sammy had a contract with them.

128

Daisy said that she could take care of it.

You and Tate were the ones who believed in me, said Isaac. *I'll never forget that. I trust you. I'll do what you think is best.* Una nodded in agreement.

Daisy felt the awful burden of their unconditional trust. They were like a pair of children. She thought with a sudden pang of her own mother: this is what it must mean to be a parent – the anxious determination not to propagate the bitterness and grief of your own life, the difficult balance between preparing someone for life in the real world of blame and hatred and disappointment, and the deep wish to spare them even the knowledge of unnecessary misery. She wanted Isaac and Una – especially Una – never to feel pain. The task seemed impossibly heavy. At that moment, it no longer mattered to Daisy if Heath lost or won, lived or died. She owed it now to Isaac and Una and Esme that she repay their trust. She was embroiled in their destiny now; it was no longer just an instrument for her own. 'I'll go and talk to Sammy,' she said. 'I'll let you know what happens.'

Daisy burst in on Sammy in the back room he used as an office. She swung the door open without knocking and caught him open-mouthed, telephone receiver in hand. Seeing the expression on her face, he frowned and set the phone down with a clunk. 'Wasn't expecting to see you in today. To what do I owe the pleasure?'

'I'm firing you as Isaac's coach.'

'Well, this is all a bit sudden. Don't you think you're being a bit hasty? We're all gutted about the Ojemba fight, but six and one is a fair old record. You know how good he is. He'll bounce back.'

'It's not just about that, Sammy. He's outgrown you. Isaac is straight as an arrow. He needs to be around people who are straight . . .' She let the sentence hang unfinished.

'Meaning I'm not straight? That's a bit harsh. In this game, there's not many of us who haven't stooped at some time to skulduggery. But I'm far from the worst.'

'We don't need to go into it, Sammy.'

'I'd like to know what you're trying to say about me.'

Daisy didn't want a scene, but Sammy was determined to make this as difficult as possible for her. 'The Geoff Sugar fight? Ring any bells? You were in his corner.'

Sammy squinted as he tried to capture his recollections of the fight. 'Ancient history. Too many punches to the head to remember that far back, Daisy. *Pugilistica dementia*. It's buggered me for pub quizzes.' Sammy pretended to lose the thread of his thoughts. 'What were we talking about?'

'Geoff Sugar. You doctored his gloves. Tate lost his eye.'

'Oh, honestly.' Sammy shook his head in exasperation. 'You've been talking to Loverboy, haven't you?'

'I watched the tape of the fight.'

'Well, since you mention it, it does sound familiar. Do you remember it, Tate?' Sammy inclined his head and looked past Daisy to the far corner of the office.

Daisy turned around. Tate was sitting in the armchair behind the door. He looked rested and fit, tanned and somehow younger. He had let his hair grow a little longer and it softened his lean face.

'Hello, Daisy,' he said.

'You . . .' She was taken aback. Something about Tate was different. There was a lightness about him, as if he'd shed some invisible burden he'd been carrying, the air of anxiety that had crackled around him like the onset of a migraine. 'Sammy doctored the gloves. I'm sorry to be the one to tell you, but it's better you know.'

'It wasn't Sammy's fault,' said Tate.

'It was Sugar what done it,' said Sammy. 'I wasn't to know. I was a jobbing cornerman. I was in it for twenty quid and a ringside seat. Terrible situation. I was cut up about it. We all were. What with Tate losing the eye and all.'

'But why wasn't there an inquiry? Why didn't the Board do anything?'

'Some things are better hush-hush,' said Sammy. 'Tate's been taken care of. Ron's looked after him. I've looked after him.'

'No,' said Daisy. She glanced at Tate, wanting to see some anger in him, furious on his behalf, impatient with his placidity.

'We kept it quiet,' said Tate mildly. 'It was the best thing.'

'Who said? Sammy?' There was no denial. 'He's envious of you, Tate. Do you see that? He envied what you had, and he fooled you into betraying your own talent.'

Sammy clucked his tongue and went over to the low grey filing cabinet that stood in the corner of his office.

Tate looked at his hands. He said softly, 'Envy me? Who'd be that stupid?'

Sammy clanged the drawers. 'Here's your blooming contract. Do what you want with it. You'll live to regret it, though. Too much smoking the wacky baccy with Loverboy. It's made you paranoid. He thinks he's a matchmaker too, you know. He couldn't match the cheeks of my arse. Tell him that. From me.'

Daisy took the proffered contract. She kept her composure until she had left the gym, but outside she had to stop and lean against a wall because her legs were shaking. She was dry-mouthed. When she had recovered a little, she walked along the canal for a while to give her racing thoughts time to slow down.

Two men were using boathooks to dredge objects from the murky water. They'd landed a fridge door and two children's bicycles all strung with weeds, reeking and riverish. Daisy kept walking.

'Daisy?' It was Tate's voice behind her. He approached her shyly. The fish-scale over his left eye glimmered with the day's dying light.

'Where have you been?' she asked.

'It's a long story,' he said.

'I don't understand you. If someone did that to me . . .'

Tate stared at the canal. 'Costello visited me in hospital. Promised me fifty, ended up giving me five. You know how it is. Boxing.' He shrugged. 'I'm tired of being angry about it. I've been angry for years. I felt like boxing owed me a living. I've lost friends because they've nagged me to quit. I couldn't let go of it. But I couldn't fight, and who was going to let me train a champion? You know? Sammy gave me work because he was sorry for me. I was all right with the real cynical losers, but whenever someone a bit talented came along, like Wes, I turned into a monster. Because he wasn't me. Because I'd fucked up my chance.'

They fell into step. There had been times, Tate explained, in his years at the gym, when he had come across young fighters of genuine promise. He had been merciless with them on the padwork, called them lazy if they slacked off from pounding the heavy bag, made them spar with the biggest, hardest punching fighters, and told their opponents not to hold back. On two occasions, the boxers had simply lost interest, declared Tate a psycho and stopped coming. Then there was Wesley. Wesley got the message. Wesley understood, or was needy enough to accept Tate's love as the real thing. Tate would bash him up in the ring, throw things at him when he felt he was being lackadaisical, push him to train so hard that several times he threw up. It was a side of Tate, normally so laid back, that puzzled the other boxers. They had heard him shouting himself hoarse at Wesley: 'I'm not going to be with you in the ring! You've got be your own sergeant major, you've got to kick your own arse over the obstacle course!' And most tellingly: 'You're wasting your god-given talent!'

'That night he lost to Heath was when I started to unravel proper. The night you . . .' He wasn't sure how to describe it. 'Saved me, I suppose. Then Isaac. All the hope of that and then Sammy took over. I kept asking why. Why? I was always look-ing for reasons. For reasons and someone to blame. But I've let it all go. I don't even ask why any more. I'm not angry about the eye. I was washed up anyway, Daisy, drinking.' Tate sighed. 'I shouldn't have been allowed to box. It was bad luck, that's all. Bad luck. Who knows? Might have ended up worse off if I'd carried on boxing in the state I was in. I don't regret it. Bad luck is all. Maybe not even that. Maybe it was for the best.' He turned his head. 'Want to know something I *do* regret?'

Daisy felt herself blushing. She wanted to say *No*.

Tate stooped to rummage in the bag he had set down on the towpath and held something up to Daisy, who squinted at it in the fading light. 'The mafia book?' She started to laugh.

'I must owe a thousand quid in fines.'

'Luckily, you're speaking to the right person.' They set off together westward, past the supermarket and the painted narrowboats, towards the setting sun, whose shirred reflection shone in the still water as it descended in the orange sky. 'Did you actually read it?'

'Four times.' There was that palpable change in Tate. He seemed easier with himself, comfortable at last in his own skin. Daisy envied his calm. 'So,' he said, 'what are you going to do now?'

Nineteen

Ron Costello was the only child of loving parents. His father Artie had run a dry-cleaning and invisible mending business in the East End. By the mid 1970s, he had built up such a reputation for the delicacy of his work that he had become the dry-cleaner of preference for some of the most powerful people in the land: after all, the British Establishment is founded on fancy dress. Artie's customers brought him formal regimental uniforms, judicial attire, ecclesiastical vestments. Costello senior pioneered special procedures for cleaning ermine, velvet, horsehair, fur and brass buttons. The rumour was that he even received consignments from Buckingham Palace – personal items that he'd had to sign the Official Secrets Act to be allowed to clean. At the state opening of Parliament, Artie would watch the Lords processing into Westminster and admire his own handiwork. He was justifiably proud that in one generation, his discretion and resourcefulness had brought him not only wealth, but a position of eminence in his profession. On the proceeds of the business, Costello Senior was able to move out of London to a pleasant little village in Kent and send Ron to a series of private schools, entertaining the hope that his son would achieve great things.

But Ron was a puzzle to his mystified parents, a cuckoo's egg. He grew up tetchy, vain and violent. He terrorized the village infant school: 'Ronald's poor self-control has been a source of friction with the other children.' He was turfed out of his prep school after the masters found him running a protection racket: '. . . my personal regret that your son's charisma has blinded me to the extent of his ruthlessness.' And he was ordered to see a psychiatrist after an apparently motiveless attack on a man at a car-wash.

It seemed as though Ron's dandyish sartorial choices were all that remained of the ambitions his father had cherished for him; but over time, Ron was one of those to whom boxing offered a second chance – a chance to make his way in a world where poor impulse control, a ruthless and charismatic personality and the almost total absence of empathic awareness were positive assets.

It would be hard for anyone to feel their way into the minimalist interior of Ron Costello's emotional life. Most people's internal worlds are messy and crammed with objects that induce shame, and joy, and sadness. Ron's was like a hotel bedroom. You might be in there for days, and still be no nearer to understanding what drove him. All that conscienceless energy. Where did it come from?

Ron's rise in boxing was in keeping with his character: he was savage and undistractable, and consistently underestimated by people who found him comical.

In its grandiosity, its disregard for accepted behaviour, its enslavement to appetite, so much of what we call evil is funny. It just ceases to be amusing when its fist is closing round your throat, and its absurd uniforms are goose-stepping down your avenues, or its warm breath is whispering threats at you through a spy-hole.

There was often laughter around Ron Costello, but it was the laughter of farce that turns us all into psychopaths for an instant. That withdrawal of empathy that makes someone else's physical humiliation funny gives you an inkling of the arid space inside Ron Costello, like a desert under a rolling bank of cloud, changing swiftly between rage, and boredom, and euphoria.

Ron was so desperate to be given a high-roller's suite when he went to Las Vegas that January that he sent Terry Mansour out ten days early to schmooze the appropriate contacts. Terry shared not only his boss's taste in bespoke suits but also his fondness for voyeuristic sex acts that bordered on the non-consensual. Ron was obsessed – a word that somehow only reveals its full plumage when applied to a person like him – with being BIG in the States. That's how he thought of it: BIG, like that, and if you could spell it with stars and stripes and an oompah band, and dangle a woman in a feathered head-dress and a glittery bikini from the letter G, you would be closer still to the word he saw in his imagination.

Ron loved riding in a limo down the strip, air-conditioning turned way up, smoking a big cigar; having his picture taken with bemused celebrities at the MGM Grand and Caesar's Palace. Terry also liked Vegas, but Ron clicked with it: he saw its deeper meaning, a triumphant Sodom, unrestrained by the limits of reality or taste, hotels that replicated Venice, New York, Camelot, in a thirsty desert. Ron even dreamed of having his own hotel there. He'd thought about it a lot: Churchill Towers he would call it, in honour of Winston, the greatest ever Briton, the last Prime Minister to be able to stand nose-to-nose with the Americans. Ron would fill it with Churchill memorabilia and dioramas of crucial World War Two battles, and staff the bars with Churchill lookalikes serving blood, sweat and tears cocktails. The fruit machines would be designed to embody the overall theme – with odds that reflected some of Churchill's wartime gambles and a computerized voice that would remind the player: 'You have just lost ten thousand civilian lives.' And the best part of all was this: the whole thing was to be housed in a giant crystal edifice shaped like the great man's famous salute – an enormous victory sign, no doubt, but also two giant fingers which, in the absence of a deeper philosophy, encapsulated Ron Costello's message to the world.

Not for the first time, Ron outlined the idea for Churchill Towers to Terry as they drove in from the airport. Terry listened respectfully, then said, 'I tell you what else would be good, Ron. Hitler Towers, shaped like a, like a . . .'

'Like a big arm, yeah.' Ron made a tentative Nazi salute. 'Hitler Tower, really, because you'd only need the one.'

'Depends how you did the fingers,' said Terry.

'Not really,' said Ron. 'It's just one structure. Look, he didn't Sieg Heil like that –' This time Ron splayed his fingers as he saluted. 'See? That's just waving.'

The driver of the limousine angled his mirror to get a better look at his two passengers. They cruised along in silence for a minute or two before Ron spoke again. 'Purely on greatness terms, purely on greatness, there should be an Hitler Tower.'

'Oh yeah,' said Terry. 'I'm not saying I agree with what he done . . .'

'No,' said Ron. 'Purely on greatness.' He paused for a moment. 'The trouble is, the Jews would never let you build it.'

One big difficulty besetting Ron's American ambitions was that he was, in relative terms, a nonentity. Hype it how he might, Ron could rarely persuade the people in charge of the world rankings that he had his hands on a superstar. He had a couple of gimcrack versions of world titles, some useful super-middleweights, but no fighter whose gifts or charisma would persuade the average punter to disfigure his house with a satellite dish; no one that eleven-year-olds would want to wake up at three a.m. to cheer for; no one, in fact, who could win Ron much credibility with the Vegas big boys.

Everywhere, of course, Ron was met with a cordial welcome, but he could never shake off the feeling of being a country cousin. He and Terry were kept waiting for meetings, and when they finally got in to see someone, he would invariably get their names mixed up, call Ron Terry, and Terry Ron. Ron hated it. Ron being Ron, he would rather be feared and loathed than condescended to by his wealthier and more powerful US counterparts.

Still, these trips were never a total bust. Ron and Terry matched some of their boys with lucrative but rather inconsequential fights, got two fighters undercard places on the bills of world title contests and worked off their disappointments with well-remunerated call-girls.

Back in London, Ron could play the tyrant again. But there was something hollow about it now. He longed for a seat at the top table. It was hard, after Caesar's Palace, to summon up much enthusiasm for Goresbrook Leisure Centre. Everyone knew Las Vegas. Who on earth had ever heard of Becontree?

At least, Terry enthused, terrestrial television was getting excited about boxing again. Terry had a point. Satellite broadasters paid well, but the boxers remained largely unknown to the general public. Most people had no idea who was the current British heavyweight champion, never mind the lighter weights. Greed and short-termism had made the sport a marginal interest.

But now the BBC was looking for promoters to help put together a series of live boxing matches to be broadcast late on Saturday nights. Ron was more cautious than Terry, but he felt it augured well. They could build up some of their fighters with domestic exposure, work up a head of steam, get the tabloids behind them. Then he would have something to show the Americans. BIGness couldn't elude him for ever.

Preliminary meetings were promising, but the young executives in charge of the programme – a woman called Karen and a man named Dinesh – turned out to have rather funny ideas.

Dinesh was waving a copy of *Boxing News*. 'We like this deaf kid.'

Ron took the paper from him. 'Let's have a look at that. Him? Plum? Blown-up bantamweight? No chin? Lost to the Ghanaian boy at Ally Pally?' Ron, of course, did not say he didn't promote him, but disparaged him instead and tried to press the claims of one of his own stable of boxers.

'We think he has crossover appeal,' said Karen. 'He's stylish, the whole disability thing, he's got a woman trainer. We're talking about someone who will appeal to the whole family.'

'Joel Heath's got family appeal,' said Ron. 'Loves his little

girl – tattooed her name up his arm in . . . What do you call
'em, Terry?'

'Runes.'

'Yeah, Sanskrit runes. All up here. Loves her to bits.'

'Without wishing to denigrate Heath,' said Dinesh, 'we've
all seen fighters like him. He appeals to people who already
like boxing. That's not going to do anything to change the fact
that the sport is . . . moribund.'

'Preaching to the converted,' glossed Terry.

'Yes, thanks, Tel,' said Ron, 'I know what "moribund"
means.'

'I think what Dinesh and I are saying,' said Karen, 'is that
we are looking for someone different. Heath is edgy, which is
great. We can't have enough edge. But we think Plum might
have something special, that X Factor, rising from adversity.
To be frank, he's someone we look at and see a potential
Sports Personality of the Year.'

'He's someone,' said Dinesh, 'who the public can take to its
heart.'

Karen smiled at him. 'Exactly.'

'How long have you been keeping this up your sleeve?' said
Ron, with as much 'edge' in his voice as Karen could possibly
have wished for. 'Plum's a nothing, a nonentity. When did you
get this mammoth hard-on for Isaac Plum?'

Both Dinesh and Karen now seemed reluctant to speak.

Ron brought his meaty fist down on the table. 'Come on!'

'I was . . . er . . .' stammered Dinesh, 'flicking through
Boxing News before you came. And I saw the article.'

'*Today?*' Costello's voice cracked into an incredulous falsetto. 'You mean you've never even fucking heard of him before
today?' He paused. The muscles in his jaw were visibly clench-
ing and unclenching. He stood up suddenly and slammed his
hand down on to the table. 'And now he's Sports Personality
of the Year? In your minds? A pair of fucking kids?' Ron
picked up a mug and used it to punch in the screen of Dinesh's
computer. 'A. Pair. Of. Fuck. Ing. Kids.' A shard of glass cut

his hand and he slurped blood from the wound.

Dinesh whimpered as he gazed at the floor, trying to avoid Ron's stare.

Terry spoke in a low, admonitory voice, trying to claw back the covering over Ron's exposed lizard brain. 'Ron,' he said. 'Ronnie. You're switching.'

Ron went over to the open window and took five deep breaths, in through the nose and out through the mouth. He closed his eyes as he made the final exhalation, and then opened them and turned back to the room. His voice, while still irate, was now under control. 'You want *lovable* boxers? Boxers aren't lovable. Boxers are trained to brutalize each other. Boxing isn't about the Ali shuffle and playing the Widow Twanky in panto. It's about climbing through the ropes and squaring up to a man who wants to give you brain damage. And that's why people fucking love it. Because all day long that key in your back is wound tighter and tighter. Given up smoking? Round it goes. Got a speeding ticket? Round it goes. Missus moaning at you? Round it goes. Didn't get a rise? Tubes on strike? Round it goes, round it goes. And at the end of a day of that, you need to beat the shit out of someone. It's a biological necessity. But you can't. Because it's against the law. So what are you going to do? Because that key is wound so tight that if you don't hurt someone, you're going to die. Well, some people do die. They hold it all in and it kills them. Other people kill other people. They go to prison. Or you take drugs, or beat your wife. Or you can go to the boxing, thank God, and watch a licensed professional beat ten colours of shit out of the taxman, or your boss, or your mother-in-law, or whoever else you want to imagine coming out of the blue corner. And that spring unwinds inside you, and you wake up the next day ready for the bills and the train-strikes and the shit that would otherwise kill you. So don't tell me about lovable. Ninety per cent of people are fed up of being *lovable*. They want to be fucking killers. And *that's* what we're charging them for.'

A profound, inexpressible joy flooded Dinesh as it became clear that he would escape serious injury.

'Come on, Terry,' said Ron. 'I've had enough of this.'

The two men left the office and headed for the lift.

'I've got to say,' said Terry, 'I'm very impressed with your self-control.'

Back in the office, Dinesh swept up the broken glass. The brush smeared Costello's blood in streaks over the top of the desk. He shook his head and reached for some tissue paper.

'I know,' said Karen. 'You're thinking it too.'

'Thinking what?'

'We've got to find a way to work him into the coverage.'

The following day, Ron received a letter from Karen which said: 'Thanks so much for coming in to see us. Dinesh and I though the meeting was fantastic. We wondered if you'd had any more thoughts on the availability of Isaac Plum.'

Twenty

Where had Tate been? Sammy was partly right. Sammy's cunning and the disappointment over losing Isaac Plum had indeed set him off on a bender of epic proportions. It lasted a week. This time no one saved him. No one pleaded with him to stop, no one tried to break his fall by appealing to his sense of guilt; there was no one to call him feckless. The indifferent world had its back to him, had always had its back to him. A voice said: Suit yourself. Go in the tank. Choose your poison. Heroic drunken failure? Sure, we're serving plenty of those. Have a double. Double drunken failure. On the rocks?

Tate was falling, past the exitless blank walls of an elevator shaft, down and down and down.

Then he stopped drinking. Hung over – he would be for three days – he packed a bag and bought a ticket to Guatemala City. He had wanted to go to Guyana, his late father's birthplace, but he was so drunk that the travel agent misheard him. It came as something of a surprise to Tate that there was a country called Guatemala. Still, it was on the same page of the atlas as Guyana. There was some consolation in that.

He sobered up in Guatemala City, staying in a fleabag hotel near the Plaza Mayor, which he would wander round every day after eating beans and rice and reading a book about the mafia that he had borrowed from Daisy's library. After a week of this, he felt like going to a bar, but found his way to an English-speaking Alcoholics Anonymous meeting instead. There were about a dozen people, mainly US expats, and a black man in his sixties who spoke English with a Caribbean accent that made Tate homesick for London. They got talking afterwards and Tate asked where he was from.

'Here,' he said. His name was Edgar Ubaldino.

'Guatemala?'

'Livingston.'

Tate went to visit. The north-east of the country had a Caribbean coast that was predominantly black and English-speaking. He got a room with a family, lived for peanuts, started running in the morning with whichever local children wanted to tag along behind him, ate well, and napped in the steamy afternoons. It reminded him of his one childhood holiday to visit his father's family. Whenever he felt like drinking, he rang Edgar from a crackly payphone outside the general store. Whatever Edgar was doing, he would drop it and listen patiently. Tate, who could be taciturn in person, found it easier to pour his heart out over the phone, the handset hot against his ear, gazing at his bare feet on the sun-bleached boards. He fed handfuls of quetzales into the coin slot and talked about all sorts of things: his parents, Sammy, boxing, Isaac, Daisy – Daisy a lot.

After he had been there a month, he went back to the capital and had supper with Edgar. He told him he wanted to see more of the country.

'Fine,' said Edgar. 'But get yourself a mobile phone. Whenever you feel like drinking – and you will – call me.'

Tate travelled by beaten-up buses with engines that strained on the mountain roads to Huehuetenango, Chichicastenango, Lake Panajachel, and across the border to Honduras. He loved the green hillsides, the ramshackle buses, the twilight fogged with woodsmoke from cooking fires, the clear bright air of mountain towns, the volcanoes. And everywhere he had the same thought: why didn't anyone tell me about *this*?

In Antigua, the old capital, a twenty-year-old student from Farnham seduced him after chatting him up in a café. She smuggled him back to the house where she was lodging with a local family while she studied Spanish in the town.

'You're lovely,' she said, snuggling up to him afterwards.

'I'm old enough to be your father,' he said.

'I already have a father,' she said.

He had to sneak out at six a.m., before the family got up for breakfast. Walking back along the deserted cobbled streets, heady with bougainvillea and fringed with crumbling colonial churches, he thought: *Who am I?* He didn't have the faintest idea any more. And yet he had never felt better.

All in all, Tate was away four months. He left Guatemala and travelled all the way down to Tierra del Fuego, before looping back up to Guyana at last; but he made sure he flew home via Guatemala City so he could say goodbye to Edgar in person. 'What am I going to do without you?' he asked.

'Get a sponsor at home,' said Edgar. 'And come back and visit. The world is smaller than it used to be.'

'Not to me it isn't,' said Tate. 'It just got enormous. And all this time I've told you everything about me. I hardly know anything about you.'

'What do you want to know?'

'I don't know where to begin.'

Edgar smiled. 'Then don't. Just pass it on.'

Back in London, Tate thought about college and he thought about going away again. In the meantime, he looked for work. He ended up giving boxercise classes at a gym near Chalk Farm. He was a good teacher, and City types preparing for white-collar tournaments started paying high prices for his services as a personal trainer. But the Chalk Farm gym was crowded: up until seven-thirty every weekday evening it was restricted to members of the youth club – children as young as seven and eight bounded around the rings while Tate's impatient stockbrokers chafed to get started. Tate would have to take his clients running up Primrose Hill while the young club members snapped towels at each other in the showers. 'There must be another boxing gym that will have us,' said Raimundo, a venture capitalist from Brazil who was getting in shape for a fight against the creative director of an advertising agency. The modest and unflashy violence of their short bouts was some kind of compensation for lives they felt to be pedestrian. Gloved up, wearing headguards, tense with adrenaline, they were briefly heroes.

'I'll ask around,' said Tate. And so he went to Sammy's.

Not much had changed. A few ripe bags had dropped off their frayed twine and been reattached elsewhere. A few posters had migrated. There were three nice photos of Isaac Plum in action.

'And who do we have here? As I live and breathe. An apparition!'

'Hi, Sammy,' said Tate. Sammy looked nervous, as though he was having trouble keeping that big grin on his face. Tate wandered with his old partner to the back-room office. 'My picture's gone,' he said, gesturing at a bare patch of wall.

'It is. That's right. We needed the space. Some of our boys are doing rather well.'

'Like Plum, you mean?'

'Like Plum, and one or two others. But . . . now you're back . . .' Sammy opened a drawer and rummaged through it.

'I'm not *back* back, Sammy. I don't want to coach the pros.' Tate sensed Sammy's relief that he had no desire to rekindle their old professional relationship. 'I've got a white-collar thing in Camden. We need some space. I reckoned, charge them gym fees and you could turn the place over to us when you don't need it. Weekends. Mondays were always quiet.'

'Here it is,' said Sammy, holding up the picture of Tate, faded and worn thin where it had been folded. 'I'll get some pins.' The phone rang; it was Vovan, the part-time trainer, to say he had the flu and couldn't make it in.

Tate took the photo from Sammy's outstretched hand and sat down in the chair. Poor Tate, he thought, looking at the picture of himself with tenderness but no self-pity: there's some surprises waiting for you – and some bad, bad choices.

Just then, the door swung open and Daisy confronted Sammy.

*

'She's got the wrong end of the stick,' said Sammy as she left. 'She'll see sense and bring the boy back here. I just hope it's not too late.' He looked at Tate. 'The eye, you know – none of us knew. It was Sugar on his own. Crazy.'

'I know,' said Tate. 'It was my choice to keep fighting. I could have gone down.'

'Ron was gutted too.'

'I bet he was.'

'I didn't, what she said, *envy* you. Admired you is all. You had a gift, Smoke. I never did.'

'It was a burden, Sammy. I'm happier now without it. I'm better off outside boxing. This white-collar thing, it's just a stop-gap. I'm looking at other possibilities.' *Possibilities*. Tate almost smiled as he said the word.

'I'll check the schedules. See if we can squeeze you in.'

'Thanks,' said Tate. He already knew the answer would be no.

At the canalside, Daisy talked to Tate about her fears for Isaac.

'Keep him away from Costello,' was Tate's advice. 'It means going the long way round. Building up a record that they can't ignore. But it means he'll keep his independence. No stupid compromises. It's tempting to go for the short-cut. Especially when they won't give you the fights you deserve.'

'But with this loss, he'll never be unbeaten.'

'Ways round that.'

'Like what?'

Tate smiled. 'I had a couple of losses early on, like his. Loverboy took me to the States. We called it our Bum of the Month tour. Robbed a few graveyards for my opponents. I'm pretty sure there was a couple of them hadn't been in a boxing ring before. Not the noble science, but it's that or Costello.'

'Want to come?'

And that's what they did. The three of them got a cheap flight to Chicago and drove south. Isaac fought along the way –

modest opponents with dubious pedigrees, men who came into the ring with adverts for pizzerias and local garages daubed in paint on their naked backs. All the way along the Mississippi they travelled, notching up easy victories as they went. With Isaac at eleven and one, they reached delta country: scrubby flatland lined with catfish farms and clapboard houses, where they'd come for his final fight at a riverboat gambling complex in . . .

Twenty-One

'. . . Tunica, boss. TKO in the second.'

'Let me see that.' Ron snatched the *Boxing News* from Terry with a fat, damp hand. They were braising themselves in the dry heat of the Valley Hall sauna. Their dinner jackets hung in the tin cupboards in the marble hall above them. There was boxing later. Ron read aloud. '"Isaac Plum. Hero or hype? From our US correspondent."'

'"The deaf dazzler from Ye Olde England continues to shine against an array of mediocre talent . . . Not much more than a sparring session for the too-powerful Plum, it was still enough to showcase the classy talents of the wordless assassin whose quick hands have set the fight world talking. 'Toussaint Henry showed a lot of heart to come out after a difficult first round,' said Plum through his trainer and interpreter Daisy Adams, paying tribute to his journeyman opponent after the fight was stopped in two . . ."'

Ron had read enough. He shook his head. 'He's fought no one, you know that? They've taken him over there to fluff up his record against a load of stiffs. It brings shame on British boxing. It demeans the sport. No wonder the Yanks won't give us the time of day.' Ron stood up and adjusted himself under his towel.

'Shameful,' agreed Terry, following Ron's hairy back out of the hot room, through the changing area and through the plastic flaps of the steam room. The two men were enveloped in clouds of hot mist. Ron's flip-flops clacked against the tiles. Even sound seemed to slow down in the enervating steam. 'I thought Sammy trained him?'

'Nah,' said Ron, setting himself down on a marble bench. 'Silly bugger let him go after the Ojemba fight. Said he was shot. I said, "I don't know if he's quality, but he's far from shot."'

'Sammy's getting choosy in his old age. That's a bit of bad luck. It would be convenient if Sammy had him. He owes you a few.'

'You're having a laugh, incha?' The heat made Ron tetchy. 'After the work he's got off me over the years? More than a few.'

Terry reached down to refresh his face from the hose of cold water that trailed across the floor like the coils of a black mamba and inadvertently brushed the big pumpkin of Ron's stomach. He was quick to apologize: 'Sorry, boss.' Terry had witnessed too many scenes of Ron's switching to let himself forget that his boss had a fat man's prodigious strength and, when he unleashed it, the wild fury of a cornered baboon.

Ron hadn't even noticed. Deep in thought, he raked the sweat off his chest with a cupped hand. 'We'll get him anyway.'

The man on Ron's right couldn't restrain himself any longer. 'Excuse me, mate. You want to take your watch off. This heat and damp'll ruin it.'

Ron was suddenly alert. His eyes bulged like ping-pong balls and a lightning flash of purple vein pulsed at his temple as he brought his face to within an inch of the stranger's and spoke to him in a voice that was quiet but pregnant with menace: 'This chronometer, my friend, is precision engineered to withstand two hundred atmospheres of pressure. The bezel is tested to destruction by Swiss craftsmen. The crystal housing is the same as what they use in the binnacles of nuclear submarines. Right now, this timepiece is a lot healthier in here than you are. Now piss off.'

The man backed away into the mist.

Daisy, Tate and Isaac had two free days in New Orleans before flying home. Isaac bought presents for Una and Esme. Tate went on a voodoo tour of the cemetery. And Daisy stayed in her hotel room with a carrier bag of receipts, trying to figure out how much the trip had cost. She thought with regret of the money she had spent on the gun.

Isaac slept like a baby the entire homeward flight, his head lolling back on an inflatable neck pillow he had acquired in the city, along with a hand-held massage device and a radio for Esme that was shaped like a paddle-steamer. He was a gadget addict, with a child's appetite for novelty. It had taken both Tate and Daisy to shift him, once ensconced, from a ten-thousand-dollar leather massage chair.

'It's going to be like Christmas when he gets home with all that stuff,' said Daisy.

'I suppose.' Tate paused. 'We didn't have Christmas.'

'Meaning?'

'My family was very religious.'

'Religious how?'

'They joined this charismatic church when I was nine: eight hours of Sunday school, learning the Bible by heart, no Christmas presents.'

'Wow. And I thought my family Christmas was bad.'

Tate told Daisy about his family. 'Didn't see eye to eye with my dad,' he said. He meant that he hated him: hated him for being a hypocrite, for the beatings he'd had to endure for small infractions of house discipline. He hated him for leaving his mother, for blaming *her* when he left, declaring, 'I want to become a people!' when Tate's weeping mother begged him on her knees to reconsider his decision. Tate had been eleven. He understood that his mother was unable to have more children. He felt that in some way he was to blame.

And yet, Tate said, for all that hatred, he knew that his father had taken enormous pride in his achievements, telling acquaintances in Georgetown, 'That's my boy,' as he waved a photo of the Olympic squad he'd clipped from a newspaper.

The clipping had been in a jiffy bag of things sent by Tate's half-sister a few months after the old man's death. The clipping, a prayer book, a pair of wooden Eskimo sunglasses that Tate had carved in Cubs before he got kicked out for fighting, a photo of Tate's father in his Sunday best – this was all Tate had left of the old man. Tate's father had five more children in Guyana, then came apart in his forties and died a drunk: all that severity, all those laws and judgements, a corset of restraint that failed to control a wayward spirit.

'What about your mum?' asked Daisy.

Tate explained that his mother Evangeline had despised boxing, literally prayed for Tate to find some other use for his god-given ability, and when it became clear that the boy was unpersuadable, she refused to take any interest in his career, and banned boxing talk from the table. More than once, Tate had had to rescue his amateur trophies when, after a particularly ferocious argument, his mother had put them out with the garbage.

Isaac shifted in his seat without waking up. Tate marvelled at the ease with which he slept. 'Wish I could sleep like that,' he told Daisy. 'He's in the shape of his life. At his age, at that level of fitness, his body's like a high-performance car. It's like a different machine to what everyone else has. Runs better, sleeps better, eats better . . .' Tate trailed off uncomfortably.

'Yes,' said Daisy, 'I think I know what you were going to say. Shags better.'

'. . . everything better.' Tate cleared his throat. 'Trouble is – you don't notice it until it's gone. He doesn't wake up feeling healthy. He just feels normal.'

Tate picked up the in-flight magazine. He always seemed uncomfortable when the subject of sex came up.

Una surprised Isaac by meeting him at the airport with Esme. Isaac wept to see them. For a while he was comically torn between wanting to embrace them and wanting to tell Una about his victories. He carried his daughter triumphantly through the arrivals hall while Una pushed the trolley. Tate and Daisy watched them go, then went their separate ways.

*

Loverboy Edwards agreed to help them out and Isaac's training continued at a gym above a pub in Herne Hill. It was more rudimentary even than Sammy's, and the ceiling was too low to admit a raised ring, but it was perfectly adequate for Isaac. Tate and Loverboy shared the training between them. Daisy appeared less and less. A change had come over her. In spite of her pride in Isaac, her affection and respect for Tate, she sensed that the time for her to move on was drawing closer.

Slow, hard-won and unmistakable, a kind of peace had descended into Daisy, simultaneously expanding and sharpening her awareness of the life she was in, and she felt the murmuring of much older hopes and discontents, from a time before her obsession with Heath, or even her life with Stuart. *What do you want?* The question didn't ring so mockingly, stirring up dust in a tomb, but held out the promise of an unimagined future. She felt that she owed it to Isaac and Tate not to leave them in the lurch, and to put Isaac's career on as secure a footing as possible, but tentatively she began dropping hints about leaving.

She broached it one day at the gym with Tate, as he sat with her at ringside, watching Isaac and Loverboy work.

'I can't do this for ever,' she confided to Tate. 'I'm the wrong person to do this job. Someone else should take him from here.'

There was no one else, Tate told her. Loverboy would soon be too old. All the others were crooks.

'I fell into this, Tate,' she said. 'I keep asking myself what I'm doing here.'

Tate pleaded with her to give it a little more time. 'You're the only one he trusts,' he said.

In the ring, Loverboy glowed with the vitality of a much younger man as he worked on moves with Isaac

'Amazing, isn't it?' said Tate. 'I take back that thing about Loverboy being too old. I don't know what he grows on that allotment, but I wouldn't mind some of it.' He sat with her in silence and watched Isaac for a while, slippery as a dolphin, weaving around the old man. 'Have you noticed,' said Tate, 'he gives a little of his gift to everybody? Whatever Isaac's got, it rubs off on people.'

'Yes,' said Daisy, 'amazing what joy can be spread by thumping someone.'

'You know what I mean . . .'

'Tell me something, Tate. This isn't a complaint, because you've done a great job, but you're spending less time in the ring with him. I just wondered why.'

'My eye,' he said. 'It would just take a tap. I'm too old to learn braille.'

It struck Daisy that perhaps Tate too was envisaging a life for himself outside boxing, but Tate wouldn't elaborate, was only willing to admit that he was keeping his options open.

They negotiated a modest deal with the BBC to broadcast three of Isaac's fights. He would make his first television appearance fighting for the Southern Area Title against a non-Costello fighter called Bradley Keach. After the tour of the States, the pre-fight ritual had taken on the reassuring predictability of a family Christmas with, so far, none of the trauma or buried antagonisms.

Isaac, as challenger, came into the ring at ten o'clock on the dot to the sound of 'Kiss'. For the first time, Daisy could hear a crowd cheering for Isaac Plum, and he felt it too – as vibrations in the canvas that transmitted themselves up through the thin soles of his boots.

Tate and Loverboy had arranged to work the corner together, leaving Daisy solely to fill the role of interpreter.

Isaac seemed tight at the opening bell and perhaps overawed by the occasion. He fought cagily, but was probably just ahead on points when he went back to his corner.

Daisy's job was made more difficult by Loverboy's tendency to slip into patois when he got excited. 'Lickle bups with the lef' hand, trick him so. Den, 'it 'im stooshus right-hand-dem gaan-to-bed!'

Tate moved the old man tenderly to one side and calmed Isaac down, telling him to relax, soothing the boy with his soft words and easy manner. Tate understood all about nerves.

At the start of round two, it was as though Isaac had uncorked a magic flask. He poured it on, intoxicating Keach and the crowd with his dexterity, punches from all angles, dipping and swaying to make his opponent miss by millimetres, stepping like a cat around him on those quick, light feet.

The television audience could hear the commentator screeching excitedly: 'Keach is the notorious power-puncher, but Plum is neutralizing him by quite literally standing in Keach's shorts!'

Keach lasted two and half minutes of the second round before the referee intervened.

Daisy joined Isaac in the ring as he received the belt. She translated his standard thanks and commiserations, but this time Isaac departed from his script to catch her out.

'"There's only one word for the way I feel . . ."' said Daisy into the microphone on Isaac's behalf. Isaac spelled it for her on his fingers. Daisy looked uncertainly at him, but he was adamant.

'". . . *voluptuous!*"'

Twenty-Two

Money at last for Isaac, and growing acclaim. He was hardly a household name, but his odd conjunction of talent and disability spread his fame far beyond the usual boxing circles. Tate was right: Isaac's gift – whether you considered it to be his considerable skill, or his exceptionally free and open nature, or the two in conjunction – was benignly contagious. And for all the reasons that Dinesh and Karen had explained to Ron Costello, Isaac was felt by them to be a star-in-waiting.

Daisy worried a little about how huge success would affect him when it came. She knew how fame could shark out unpleasant dormant traits in otherwise likeable people. But Isaac's personality was robust, his marriage strong, and, deprived of words, he read people very carefully: their expressions and gestures spoke to him without their being aware of it. And yet, Isaac had a childish love of luxury and a poor man's unsatisfiable yearning for money. To get to Isaac, the most promising line of attack would be an appeal to his cupidity.

A week after the Keach fight, with future plans for the title defence still unannounced, Isaac returned from his morning run to find a brand-new Mercedes sports car siting outside the caravan and done up with a big white ribbon. Una stood on the front step, juggling Esme and looking uncomfortable. A strange man stood beside her.

Isaac slowed to a walk as he drew near. It was a hot and sunny day. He put his hands on his head to open his lungs as he caught his breath. *What's this? Who's he?* he asked.

A signing bonus, the man replied.

Isaac had grown accustomed to the mistakes and quirks of Daisy's signing, and he had learned to compensate for her, to intuit some of what she was unable to say. But this man's signing was crisp and fluent, and included the informal idiomatic signs that deaf people use only among themselves.

Deaf? asked Isaac

Deaf mum, the man replied.

Like her, signed Isaac, and pointed at his daughter.

After he'd satisfied himself that the visitor meant no harm towards them, Isaac excused himself and had a shower. When he emerged, the man suggested they all go for a drive. *Someone I want you to meet*, he said. He wouldn't tell them who it was, but the three of them chatted amicably as they drove, exchanging sign-names – the nicknames that deaf people use to save laborious finger-spelling when they communicate. Isaac's, of course, was Plum. Una's was One. Peter's was Naughty.

What about the baby? asked Pete.

She's too young to have a sign-name, Una said. *You can't have been 'Naughty' when you were her age.*

It's naughty from Naughton, my last name, said Pete.

Oh, said Una, visibly reassured.

Pete had said he'd better drive as he knew the way. Isaac was sitting in the front and playing with the electric windows, the heated seats and the air-conditioning.

They drove for almost an hour. Pete suggested stopping for a burger, but Isaac and Una wouldn't touch junk food. *Right*, said Pete, *very sensible*. Their bonhomie was starting to wear thin. Una was afraid to ask where they were going.

Pete turned the car down a private avenue lined with tall, shady trees, and parked in a semicircular driveway outside a large old house of red tiles and Kentish flint. Ron Costello emerged from the back of the house in knee-length shorts and a Versace shirt. He kissed Una's hand and paddled Esme's cheek with his fat thumb. 'What do you think of the car, champ? Come out to the pool, we've got the barbecue going.'

Pete obediently translated everything Ron said, all trace of his own personality having vanished.

There were three staff and half-a-dozen guests lounging and sipping drinks on the verandah. Ron introduced Isaac to them as 'the next undisputed welterweight champion of the world'. He nudged Naughty Pete. 'Make sure he got that bit.'

The pool was Olympic-sized, its aquamarine waters filtered and returned through the mouth of a huge medusa. 'What about that, Una, eh?' said Ron. 'A Versace pool!'

Una longed for a swim. Ron's girlfriend Janice took her indoors to find a costume. 'You're a slip of a thing, aren't you?' said Janice. 'However did they get that baby out of you? I hope I have something small enough.'

Ron's twin boys, Daniel and Solly, a pair of gloomy sixteen-year-olds, were detached from some electronic equipment and brought outside to meet the champion. They towered over Isaac.

'Look at the pair of you, sitting indoors on a day like this. Lardbuckets. You want to take a leaf out of the champ's book. He could go through your belt-loop, Solly.'

'Look who's talking,' said Solly.

'Can we go now?' said Daniel.

They trooped back indoors to darkness and high-tech destruction, pursuing each other round some infernal virtual labyrinth.

'"Their mum doesn't look old enough,"' said Pete, translating for Isaac.

'Eh?' Ron was preoccupied with his barbecue. 'Oh, Janice isn't their mum. Their mum's passed. Brown bread. Sad story.' He pressed down a chicken breast with a spatula.

Una emerged shyly in one of Janice's bikinis, her pale face half-hidden behind a pair of borrowed sunglasses.

Film star, Isaac signed. She gave his arm a loving punch.

After lunch, Janice took Una and Esme to pet the horses.

Ron led Isaac and Pete to the library. He showed a short corporate video about Costello Promotions on his plasma-screen television while Pete translated. When it was over, Ron poured himself a glass of brandy. 'Tell me honestly,' said Ron. 'Do you like this place?'

'"It's beautiful,"' translated Pete.

Ron swirled the brandy in his glass and teased his nose with the aroma. 'Cigar? No, of course not.' He gave a throaty chuckle. 'I'm glad you're here, Isaac. I'm glad you've seen where I live. A lot of people have the wrong idea about me. They think I'm some kind of monster. But most people never get to see the side of me that you've seen today.' Ron was getting a little teary, as he tended to when he talked of feeling misunderstood.

He went on: 'There are three things that are important to Ron Costello: family, family and family.'

'Sorry. I got "family". What are the other two?'

'It's just family, you fool,' Ron snapped at Pete. 'That's what I'm all about.'

'I'm just translating, Mr Costello,' said Pete.

'Oh, right. What I mean is, family three times over.'

Isaac looked puzzled. '"How many families do you have?"'

Ron warned his translator in a softly menacing voice, 'Peter.'

Pete took a moment to iron out the misunderstanding. Isaac made an 'Aha!' face and said in that bleary voice of his: 'Famly, famly, famly.'

'Yes!' said Ron. 'You and me, Isaac, we're both family men. We appreciate the same things. I like you, Isaac. And when I like someone, I like to share my good fortune with them.'

'"Thank you,"' said Pete. '"Now I wish I'd come in a bigger car."' Isaac did a light-hearted but untranslatable mime of himself denuding Ron's house of its valuables and driving them away in a lorry.

'The champ's not stupid,' said Ron. 'He knows what I'm talking about. I want us to be partners. I want to manage and promote you. We could be very good for each other.'

'"Thank you for lunch, Mr C. And thank you for showing

us your mouthwatering – erm, beautiful life. I feel like a real success coming here. It's a lovely feeling. If I was at the beginning again, I'd definitely start with you. But the thing is, I'm not at the beginning, and when I was, it was a big problem to get people to recognize me and take me seriously. Only two people believed in me. I know you love your family just like I do. But D-A-I-S-Y, Daisy, and T-A-T-E, they are my family."'

Ron went over to the drawer of his walnut desk. 'This is a contract. Take it with you. Read it. Think about it. If you decide to sign it, I will immediately give you the car you drove down here in, and guarantee you fifty thousand pounds a year for the next three years, exclusive of any prize money. That's how much I believe in you, Isaac.'

Isaac thought for a moment, then shook his head.

'"Thank you, but no thank you."'

'Tell him, Peter, that *no* is bad for my health.'

'"Yes, then."'

'That's more like it.' Ron clapped Isaac on the back and insisted he put the contract in his pocket.

Isaac and his family drove back to the caravan without communicating with each other, or Pete.

As the car departed, Isaac gave its paintwork a forlorn pat. The next day, he returned Costello's contract without a signature.

Twenty-Three

Now strange obstacles began to thwart Isaac's progress. At first they were low-level inconveniences, unremarkable for life in London, and even taken together they didn't seem to amount to a pattern of harassment; but over time the pressure mounted. Daisy's car was vandalized. The gym they used near Dulwich, having never received a complaint from its neighbours in fourteen years, was now visited six times by the council's environmental health officers. Then policemen showed up at Loverboy's allotment one Sunday and poked around among his plants and seedlings.

'Just a routine visit to have a look at what you are growing here, sir.'

Loverboy showed them his tomato plants, his purple-sprouting broccoli, his mangetouts and jerusalem artichokes. The officers were more interested in the contents of one of his polytunnels. 'What might this be?'

'*Eleutherococcus senticosum.*'

'Come again?'

'Siberian ginseng.' Loverboy snapped off a bit of the crinkly shrub. 'Take it. Put it in your tea. Your wife will thank me.' The gesture disarmed the policeman for a moment.

'I'm afraid I can't accept that.'

'I'm sorry, officer, of course – undue influence. Impeccable character of the British bobby.' Loverboy wiped the red soil from his fingers with a rag. 'Tell me something: you think because I have dreadlocks I must be growing draw? Or are you here to steal the secret of my prize marrow? Someone tell you black men grow a big marrow, officer?'

The policemen looked uncomfortable and retreated smartly to their waiting vehicle.

These minor hassles and setbacks – plus the managers who agreed in principle to bouts with Isaac and then suddenly got cold feet, and even the relative scarcity of sparring partners – all these alerted Tate and Loverboy to the reality of what was going on, but they tacitly agreed to keep Daisy in the dark lest word should get to Isaac of Costello's manoeuvrings.

And there were more dispiriting occurrences. Twice, fighters dropped out of contests with Isaac barely days before the weigh-in. The promoters in each case had no overt links to Costello, but that guaranteed nothing, and even Sammy couldn't be persuaded to put up replacements. 'Can't help you,' he said.

'But what about – ?' Tate rattled off five names, adequate welterweights who would earn decent money for the fight and help by keeping Isaac on television and in the public eye. Sammy had excuses for each of them.

It was galling for everyone, but agonizing for Isaac, who had trained so conscientiously and hungered for these opportunities. To Daisy, Tate dismissed it all as typical boxing snafus. With Loverboy he was more frank. He worried that the disappointments would upset Isaac's admirable equilibrium. 'We can't keep doing this to him. After a while he'll lose motivation, training so hard for fights that don't come off.'

Loverboy agreed. They almost never mentioned Costello's name in conversation: it was like the superstitions of trawlermen, or Russian hunters who know that saying the word 'bear' in the forest brings on just the encounter they most wish to avoid.

'Europe,' said Loverboy.

Tate pondered: he had a point. It would mean vacating the Southern Area Title, but victory would take them, in one audacious leap, out of Costello's clutches altogether.

Loverboy and Tate told Daisy of their idea and they started looking into it. They had preliminary talks with a promoter in Italy. Somehow, a boxing magazine got wind of what they were up to. The magazine was hungry for news about Isaac and they rang Tate out of the blue. Tate talked to the reporter for about ten minutes. He took the line that he and Loverboy were looking overseas for fresh challenges. There was nothing on the domestic scene, he said, that would really advance Isaac's education as a champion. It seemed wiser to Tate to sound unpatriotic than to give a hint of the real reason.

The day after the article appeared, a box of dead rats was delivered to Isaac's caravan. Isaac got back from his morning run to find Una in tears. The box, tied with a black silk ribbon, seemed to have arrived from nowhere. The six rats, fat and black, were curled plumply at different angles in the bright red tissue paper, as though they were half a dozen expensive mangoes. Two of the rats were on their backs, their feet drawn helplessly towards their bodies, their yellow teeth bared in an exhausted grimace.

Isaac was shaken and went to Daisy, coming clean with her about the episode with Costello and the unsigned contract. Daisy called an emergency meeting with Tate and Loverboy and demanded to know what was going on.

'Chances are it's not who you think it is,' said Tate.

'Costello, you mean?' asked Daisy.

Loverboy picked up the box and was on the point of heaving it into a garbage bag.

'What are you doing?' said Daisy sharply.

'Getting this out of my gym!'

'It's evidence,' said Daisy. 'I want to give it to the police.'

At the word 'police', a rapid glance passed between Loverboy and Tate: the look of mariners who know the sea so well they have an instant and exact apprehension of the approach of danger.

'It's the article, Daisy. Somebody thinks that I was dissing British boxing and they're taking it out on Isaac.'

'So this is another of those snafus? Come off it, Tate. I'm not stupid.'

'Well, it's not exactly normal, no . . .'

'Did you have any idea that Costello was interested in signing Isaac?' she asked.

'No,' Tate admitted. 'But it doesn't surprise me. That's his way. Finger in every pie.'

Over Loverboy's strenuous objections, Daisy insisted on involving the police, but they drew a blank, agreeing with Tate that the most likely culprit was someone who had taken exception to his remarks in the article.

But Daisy remained unsatisfied. She confronted Tate in private, told him she had always known he was an appalling liar. He was concealing something from her, she said, and asked him, if not for her sake, then for Isaac's, to be straight with her.

'I don't *know* who it was from any more than you do,' said Tate.

'But look,' she said, 'the contract, the car, the cancelled fights, now this – isn't it obvious?'

'It's not obvious.'

'If this is some pride thing, something between you two and Costello, then it's not fair on Isaac. And if Costello can get him the fights, why not just make a deal with him? Why do we have to fight *everyone*? You made a deal with him once.' Daisy regretted those final words as soon as she had said them: Tate's dead eye was an unspoken reproach.

'Say it is Costello,' he said. 'Say it was him that sent it. You want Isaac's future to be in the hands of a man like that? That's only a fraction of what he can do. I'm serious, Daisy: from Ron Costello, a box of rats is a love-tap compared to the shit he can bring on. Do you get me? It's not about pride. I've done too many stupid things to care about pride at my age. This is about survival. If we keep our nerve we can get right past Costello. Loverboy and me are the ones taking the risk. He's never going to harm Isaac – Isaac's the prize. And you're safe – Costello doesn't know you. He works on weaknesses in people, gets them that way through greed or fear – whatever it is, he finds a way to work them open. I know you, Daisy. You're straight. There's nothing for Costello to get his claws into.'

Tate's expression of confidence silenced Daisy, but not for the reason he had intended. She was gripped by a corrosive sense of shame. She had come into his world on a lie. She felt the impossible burden of too many secrets. She wanted to be known again, and open. But her veneration of her dead husband and her lost life had shut her away in the dark, and made her careless of the living that she had come to love. Nothing in her life had made her feel so unworthy as Tate's misplaced trust. She felt hollow. She, who had thought of herself with pride as Isaac's most principled defender, now saw she was his greatest liability.

As time passed, her sense of guilt made her paranoid. Daisy felt sure she was followed on her way to and from work. She thought her phone was bugged. She grew alarmed at strange new faces in the library. She was going mad. She tried bringing it up with Tate. He ridiculed the suggestion: even you-know-who wouldn't go that far, he said. Daisy felt better, but as soon as she was back at work, the anxiety returned. She hadn't been truthful with Tate. He had no idea of the risks she had taken. Those omissions, which had just seemed prudent at the time, now appeared to be a terrible betrayal. This constant worry on Isaac's behalf, and a nagging sense of guilt, were her punishment.

Two men in particular appeared in the library every day with a consistency that she felt couldn't be imaginary. The only explanation for their presence was that they were agents of Costello. Neither of them ever borrowed books. One, 'Mr Brown' – whom Daisy had named after the preferred colour of his corduroy trousers – would arrive as the library opened and browse on the shelves until about lunchtime, when he was relieved by 'Mr Bogarde' – so called because he always read the same book, a biography of Dirk Bogarde, which he replaced on the shelf when the library closed. There was never any communication between the two men, never anything that would draw attention to them – though sometimes they would drift off to where they couldn't be seen, to discreet corners of the reference section – and every day, between twelve-thirty and one, the changeover. Only Daisy, in her heightened state of paranoid awareness, could have noticed the patterns.

Finally, she could bear it no longer. She took Simon Black to the old card catalogue room, out of Bogarde's sight, and explained all her suspicions to him. He didn't dismiss her worries at all, but listened carefully and then quizzed her when she had finished.

'For two weeks,' she said. 'Every day like clockwork. It's giving me the creeps. I know they're following me. But it sounds so crazy.'

'I don't think you're crazy at all,' said Simon Black. 'I think you did the right thing in telling me. You wait here. Act normal. I'm going to go outside and call the police. On no account confront them.'

'Are you sure?'

'Absolutely.'

Daisy felt hugely grateful to him for being so decisive and wished she had told him a week earlier.

Black took his coat from the back office and called to Jorge at the desk. 'I'm doing a coffee run, Jorge. Fancy *algo*?'

'Yes please, Simon. A latte. Thank you.'

Black walked unhurriedly toward the exit. Daisy noticed Mr Bogarde's eyes lift from the page and follow Simon to the door. He appeared to clear his throat into the sleeve of his jacket and then stood up. Black broke into a run. Bogarde threw the book aside and sprinted after Black with an astonishing turn of pace, rugby-tackling him just by the exit and slamming him into the plastic upright of the electronic security barrier. As it snapped, Mr Brown arrived from the lobby and pinned Black's struggling body to the ground.

'Leave him,' Daisy screamed. 'He's done nothing to you. I'm calling the police.'

'We are the police, love,' Mr Brown reassured her. 'I'm arresting you on suspicion of murder,' he continued, as Black thrashed on the ground, his face in a paroxysm of fury, spittle flecking his beard.

'You have the right to remain silent,' began Mr Bogarde rather breathlessly.

'There's been some mistake,' Daisy said.

No mistake, as subsequent events confirmed. The police had been investigating Simon Black for months. He was charged and held on remand for killing his parents, a pair of elderly academics who had inherited a fortune from Mrs Black's American father.

Daisy told Tate that it was simultaneously shocking and a bit of a relief.

'Weird,' said Tate. 'Someone you went out with.'

It took Daisy a moment to recall her ancient fib. 'Oh yeah, but you know it wasn't really a relationship. I always knew there was something a bit funny about him.'

Twenty-Four

For so long, Daisy's life had been fixed on a single point: like a mediaeval map with Jerusalem at its centre, her world had seemed to radiate from that tiny bloodless wound in Stuart's chest. Now she was forced to acknowledge that the planet was peopled with other dramas, unrelated to her, or Stuart, or Ron Costello, or Joel Heath.

Joel Heath: she noticed with astonishment that even that name, which had once been a constant affront, binding her to that moment in the past when their lives had intersected, no longer affected her with such power. She couldn't think about him with equanimity, but his aura, his potency, had almost gone, like a crippled autumn wasp buzzing faintly, growing weaker and weaker.

The truth was she might have noticed sooner, but Joel Heath had dropped out of sight as a boxer.

Heath had found his new religion empowering for a while: it articulated his sense of anger and victimhood, subsumed his plight into a larger grievance against an unjust world. But he was a weak personality and there were plenty of reasons not to stick to its demanding disciplines: the prayer times were inconvenient; training during Ramadan was much harder if you observed the fast. And, with increasing success, he lost one of his chief motives for worship: he had less and less to be angry about. By the time that success had begun to desert him, the desire for submission to God had long been supplanted by desires for things that were more immediately gratifying. A few excuses early on facilitated subsequent failures of resolve;

these were cumulative, until there was no longer any pretence of observance. Heath fell away from Islam, not as an apostate, but rather in the way that someone abandons a New Year's resolution. And much the same thing happened to his training routine.

One of the difficulties for Joel Heath was that there were so many things he would rather do than boxing. Eating, for example: meals at the kind of fancy restaurants that footballers went to – one in particular with £10 cocktails, sunken bars and freestanding toilet cubicles shaped like giant fluorescent eggs. Or shopping: there were shops on New Bond Street that sent him slavering for *stuff*, a whole realm of beautiful possessions that he'd had no idea existed. But most of all, Joel Heath loved taking drugs. Cocaine in particular made Joel feel like the boxer he no longer trained hard enough to be. It burned through him like the taste of glory, like a knock-out punch, a gunpowder trail of crackling silver dust, setting off fireworks in his brain all night – or, at least, until the drugs ran out. And at first, anyway, when he was winning, they didn't. There were plenty of 'party organizers', young men with their names and mobile numbers on printed business cards, more than willing to give *gak* to the champ on tick; even free, for a while. Heath would sit up all night, firing his septum with fuses of cocaine until dawn had broken and only he was left, wired and whey-faced, still in no mood to stop, not ready to face the psychic bill for all the damage. He had a predisposition towards it. He wasn't reflective enough to experience the come-down as anything other than an unpleasant physical nuisance. There was no guilt or paranoia, no feeling of self-disgust to alert him to the presence of a problem. He could go on for days.

It didn't do much for his boxing. Tate had been right when he observed once that Heath was nothing special; but at least he had had the initial hunger and a hoodlum's useful familiarity with violence. Now he started having problems with his weight. Cocaine is a terrible bloater of bodies. There's a certain puffy look some celebrities acquire as they head for super-annuation, as though their metabolisms, fed up with the star-vation diet that accompanies binge drug-taking, have decided to reorganize, stuffing the body with extra calories here and there, as hamsters do, just in case it's a long wait for the next mealtime.

Heath had to move up. He was losing at welterweight on points. He couldn't fight the boys from Losers Inc. for ever. Now he lost by knockout and stoppage at light middleweight and middle. The opponents were taller and stronger. Heath had neither the chin nor the punch to live with them.

The solution? More drugs, of course. At least the illusory feeling of success, and the chance, while high, to recast each bruising defeat more favourably, to persuade himself it had been another fluke, to figure out how to win the rematch.

And then the fights dried up. Heath gave up his rented Docklands flat and moved in with a friend. The drugs got cheaper too. Not coke and valium, but crack and heroin, and strong weed for come-downs. Heath signed on, drew benefit, got high, sold his only belt and was abandoned by his wife. Sometimes he went round to her house and begged to see his daughter. Other times, he went round high, and raged and broke the windows. She wisely got a restraining order; she had started seeing a slightly older car salesman who had his own house and a good salary. The last time Joel Heath came round, the car salesman was there, answered the door, knocked out two of Heath's teeth and called him a loser. Heath was led away in handcuffs still protesting his love for his wife and child.

The front door of the house Heath shared was fastened with a lock, three bolts and a metal pole, or police bar, that fitted into a special box in the door and connected to a steel ring in the flooring. There were some bills outstanding with local dealers and Heath wasn't taking any chances. Lately, the first line of defence had become keeping the curtains shut and not answer-ing the door at all. One morning – the exact day was unclear and probably irrelevant to him – Heath was roused from sleep by a persistent ringing. He did a mental inventory: the locks were all in place; and put the coverless, sweat-stained, pillow, over his head. The noise didn't stop for twenty minutes. Finally, Heath cast the pillow aside in fury, took a short crowbar from beside his bed, slid the police lock back an inch and opened the door a crack on its reinforced steel chain. A blade of sunlight fell across his wincing eye. 'Ron?' he said in amazement, now thoroughly confused. He rapidly drew back his armoury of bolts.

'I've been ringing for twenty minutes,' said Ron. 'I asked for you at the gym. They said you hadn't been there for *munfs*.' Ron paused on the threshold. 'This place smells like a fucking *shithole*. What have you done to it?'

'Party last night,' lied Heath unhappily. 'Friends came over and trashed the place.'

Ron stepped gingerly, picking a path for his Italian shoes through the rags and pizza cartons, the glasses of cheap booze packed with drowned cigarette butts like floating leeches. 'How can you fucking live like this?' asked Ron incredulously, flicking over a box of congealed chow mein with his distressed morocco toe. He looked at Heath's naked torso, and the paunch which bulged over the elasticated band of his tracksuit bottoms. 'And you're fat.'

Heath pinched his gut with fingers like callipers. 'Two weeks at the gym,' he pleaded. 'This'll melt away.'

'I can't think straight in this pigsty,' said Ron. 'Put some clothes on. I'll be in the car.'

'Fuck, fuck, fuck,' said Heath, running up the stairs and rummaging around his room for something clean, for something that resembled clean. He remembered one of his New Bond Street shirts, a legacy of better days – an augury of better things to come? – and yanked it from a drawer. There was blood all down the front and what looked like a blob of pus on one of the collar points. Heath sniffed it: it was mustard.

Five minutes later, Heath came out of the house in trainers, stained jeans, a sweatshirt and a pair of broken sunglasses. He smelled like spoiled milk and there were beads of sweat standing out on his forehead.

Ron's car was waiting – a huge sports utility vehicle in gleaming black, with blacked-out windows. It was massive, and absurdly high, like a tank, like a great chariot of death.

'So what the fuck,' said Ron, 'has happened to you?'

Heath rubbed his red and streaming nose with the back of his hand. 'A few bad months, Ron. Tracey fucked off, took Joelene. I'm over it now. I'm clean. I'm ready to start fighting again. Have you got anything for me, boss? I need an opponent. I need to get motivated.'

'That's why I've come,' said Ron. 'We need to discuss your future.'

Ron manoeuvred his huge black vehicle into the faster-moving line of traffic.

Twenty-Five

Simon Black's arrest had a strange effect on Daisy. After an initial sense of liberation, she felt increasing unease, and an eerie foreboding she found it hard to shake off. One night she dreamed that she was dropping a dead body into the Thames. When she woke up, the furtiveness and shame clung obstinately to her. Whose body was it? Stuart's? Her own? Her dead child? Or Heath's?

The dream of the dead body haunted her for days. It seemed ominous: the strange, genderless corpse that she zipped into a bag and dropped over the side of Vauxhall Bridge. Then it began to dawn on her that the dream could bear a more positive interpretation. Like the card of the hanged man in the tarot, death could be a symbol of change. Perhaps some of her past had been tossed overboard; perhaps the old Daisy had had to die.

She saw more clearly now that the strain of her life, her accumulated small deceptions, the power of her hatred, had led her to find Costello's plots where there were none. Real evil was more sudden and unexpected, like Simon Black: rewarding thirty-five years of loving parental attention with strychnine and a shallow grave in France.

The newspapers loved the story. They depicted Black as a psychopathic voluptuary, a public school boy gone bad. He had spent a small fortune on rare books in the two years since his parents' disappearance. His free spending was what had first alerted an aunt to the possibility of foul play. She had notified the police. The undercover officers at the library had been detailed to keep Black under surveillance while gendarmes and detectives from Scotland Yard conducted fingertip searches of the woods around the Blacks' holiday home in Provence.

All these details came to light later, during the trial and in its immediate aftermath. In the meantime, Simon Black was being held on remand. Jorge claimed, typically, to have seen it coming.

Daisy wrote Black a friendly letter, wishing him all the best and telling him he was missed – which was the honest truth. Jorge had been promoted in the hasty reorganization that had followed Black's arrest and had become absolutely insufferable. He kept a respectful distance from Daisy, but lorded it over his new subordinates, Godfrey and Caroline.

Black wrote Daisy a long letter back. He made no mention of the trial, but said he had got the job of prison librarian, which he was enjoying, and was glad to have the time to get back to his much-delayed doctoral thesis, a dissertation on a minor Jacobean dramatist. However, specialist books were hard for him to come by, and he wondered if Daisy could track down anything that might help him: a concordance, critical commentaries, variorum editions.

It took Daisy a while to get round to it, but she found she couldn't ignore his request indefinitely. One free afternoon at home, she switched on her computer and prepared to scour rare book sites on the internet. But, instead of searching immediately for the books, the first name she entered was Isaac's.

She had seen him only the day before, yet her pride in him made her constantly eager to find his reflection in the world. And she thought that this, perhaps, was what it would have been like to be a mother.

His name pulled up hundreds of matches: articles, rankings, unofficial sites, tributes, moving testimonials from people whom his talent had touched – the way real artistry invites participation, asks to be allowed in, insists on belonging to everyone, to exalt everyone. Of course, there were a few duff matches too. *Isaac* Stevens of Roanoke, Virginia, offered premium grade nectarines and *plums*, boxed and hand-delivered to anywhere in the mainland United States.

The match had been made for the European title. It meant a trip to face a possibly hostile Neapolitan crowd, but, as Isaac was the first to point out, his deafness meant there was little chance of his being distracted by the audience. If Isaac won – and Loverboy and Tate were as confident as their superstitious natures ever allowed them to be – she could honourably step aside, she felt. Esme was bigger; Una could travel with Isaac more. Isaac would have his own support systems; Daisy would be able to start making a new life for herself.

Romance with Tate wasn't on the cards. Imo had brought it up, having met Tate and pronounced him 'pretty sexy for a man with one eye'. Daisy told her she had ruled it out; but the fact that she had even considered it felt like enormous progress.

Once again, she remembered her dream: the sinister bag plopping into the river. That unexpected guilt that oppressed her for days afterwards – was it guilt at finally being able to bury her husband? Of course, she thought about Stuart a lot, and with great tenderness and sadness. But she remembered funny things about him too, even annoying things, and it no longer seemed, as it had done once, that the meaningful part of her life had died with him.

Daisy cleared the search form, and as she did, the doorbell went. Downstairs, she pulled open her front door.

It was Ron Costello. He came past her into the communal hallway. 'Hope I haven't disturbed you. Needed to talk to you in person. Daisy Adams, Daisy Polidoro – what are you calling yourself these days?'

'I'm busy,' Daisy said. 'I've got people round.'

Ron was already going up the steps, his head turning the corner that led to the first landing; he leaned back to meet her startled gaze and smiled. 'Liar,' he said.

Daisy came back into her flat. She stood with her back to the open door. Ron was parked on the sofa, the flaps of his black leather coat spread out under him like the wings of a cockroach.

'Daisy, Daisy,' said Ron in an almost avuncular tone. 'Do you find it a pain when people make jokes about your name? Sit down. Relax. I wouldn't come myself if I wanted to do you an injury. That would be silly. We're neither of us silly.' Ron looked around the room. 'Nice place. Small, but you've done it nice. Me, I could never live in a flat. The noise, the neighbours, the vermin.'

'What do you want?' Daisy tried to summon a feeling of composure from somewhere. The image that came into her mind was of Isaac, taking calm breaths between rounds, in the last seconds before the triple flash of the ring lights sent him out to fight again.

'A cup of tea would be nice,' said Ron. 'Herbal if you've got it. Any of that rooibusch? No? PG'll do.'

'You know what I mean,' said Daisy. Ron was smirking, silent. 'I'm calling the police.'

Ron grasped her wrist as she reached for the phone. 'Ground rules,' he said, 'no threats. It's just a waste of time. There are people you threaten and there are people you buy. You and me, we're the second kind. I'm here to buy.'

'I'm not for sale,' said Daisy. 'Neither is anything I have.'

'Really? What, that laptop, for example – if I offered you ten thousand pounds for it, you mean you wouldn't sell? Of course you would!'

'You didn't come round here to buy a computer.'

'No, that's true. But the principle's the same: you've got something I want. What's the price?'

'I told you . . .'

'Oh, I understand how attached you are. He must be like a son to you. Do you have kids of your own, Daisy?'

Daisy shook her head.

'No? I've got two boys, twins, Solly and Daniel. The apples of my eye, they are. I don't know what I would do if anything was to happen to them. I really don't. I'd have to kill someone.

Hostages to fortune, kids are, in a way. Loving someone that much. It's hard. You worry. This world, it's full of nutcases.

'James Bond – he had the right idea. Never settle down. Shag birds left, right and centre, but never stick around long enough for them to become a liability. He couldn't have taken the risks he took if he'd had a family. Moneypenny and Q, they're his family. Your mum's alive, isn't she, Daisy? That gaff in Finchley. You should visit her more. I think she gets lonely in that big house.'

'You said no threats.'

'Who's threatening? Friendly advice is all. Kids break your heart, Daisy. Ask your mum.'

'You've had a crack at Isaac. Nothing I can say will change his mind. He likes the team he's with.'

'You underestimate your influence on him. He calls you *family*. To my mind, that's the highest praise there is. I understand your reluctance. The press I get. I'm here to persuade you I'm the best thing for him. If you believe it, then he will too.'

'But I don't believe it, Ron.' She hated saying his name.

'I've got America going nuts for the kid. There are four welterweight champions, all Yanks. Different sanctioning bodies – alphabet soup and all that. Give me the word and I can put him in the ring with any of them in one month's time. And I tell you, he'll beat them – Reuben Mendoza, Shane Jackson, Iran Zebulun, the Croatian kid . . . what's his name? . . . Chris Panic. Worst-case scenario: he fights, he loses. He's still set up for life. The money he'd earn, he'd be well taken care of. Can Tate promise him that? Can Loverboy promise him that?'

'He's fighting in Europe. He's getting good money for it.'

'Forty grand? I don't call that good money. After tax, it's a pittance. Come on, Daisy. No one cares who's European champion. It's always some ugly Turk from Germany. And the boy he's fighting, Maurizetti, he's a warrior, he can bang a bit. Shane Jackson is an easier night's work for much more dosh. You follow me?'

Daisy's head was spinning. Ron was fencing with her, slyly

picking apart her defences, wearing her down. 'You've got everyone else,' she said. 'Why Isaac too?'

'I've got to have him,' he said. 'Simple as that. He's the first non-heavyweight British fighter in ten years that the Yanks have given two shits about. And the more you tell me he's not for sale, the more I want him.' Ron seemed bemused by the irony. 'Perverted, ain't it?' Some of the urgency had gone out of his voice. He was calmer. She thought that maybe he would hear a polite but firm refusal.

'I'm flattered by your interest. I know Isaac was too. Who knows, some day, maybe down the road . . .'

'No!' Ron barked at her. 'Now, Daisy, now. It's got to be now. This is the moment of glory. Isaac Plum conquers America. The balloon goes up. I want to be standing behind him, not coming along months later like some glorified matchmaker while someone else gets all the credit for spotting him.'

'But someone else did spot him first.'

'I know. I don't care about that. I just want the credit for it. Daisy, I've been very patient, I've worn myself out with chat. Let me be perfectly straight with you: how much for Isaac Plum's signature? What will it take?'

'Nothing you're in a position to offer me.'

'Don't bet on that . . .'

'Nothing. There's nothing I want. I'd like you to leave now, please.'

'You're starting to piss me off,' said Ron. 'I wanted this to be simple and polite. Now you're forcing me to go against my loving nature.' Ron stood up and gathered his coat around him. 'And you've offered me nothing to drink. You've brought this on yourself. Regrettably, I've got to open the ugly box.'

Twenty-Six

Daisy closed and bolted the front door after him and listened for his heavy feet on the stairs, descending. Then she went to the phone. But who to ring? Tate? Imo? Loverboy? The police? What could she tell them? Costello had threatened her so obliquely. She wondered if she ought to text Isaac and Una, alert them to the possibility of a visit from him. She needed to get out of her flat: that she was sure of. She grabbed some clothes and stuffed them in an overnight bag. What else? Her mobile phone and charger; sponge bag and toothbrush; the car keys. She would go to her mum's, think, take stock and get in touch with Tate and Isaac. Her mind felt clear and focused. This was what came of years spent preparing for the worst. She thought again of Isaac. She needed to emulate his coolness: the clarity and attention he gave to Tate and Loverboy's instructions. One last look round the flat: all in order. Good. She took a deep breath and opened the front door.

Ron Costello stood there, uncharacteristically rumpled and breathing heavily. 'Nice timing,' he said, and pushed past her. The stairway seemed suddenly full of a maul of struggling men. Arms and legs tangled on the bannister. 'Stop it,' Ron ordered, and with a couple of sharp blows from his fist the maul diminished, resolved like vapour into a single image: one person stumbling, limp, prising weakly with his hands to free his locked head from Costello's armpit. Someone whimpered. Costello wrenched the man's head and with a kick sent him sprawling across the room. Costello took a breath and smoothed his hair, and then fetched his victim a kick in the face.

The bag slipped from Daisy's hand. 'Isaac?' she cried.

Costello moved round the flat, checking the locks on the windows. 'Not Plum, no. I'm not that daft.'

It took Daisy a moment to recognize the bloody face. Heath. He lay flopped on the carpet, his arm thrown back over his forehead as though shielding his eyes from the light. He was barely conscious, and breathed in shallow, stertorous gasps.

His face seemed to have aged in the months since she had seen him last. His last bruising defeats, or just heavy sparring, had altered its shape. His nose, his brow, were coarser, less regular, and bloodied where Ron had kicked him.

'Got any newspaper?' Ron bustled about the kitchen. Daisy could hear him yanking drawers open. 'This'll do.' He came back into the sitting room with two big black rubbish bags which he slid under Heath's head. Daisy noticed that Costello had put on leather driving gloves. 'Don't want him bleeding on your kilim,' Ron muttered. 'I meant to mention that before – big fan of Turkey myself. The place, not the meat – I find it too dry.'

Heath struggled a little, as though trying to get up, but ineffectually, with very slight movements, like a dog dreaming of catching rabbits. His limbs gave way again and he dropped back on to the plastic bags.

'So, tell me, Daisy, did Stuart want kids? Nice Italian boy – must have wanted kids.'

Daisy felt her face burning.

'Could you not have them?' Ron leaned closer to her and whispered as though he didn't want Heath to hear them. 'Was you barren?'

Daisy found herself shaking her head.

'What? Just left it too long? You Bridget Jones types – career this, career that. Can't wait for ever, you know. It's biology: tick tock, tick tock. You want to have your kids young so your body recovers easier. They reckon fourteen is the perfect age for a woman to give birth. Like a cow – calf pops out, she licks him clean, off they go, she hardly breaks a sweat. Nature's way. You'd be a grandmother by now. *He*'s got a kid.' Costello tilted his head at Heath. 'Imagine, shit-arse like him, a dad. It shouldn't be legal. Ironic, because you and Stuart would have made lovely parents.'

He crouched down to her and lowered his voice to a whisper. She could feel his breath on her ear.

'Heath told me he got an erection when he killed your Stuart. He goes, "Ron, I'm not gay or nothing, but I enjoyed it that much." Boxers get it too sometimes – a big old woody before a fight. It's the hormones. Does Isaac get one, I wonder?' Costello looked around the room, appraising. 'Now,' he said, 'how do you want to do this?'

Daisy said nothing. She stared at the bloody face on the bin bag.

'Daisy, Daisy,' Costello sang quietly. 'Give me your answer, do.'

Daisy got to her feet.

'We don't *have* to do it here,' said Costello. 'If you're not happy with the choice of venue, there are plenty of others.'

It seemed to Daisy that she had been wrong to place so much importance on Isaac and her life after Isaac. What was happening now, this moment, was the culmination of her life. She thought that Isaac must feel this every time he stepped into the ring and felt that breathless, collective hush, its spirit of religiosity. And she thought of those pregnant moments in the ring, seconds before one man became a blood sacrifice. She understood that it was some kind of god who was being invoked in those rituals: the first god, the god of primal darkness, who promises neither salvation nor a life hereafter, who is simply that dark thing we cannot face, to which we can only sacrifice.

'No,' said Daisy. 'Let's do it here.'

Daisy went to the bedroom and got out her gun. She had packed it in a plastic bag which she had hidden in the deep side-pocket of a winter coat she never wore. She unwrapped it and sprang the clip, which she loaded with the full ten shells and then slid it into the gun butt. She cocked the weapon and checked to make sure there was a bullet in the chamber.

Ron was kneeling on the carpet, raising one of Heath's eyelids with his thumb. There was virtually only white visible, a millimetre of grey iris peeking down from beneath the top lid. 'Blimey,' said Ron when he saw the gun, 'you *are* prepared. Where the fuck did you get that?'

'None of your business,' said Daisy.

'Two things,' said Ron. 'One: a cushion on the side of the head to prevent flash-burns from the muzzle and muffle the sound – which, by the looks of that hand-cannon of yours, is going to be considerable. And two – and this is purely a matter of taste, so I'm not going to insist on it – you may find the whole experience more satisfying if he's conscious. But, as I said, it's up to you.'

'Yes,' said Daisy. 'Wake him up.'

Ron got up, whistling, and went into the kitchen. Daisy heard him running the tap and scrabbling in the freezer for ice. He returned with a jug of iced water which he poured in a thin stream on to Heath's face. Pink drops spattered from Heath's chin on to his stained sweatshirt. He groaned and blinked, rolled over on to his hands and knees, and threw up on the plastic bag. Ron slapped Heath's head. 'Manners!'

Daisy pressed the gun into Heath's temple. The barrel made a dint in his skin.

'Going without the cushion – fair play to you. We'll have to hop it quick after. I've got Terry Menswear on stand-by to take care of the carcass. Your neighbours in? I might turn on the stereo if they are. Or better still, fireworks.'

Ron carried on talking, but his words seemed to fade out. Daisy heard instead the old jeering voice, like a thing from a nightmare, deriding her grief. *That big lump your ex-husband. That big ex-husband, your lump. That ex-lump. Stew-pot.*

Daisy took a couple of steps back. 'That voice,' she said. 'It's not his, it's yours.'

'What voice?'

Daisy allowed her extended arm to traverse forty-five degrees to the right so the muzzle of the weapon was brought to bear on Ron Costello's face. 'The voice in my head,' she said. 'The voice I thought was his.'

Ron hadn't bargained on this. 'Don't play the barmy card with me, Daisy. It doesn't scare me. I know . . .'

'What do you know, Ron? What do you think you know about me?'

There was a flash and a sound like a clap of thunder. The gun jerked in Daisy's hand. The room filled with smoke. Ron stood open-mouthed, deafened by the report. Daisy pointed the gun at his face. 'I'm going to put the next one through your eye.'

Costello glared icily at her.

She gestured with the gun towards the door. 'Go on. Get out.'

He backed towards the stairs. For once, he was silent.

After he had left, Daisy shook Heath properly awake. His brain was still scrambled. He looked at her blankly. 'You get out as well,' she said.

Heath stumbled drunkenly down the stairs. She heard the front door shut, but Heath hung around for a while, sitting on the wall of the front garden for almost half an hour, head in hands, trying to make sense of his surroundings. Once, twice, Daisy looked down from her kitchen window to see him. The third time he was gone.

Twenty-Seven

Tate was fast asleep. In his dream there were frangipani blossoms, palm trees, warm breezes. His half-sister was introducing him to her friends. He was young. He had so much time. Each friend was more beautiful than the last. 'And this is . . .' said his sister. Daisy shuffled forward in a kimono. 'We know each other,' Tate said. 'I don't think so,' Daisy said. She gave him a cordial smile and offered to shake his hand. Tate tried to explain their connection: 'Isaac? Sammy? We were in New Orleans together . . .' Daisy's mobile phone started ringing. 'Excuse me,' she said, with scrupulous politeness, 'I must just get that.'

He was in bed. It was ten to two in the morning. The phone on the bedside table had chirruped him awake. It was Daisy calling. 'I'm outside,' she said. 'It's an emergency.'

Tate had to go downstairs to undo the dead-bolt. He was wearing a T-shirt and shorts and his cheek was cross-hatched with lines from his pillow. 'I dreamed you were Japanese,' he said.

'Costello's just been to see me,' Daisy said.

Tate heard the desolation in her voice and started to wake up properly. 'Costello? Now? Shit.'

Daisy came in. 'I haven't been honest with you,' she said, in a flat, emotionless voice. 'My husband . . .' she began. The prospect of the next word on her lips uncorked something inside her and she couldn't speak for her tears. '. . . died.'

Tate moved towards her. She pushed him away and collected herself. 'Heath was involved. I wanted to get back at him. It seems a long time ago. It's why I wanted Isaac. I bought a gun.'

Tate was bewildered. 'A gun?'

'I used Isaac. I used you too. Costello knows everything.' Then she remembered the image of her child blistering in the fireplace of the old flat. 'Practically everything.'

Daisy started to cry again – the self-possession that seemed to have been holding her upright for ever finally caved in. She wept bitterly for Stuart, her lost child, for herself. Tate put his long whipcord arms around her and held her tightly. She covered her eyes with her hands and the tears seemed to leak through her fingers.

Tate peeled her hands from her face and kissed their tear-stained palms. Her shoulders shook with sobs as she clung to him.

He held her for a while, then gently detached himself. 'He'll be back. He won't give up. We need to find Isaac and Loverboy tonight – get out of the country until the Maurizetti fight. We could go back to the States. To Tunica. Anywhere. I've got a friend in Guatemala who'll help. Loverboy knows loads of people in Kingston.'

'But training? Sparring partners?'

'We'll think of something.'

They got Loverboy and Isaac to meet them at the gym first thing the following morning. Isaac seemed glum, Daisy thought, unusually subdued. Daisy wondered if he had heard some news already. He hadn't. Tate took Loverboy aside and filled him in. Daisy explained to Isaac as best she could, trying to make him understand why she had done what she had done, trying to apologize.

At half-past eight, there was a clanking from the fire escape as feet drummed along the steel walkway. Ron Costello came in, followed by Terry Mansour, Pete the sign-language interpreter and a fourth man that Daisy failed to recognize.

Ron seemed relaxed and cheerful. He was wearing a powder-blue suit with a silk lining and a waxed car coat that made him seem even burlier than usual. 'Right,' he said, with a glance at Pete, 'straight down to business.' Pete signed Ron's words so Isaac could follow. 'So nice to be working together at last.' Ron settled himself into one of the gym's steel and canvas stacking chairs. 'First, the bad news. It looks like Maurizetti is going to have to pull out of your forthcoming title clash.' He glanced at his watch. 'He's having a nasty hamstring injury a little later today. The good news is this: I've had preliminary discussions with the promoter for Christopher "Kinky" Panic, and it's looking ninety-eight per cent certain that Panic is going to put his WBC belt on the line with you, Isaac, at the end of next month, in the arena of arenas, Bethnal Green's very own Valley Hall.'

'Bullshit. Maurizetti's not training in Italy,' said Loverboy. 'We don't even know where he is.'

'Who said anything about Italy? Maurizetti's training camp is in the Catskills,' said Costello. 'But that's not important. The important thing for you to remember, Mr Octogenarian Loverboy from Dulwich, is that Isaac is now contracted to fight for me.'

'No one's signed anything with you, Costello,' Loverboy said.

'No? Let me bring you up to speed on a couple of things. There's been one or two meetings you obviously missed. Last night, I went round to young Ms Polidoro's place for a brain-storming session. We had a very free and frank exchange of ideas. I must say, I came away with enhanced respect for Ms Adams-Polidoro. Unfortunately, over the course of our discus-sions it became clear that her position as an adviser to Isaac here has been jeopardized, owing to something of an indiscre-tion in her recent past. Shall I say what it is, Daisy? Or will you?'

Daisy realized with horror who the fourth man was: Vanes's specialist, the man who had sold her the gun.

'She's told us everything already, Ron,' said Tate.

'Really? Did she tell you she bought an unlicensed firearm?

That she conspired to commit murder? Got the shooter, Terry?'

Terry shook his head. 'Negative, boss. Someone's on it.'

Undeterred, Ron went on. 'Thanks to our intervention, no murder's been committed, and there's one less broken-hearted mother for you to have on your consciences. Joel Heath is extremely grateful, seeing as how I saved his life, and is willing to say as much in a court of law. There's someone in your flat now looking for the weapon, rummaging through your knicker drawer and all Stuart's old stuff. Even if we can't get hold of it, Ruslan here will testify that he provided you with a gun. The words *a*, *like*, *stitched-up* and *kipper* are certainly springing to my mind, Daisy, though not necessarily in that order. So let me put you all out of your misery and tell you what happens now. Isaac signs for me, fights Panic and wins, as we all know he's capable of. Or Daisy, who you are all rightly so fond of, goes in the nick for a quite considerable chunk of stir. What are we talking about, Sir Terence Menswear?'

Terry furrowed his brow. 'Unlawful possession of a firearm. Conspiracy to commit murder. Attempted murder. No previous. Could be out in five to seven with good behaviour.'

'Lucky you don't want kids, Daisy. But still – seven of the prime years of your life spent eating prison food and dodging women in comfortable shoes. It's not what you'd choose, is it? Let's be honest. It's what my American colleagues refer to as a no-brainer.'

Isaac signalled to be given a pen.

Daisy forgot herself for an instant and pleaded with him in words not to do it. 'No, Isaac. Don't. He's bluffing. I'll turn myself in anyway. I'm not afraid of going to prison.'

Isaac signed his big clumsy signature at the bottom of the proffered document. Then, as he handed it back to Costello, he pretended to expire on the spot of a heart attack. He clutched his chest and sank to the floor. Only Costello's men laughed.

Ron put the contracts into his jacket pocket. 'I propose a

celebration,' he said.

'What's the gimmick?' said Tate. 'On pain of death?'

Ron tutted. 'I see my hearts and minds campaign has a little way to go. I won't push it. After the fight. You'll have a drink with me then, won't you, Tate? Sammy tells me you like a drink.'

Costello left the gym.

'That's that, then,' said Loverboy, kicking over a chair in disgust. It clattered on to the floor.

'What do we do now?' said Daisy.

Tate shrugged indifferently. 'Get ready for Panic.'

Only Isaac, of all of them, seemed strangely relieved.

Twenty-Eight

Now that Costello managed and promoted Isaac, Daisy fully expected him to sack the lot of them and surround the boy with a new team. But Costello seemed happy for them to continue working together – at least for the time being. He knew that any more disruption so close to the fight would be bad for Isaac; and there was a particular pleasure to be had in having complete power over a set of people who clearly hated his guts. Costello left his future plans vague. The implicit message was this: he could do whatever he wanted.

Faced with near-total uncertainty, Tate and Loverboy did the only thing they could and threw all their energies into preparing for the fight with Panic. The videos of Maurizetti were discarded. Instead, they studied the recent fights of Christopher 'Kinky' Panic, a naturalized American boxer who had won gold for Croatia at the Olympics four years previously. Panic was quick and strong, a relentless, attacking fighter who bustled his opponents into making errors. Panic versus the elusive technical genius of Isaac Plum was a potentially intriguing contest. It just didn't feel that way to Tate, Isaac, Daisy or Loverboy.

A few days into the revised training schedule, Loverboy announced that he would quit after the title fight, whatever the result. He said he had been thinking about retiring anyway after the Maurizetti fight, and that it had nothing to do with the new circumstances. No one believed him, but they all maintained the fiction, each one pretending that the white lie was somehow necessary for the sake of the others. The truth was that none of them had a clue what would happen after the fight with Panic.

Daisy knew she had failed Isaac. It was an awful feeling, worse than the righteous hatred she had clung to before, because she had to acknowledge her own culpability. Terry Mansour's lackey had found the gun in Daisy's sock drawer; Costello had Isaac's signature; and now Isaac had eight weeks to prepare to fight arguably the best welterweight in the world.

The familiar routines of work and training returned their lives to a semblance of normality, but it was a strained, hollow arrangement – the normal life of an occupied country, where things go on under the oppressive knowledge that there is a storm-trooper guarding the post box, that the greengrocer is an informer, that the confessional is bugged.

And yet, because of the valedictory nature of the contest – Loverboy at least would be travelling no further – because of their beleaguered sense that they could only trust each other, because of the love and the shared disappointment that united them, they did much more than go through the motions. They worked with a furious intensity. Tate and Loverboy, in particular, conducted themselves with the zeal of men avenging an old injustice. They analysed Panic's style and figured out ways to neutralize him. Tate – the anxiety about damaging his good eye seemingly cast aside – would play Panic in sparring sessions, aping the American's distinctive style, showing Isaac ways to unpick it with combinations to the body, by boxing on the retreat, allowing Panic to over-commit himself to the attack.

A week before the fight, Tate asked Daisy out for dinner. There was something he wanted to discuss with her. They ate in silence for a while and then made small talk. Daisy was aware that Tate felt sorry for her and she resented him for it.

'How are you doing?' asked Tate, when it became clear that the real reason for meeting could no longer be avoided.

Daisy was sharp with him. 'How do you think? I feel like I've ruined Isaac's life. I'm not even sure that me sticking around is helping.'

'I don't know,' said Tate. 'Maybe you were right, maybe Costello is someone we can do business with. He's getting Isaac a big payday, the signing bonus has come in already, and there's two hundred grand for Isaac in the purse against Panic. Good luck, bad luck – who knows?'

'I appreciate your trying to make me feel better, but Costello is sick in the head. Tell me honestly, Tate, if you were me, would you stay or leave?'

'I'd stay – you have to. Isaac needs you around. I'm . . . I wanted to ask you something . . .'

'An Isaac thing?'

'Yeah, an Isaac thing,' said Tate, colouring a little. 'What else?'

'Nothing. Just wondering,' said Daisy. She remembered the tickle of desire she had felt when he kissed the palms of her hands to console her.

'Something's off with him these days.'

'What?'

'It's hard to explain. Every other fight I trained him for, there was a moment where he hit his stride with about ten days to go, and me and Loverboy could ease off him, just maintain him, let him rest properly, get relaxed and loose. But it hasn't happened this time.' Tate dropped his fork on to the plate in puzzlement. 'It's like he's not firing right. I thought I was imagining it, but Loverboy's seen it too. He missed training twice last week. He said he had to take his daughter to hospital. That would never have happened before.'

'He looks good in training to me.'

'It's a subtle thing. I feel it when I'm moving around the ring with him. Usually his mind is all over you. That sounds weird, doesn't it? It's hard to explain. It's his awareness – it's uncanny. He knows what I'm doing before I do – he's four steps ahead, five steps ahead. Lately, there's gaps in his concentration that weren't there before. Sometimes now he's no steps ahead, he's not reacting quickly enough.'

'You're worried he'll lose?'

'No, not just that. I'm worried that there's something wrong.'

'If you decide that he's not ready for the fight, we'll pull him out,' said Daisy emphatically.

'No . . . I don't know. You're closest to him. Can you speak to him? See what's up?'

Daisy agreed to bring the subject up with Isaac delicately, at an appropriate moment. But the time never came. The following day was a Saturday, and Isaac was scheduled to do a short session in the gym and a run. When he turned up at nine, for the first time since Daisy could remember, he still hadn't changed into his training gear. It was ominous. Tate and Loverboy fell silent as Isaac entered the room.

I want to say something, Isaac said, and he indicated to Daisy that it was to be a sort of general announcement. He looked off to one side for a moment as he collected his thoughts. Then he tapped himself on the chest with his right index finger.

I or *I'm* or *me*, thought Daisy, and waited for the rest. Then Isaac spelled something to her with his fingers so quickly that she couldn't read it, and she thought for a moment it was a repetition of the joke he'd made after the Keach fight: *voluptuous*.

She told him to spell it again. 'Oh my God,' said Daisy, and asked for it a third time to be sure.

The word was *epilepsy*.

Twenty-Nine

Isaac had had his first blackout on a Circle Line train three years earlier, back when he was still lugging bars of chocolate around for a living, and the dream of professional boxing eluded him. The first thing he had noticed was the overpowering smell of almonds, then the colours swam together before his eyes, grew muddy and dark, and were extinguished. The next moment – or so it seemed – he came to, four stops down the line at St James's Park. He thought the other passengers had ignored him, but it turned out that one of them had used the opportunity to filch a stack of fruit and nut from his holdall.

It was – though Isaac didn't know this – a *petit mal* seizure. It raised associations in Isaac's mind with his father Francis, a window cleaner and bare-knuckle fighter who had died after an inexplicable fall from his ladder. He didn't have another blackout for six months, but when he did, he redoubled his efforts to turn professional. Epilepsy, like a harbinger of death, like a knock-down in a late round, or a bad cut that beckons to an opponent like a winking light, was what had galvanized Isaac Plum. He needed to make money *now*, he needed to exercise his talent *now*. The fit had tripped the round-clock, upended the hourglass. He didn't know how much time he had.

There was another spell after the Ojemba fight. The nasty head-punch in the fourth that had put him down had, he supposed, strained the innate weakness in his brain. It was like having a loose wire in his head, a faulty connection. He had a seizure at home the day after the fight, then another on his way back from training a week later. It was a gloomy time. He hoped he could ignore it at least long enough to bank some decent purses. A title would be nice, but not essential. Meanwhile, without telling Una the reason, he stopped driving. It was too much of a risk, particularly with Esme in the back. Just as he had taken this decision, Ron Costello offered him the contract, baited – of all things – with a car.

Isaac couldn't hide it from Una indefinitely. One day, just as he had begun training for the Maurizetti fight, he had another fit at home in the kitchen. Again, the almond smell, the kaleidoscope of colours coming together in a blur, and something else – a sensation that he suspected might be sound – and Isaac slipped to the floor unconscious. The plate he had been drying fell beside him and span, ringing on the cold tiles like a gong, heard only, if at all, by Esme.

Una panicked, called an ambulance and took her husband and child to the hospital. Isaac's first serious outlay with his winnings, after the paddle-steamer-shaped radio, was for private health insurance. With Una beside him, Isaac felt obliged to answer all the doctor's questions truthfully. Una wasn't angry with him. She understood the deep significance of the news; the two of them together had to decide what to do.

It would be nice to believe that life looked after its freakish talents, its Isaac Plums, but it doesn't with any consistency. For every Picasso, there's a Poe, found dying on a sidewalk in Baltimore, or a Pushkin, haemorrhaging to death from a ruptured stomach after his singularly pointless duel. And yet, life looked after Isaac, though with this single reservation – a reservation which perhaps those others might not have accepted as the price of genius. Isaac's gift never shone on the biggest stages of all. It remained a mysterious flicker in the minds of those who saw him in his prime, a light of unquestionable brilliance, but, by comparison with many, a parochial one.

The compensating gift was this: first, Ron's checkmate had come at just the moment Isaac was going to break the news to Tate and Daisy. Secondly, through a journalist on *Boxing*

News, Isaac sold his exclusive story to a Sunday paper; not, it's true, for as much as he would have got if he'd fought Panic and taken the title, but a good sum nonetheless – in the region of one hundred thousand pounds. This, plus the signing fee and cash bonus he had taken in lieu of the car, was certainly not as much as he deserved, but it was, as Una kept reminding him, a good deal more than nothing.

The story, Isaac said, was going to appear in the following day's paper. He didn't need to tell them that after that there would be no fight against Panic.

I'm sorry, Isaac told Daisy. *It turns out we both had secrets.*

Don't apologize, Daisy said. *I hope they're paying you enough.*

Isaac smiled. 'Nuff!' he said out loud.

Loverboy shook off his focus mitts with a mixture of relief and sadness. 'Won't be needing these again,' he said. He turned to Isaac. 'It was a privilege.'

Same, Isaac signed, and embraced his old trainer.

This is the end, thought Daisy. It had the bittersweet almond flavour of all endings, mingling regrets and gratitude, and beyond that, a new peace. *What now?* she signed to Isaac.

Isaac shrugged.

I'm glad, said Daisy, *that you don't have to fight again.*

Isaac nodded. *Same Una.*

But Tate seemed troubled. 'Costello's going to flip.'

Thirty

There were certainly no almond-scented ambiguities in Ron Costello's idea of a happy ending. 'I want her killed,' he said. 'End of story.'

Isaac Plum's epilepsy heartbreak had got a big spread in the next day's paper and was picked up elsewhere in articles and editorials. 'In a revelation sure to send shock waves through British boxing . . .' one of them began, and went on to excoriate the sport, as though boxing itself was in some way to blame for Isaac's condition. This, however – calumny or not – wasn't what was exercising Ron. The thing that he was having a hard time swallowing, the thing that was pissing him off *considerably*, was that he was going to look a fool in front of the Americans. There were six days to go before the fight, no credible alternatives to Isaac Plum and, most galling of all, Ron, who as promoter had put up the purse, now stood to lose a big chunk of it. But it was prudence as much as vengeance that dictated his implacable response. Ron couldn't be seen to let anyone flout him. It was the old loan shark's rationale: you had to collect on every debt, or the bastards would think you were a soft touch.

Ron, wrongly but justifiably, had decided that Daisy had set up the articles. He would make sure that Isaac wouldn't see another penny of his contract, but Daisy, as the architect of Ron's embarrassment, deserved a more thorough punishment. 'She's done it to spite me,' said Ron, tending, as a textbook narcissist, to find himself at the centre of other people's behaviour. It was a view that Terry didn't disagree with; but then he suffered from a broadly similar range of personality disorders.

'She has and all,' said Terry.

'Use her gun. Make it look like she topped herself.'

Terry hired someone to do the job instead. A man from Canvey Island came into London to find her. He pretended to be a repairman and carried a length of electric flex in his pocket to throttle her with. But he got the address wrong and ended up assaulting one of Daisy's neighbours. Daisy came home to find a yellow crime board outside her building. The mistake bought her some time. Tate persuaded her to take a week off work and stay at Imo's. He insisted that he could find a way to conciliate Costello. He didn't tell her what he knew to be true: that none of them would be able to evade Costello's wrath indefinitely.

Luckily, Ron had more immediately pressing problems – specifically, where to find a respectable opponent for Kinky Panic, and how to recoup his inevitable losses. What he needed was a decent fighter who didn't cost too much, and to persuade the BBC to swallow some of the overspend, as a token of goodwill and in view of their ongoing professional association.

And so, with three days left, and the challenger still unannounced, Ron Costello made his way to the old building beside the canal that was still the home of Losers Inc.

Life at the bottom never changes. The gym had hardly altered since Isaac's first visit. A couple of boxers were pounding the heavy bags. Music blared from the speakers at the back of the gym. The place smelled. It was business as usual. Sammy sat in his back-room office, conducting some transaction or other, scheming over some new project, while in the ring two relatively new faces trained together. One was Vovan, the Yugoslav who had replaced Tate as the gym's hands-on coach. With him, thinner, livelier and generally in much better shape than he'd been when Ron saw him last, was Joel Heath.

Heath was wearing the shiny training suit favoured by boxers who want to lose weight fast. It's the high-tech heir of the plastic bags that some fighters still wear under their training kit. Supposedly, the steam builds up inside and helps the fighter to sweat off the weight. They also have an important psychological dimension: the badge of a boxer who means business in the gym.

And Heath looked . . . okay. Not classy, not terribly good, but solid, respectable. Sammy had worked his magic with him. He had another certified loser on his hands.

Sammy emerged from his office and hailed Costello: 'Ronald!' He was the only person Ron permitted to address him in this way: Ron had come in for some teasing at school on account of his name and the memory of it still festered.

'Sammy,' said Ron, by way of greeting. The two men shook hands. 'Just watching Heath. He's looking tidy.'

'Yes. We've brought him on. He's doing nicely. So good news, Ronald. I think I've solved your problem.'

'Yeah?' Ron cocked an eyebrow.

'Experienced fighter. Former champion. Superb amateur record.'

Heath fired a fusillade of punches into the pads.

'Yeah, yeah. I like the sound of him.'

'A fighter you've had dealings with very recently,' said Sammy.

Ron was tired of the theatricals. 'Right, I'm getting the picture. Joel Heath.'

'Not Heath,' said Sammy. 'No, Tate Lynton.'

'*Lynton?*' Costello's voice went up an octave in a falsetto of disbelief.

At the back of the gym, a heavy bag swung out from a last concussion and Tate appeared, trim and wiry as always, in shorts and a T-shirt, and brand-new boxing boots. He spat his gumshield into the palm of his glove. 'All right, Ron?' he said.

'It's a fucking joke, right?' said Ron, still with that incredulous swoop in his voice. 'He's practically blind, Sammy. He couldn't hit a cow's arse with a banjo! He's older than Methuselah, hasn't had a fight in ten years, and he's only got

197

one eye. I'll get a Chelsea pensioner if I'm that desperate. Come to think of it, some of them have seen active service more recently than he has. God in heaven, Sammy. You're having a laugh.'

'Hear me out, Ron. Tate's in the shape of his life. And – he's got two eyes now.'

Ron looked closer. It was true. The glinting fish-scale was gone. Two brown irises peered back hostilely at Ron Costello. 'Blimey. Which one was it?'

'The left,' said Tate. 'Laser surgery. It's amazing what they can do now.'

Ron shook his head. 'What about Heath? He's looking solid.'

'Won't make the weight in time,' said Sammy. 'Also, not as good.'

Ron looked from Tate to Heath and back again. 'Let me see,' he said.

Sammy cleared the ring and gave both men headguards; he helped Tate into his while Vovan fastened Heath's. Tate stepped into the ring first, giving a quick glance at the hand of the round-clock; Heath followed.

Heath was eager to impress Costello with his rehabilitation and bulled at Tate, who fended him off with a low, snapping jab – shades of Isaac. He carried Heath a little, careful to protect his good eye and the coloured contact lens that Vanes had given him for the bad one. One direct hit would expose the deception. For this and other reasons, Tate felt no need to prolong the examination. With thirty seconds of the first round to go, Tate feinted one way, moved inside, broke two of Heath's ribs with a left uppercut and clubbed him through the ropes with an overhand right.

While Heath lay unconscious on the floor of the gym in the recovery position, reliving a childhood visit to Nikeworld, Tate and Sammy and Ron went to the office for discussions.

'The eye's a fake, right?'

'No,' said Sammy.

'Yes,' said Tate.

'Do you think you can do that to Panic?'

Tate shook his head. 'I doubt it.'

'Why should I risk it?'

'I'm cheap,' said Tate.

'How cheap?'

'Nothing.'

'Nothing?'

'You heard me right.'

'Sammy never works for free. Why's he doing this?'

'Old times' sake,' said Sammy.

Tate quenched Sammy's uneasy smirk with a cold stare. 'Here's the deal: I fight – you get to keep my share of the purse. But Daisy and Isaac are quits with you. Call off Terry Menswear. This is your pound of flesh. You get to brag about it all you like. But I pick my corner.'

Ron did the sums in his head. 'It's a deal,' he said.

Thirty-One

When Daisy heard of Tate's plan, she pleaded with him not to go through with it. Tate was adamant. 'I'm forty-four,' he said. 'I haven't done much in my life to be proud of. This is the right thing to do.'

Daisy's objections to his fighting were not entirely altruistic. There had been a time when she would have died for Isaac, and for Stuart certainly. But the scope of Tate's gesture implied a bond between them that she could never share. She fumbled around for the words that would make it clear to him. 'I can't give you anything in return.'

'That's what's bothering you?'

'I can't accept this.'

'I don't want anything from you. I'm not asking for that. I'm ashamed of how I was with you in the beginning, following you around like a lost puppy. You must have hated it. Pestering you because you were the first person in God knows how many years to be kind to me. It's pathetic. I'm sorry about all that.'

She felt that he was being disingenuous: in some corner of Tate's heart flickered the faint hope that there could be love between them. The only fair thing was for her to extinguish it utterly. 'I don't, I can't love you, Tate.'

Under his bravado, he seemed crushed.

'Look . . .' she began.

'You don't need to say anything else. I'm going ahead with it.' There was a pause and he was moved to add cryptically: 'At Pompeii, I was reading, they left a big chunk of the city under the ash when they excavated it. Some time in the future, they reckon, they'll have found a better way to dig it all up.'

'I won't be part of it.'

'That's up to you.'

Christopher 'Kinky' Panic handed his United States passport to the immigration official at Heathrow for the visa to be stamped.

'Here on business, sir?'

'That's right.'

'What line of work are you in, sir?'

'Prize-fighter.'

The official looked up from the photo in the passport – a nervous, recently naturalized Croatian immigrant – to the face in front of him, tanned and self-assured, already comfortable in the accent and deportment of his adoptive country.

'Well, break a leg, sir, or whatever the appropriate saying is.'

Panic and his entourage of six breezed into the arrivals hall to meet the drivers of their waiting limos.

'I've got you booked in for a massage. Light padwork before supper. The hotel's erected a ring in the ballroom. Imagine that: a special room for balling.'

'Whatever.' Panic slumped down in the seat. It had been a long flight.

'We looked at a huge range of fighters when we got the terrible news about Plum,' said Costello. 'We see Tate Lynton as a veteran, a master of ringcraft.'

The radio interviewer was paid to be sceptical. 'He must be the only professional boxer in the country who wears reading glasses. Not so much rusty as totalled? If he were a car, wouldn't he be an Edsel?'

Costello did his good-natured laugh. 'Fighters of Tate Lynton's quality endure. You haven't seen what I've seen in training.'

*

There was a sombreness at Loverboy's gym. Neither of them mentioned it, but both Tate and Loverboy were well aware of the possibility that Tate could lose his sight completely, or even die. At Tate's age, who knew the risks? Vanes's bogus certificate gave them no idea of the real state of Tate's brain. Better not to know, Tate thought, better not to look down. He felt good in himself. And after initial resistance to the scheme, Loverboy was impressed by Tate's sharpness.

Tate dropped his hands at the burst of the round-bell.

'I wish you'd been in this shape ten years ago,' said Loverboy, 'when . . .' The old man couldn't bring himself to finish the sentence. He simply shook his head and turned away.

Tate's good eye was blazing with adrenaline. He still felt euphoric from the exertion. He pursued the old man across the ring. 'What? When I had a chance? When I had the hand-speed and the legs to lick him? When I had two good eyes? I could have smoked his boots then? When I wasn't an old crocked has-been? When, Cleon, when?'

Loverboy turned his back to Tate, sighing, thinking, *yes, all of those things.*

At four o'clock the day before the fight, Loverboy came to collect Tate for the weigh-in. Stripped to his designer briefs, Panic looked heavier, but he was actually giving away a couple of pounds to Tate. It was Tate's deceptive build: denser and wirier than the younger man's.

Panic stared at Tate throughout the weigh-in, trying to intimidate him. Tate smiled back. He was too old to play games of machismo.

At home later, Tate noodled around, killing time. He used up the best part of an hour packing his bag, folding and refolding his trunks, towels, socks and robe – the red-trimmed black one he had worn in his heyday, with his name in copperplate and the word 'Smoke' beneath it in the same red embroidery. He remembered the Moscow Olympics and how, after getting the hardest possible draw in the preliminaries and being matched with the Cuban champion, he had put in a typically Tate-ish performance. Tate boxed the Cuban to a standstill in the first two rounds with effortless brilliance, was miles ahead on all score-cards, and seemed to be cruising to a shock triumph. Then, coming out for the third, Tate allowed himself to be knocked out by a heavy punch that had all the rumbling predictability of a supermarket trolley. It was as though something about success made Tate giddy. After his defeat, he had got up to what young athletes get up to in the Olympic village, consoling himself with a Romanian triple-jumper called Lilya and ominous – in retrospect – amounts of vodka.

Tate sat and listened to music for a while, rereading the Houdini biography that he had enjoyed so much the first time, until it came to him with a shudder that the peritonitis that had killed Houdini had originated from an unexpected punch. Tate cursed the book for its bad omen and tossed it aside. Too late – he was already rattled.

And now the dark hours for Tate began, the hours of anticipation, the hours of pacing and not sleeping, the midnight encounters with the ghosts of his old defeats, the inexplicable losses, the self-doubt, the stomach-churning fear. Out of the pit they came, the death-fights, the horrific defeats: Jess Willard quitting on his stool after Jack Dempsey had broken four of his ribs, knocked out three of his teeth and hit him so hard in the head that Willard had tinnitus for the rest of his life; Gerald McClellan sinking to one knee in the tenth against Nigel Benn, his face already convulsing from the blood clot in his brain that would leave him blind and crippled; Lupe Pintor beating Johnny Owen to death before a crowd baying for the Welshman's blood.

Tate lay awake, hearing Loverboy's voice in his head telling him to rest his body even if he couldn't get his head to go under. Premonitions of disaster unspooled in his imagination. At two o'clock in the morning, he counted back six hours on the pillow and picked up the phone. 'Edgar – it's Tate. I'm fighting tomorrow. I can't sleep.'

Edgar told him to look out of the window. 'What do you see?'

Tate pushed back the curtain. The clouds over the slick, wet roofs had parted to reveal a big bare ball of unsleeping moon.

After that, he was able to doze.

At four o'clock the next day, Isaac and Loverboy came to collect him. They drove in silence across the city. Once inside the dressing room, Isaac and Tate played backgammon for an hour. As time passed, Tate could feel himself growing tense. He was conscious of his heart thumping. He knew he had to bring himself down a bit, that if he got overwrought, he would exhaust himself before he got into the ring. He tried to get Loverboy to join him in small talk, but the old man was too tense to chat. Then Tate remembered a game he had played with his team-mates in Moscow. He made a rudimentary ball out of a spare pair of socks and a lot of tape, and he and Isaac flung it at each other. The ball had a good heft and was gratifyingly squidgy to catch. Somehow this ludicrous game with no rules kept Tate's mind occupied until it was time to wrap his hands.

Isaac and Loverboy did one hand apiece – they each claimed to have a superior method. Tate was in a good humour after the ball game. 'We'll see which one of you gets the knock-out,' he said. 'That'll settle it.'

At quarter to nine, someone from Panic's dressing room came to check Tate's wraps and make sure there was no tape across the knuckles. Loverboy avoided Tate's glance as the man initialled the tape that sealed the cuff of Tate's gloves. Poor Loverboy, Tate thought. If I get through this, I'll think of something I can do for him, he decided. Then the real significance of the thought hit him: *if I get through this*.

With the gloves signed, Tate began to work up a sweat on the pads. He cut loose with a flurry of uppercuts. His arms were rolling nicely, no tension in his back or shoulders, and he could feel the line of power from the sole of his right boot to the knuckle of his glove as he threw the left hook. Tate smiled at Loverboy. 'I wish . . .' he said.

Loverboy shook his head. 'Don't say it.'

Tate felt a tap on his shoulder. It was Isaac, jerking his thumb towards the open door.

Tate looked and saw the whip, Ernie Draper, standing in the doorway. 'It's time,' said Ernie.

Thirty-Two

Tate felt the crowd's heat on either side of him, its unified desires, its expectant breath. And then he was in the ring, buoyed up on a surge of adrenalin. Loverboy could see it and motioned to Tate to ease things down. He beckoned Tate closer and rubbed a blob of vaseline into his eyebrow: a lioness grooming her cub, a parent primping a child with spit. 'Take your time. Protect the eye.'

Panic prowled round his corner, trying to project a fearless malevolence towards his opponent. Tate dipped those old knees of his and shook his feet out. He looked self-conscious, a little clumsy.

At the instruction to touch gloves, Panic banged his hands down hard on Tate's as if he couldn't wait to get started, and smiled, flashing a sliver of red gum-guard through the chink of his grin.

And it began.

Panic flew out of his corner on the bell and tried to unload a furious right hand on Tate's head. It was a move he had been practising all week in training – a one-punch knockdown. There was a roar from the crowd at the audacity of it, the disrespect, but Tate dipped, tangled his arms in Panic's and wrestled him, tutting in his ear as he did so like a disappointed uncle, deliberately patronizing the younger man. That riled Panic, and as he broke the clinch he lashed at Tate, striking him with the right hand on the cheek and scoring the first clean shot of the fight, which was now ten seconds old.

It was clear that Panic's strategy was to hound Tate, charge at him, press him, rattle him, chase him round the ring with the advantage of his young legs. Tate was on the back foot all the time, with his guard unusually high for him, stepping constantly to his left to keep Panic clearly framed in his good eye. But this brought him in range of the right hand and Panic began scoring with it to the body and head.

A punch caught Tate's temple, a punch so fast that he was not even conscious of its impact, only that the light in the auditorium afterwards had been subtly enhanced. As more blows landed, Tate backed on to the ropes; he covered up, intermittently aware of Loverboy's voice urging him to him to move laterally, to pivot, to use his feet to get him out of trouble, but also troubled by elusive memories that he couldn't quite recall, as though he was on the edge of sleep . . .

Smoke drifted, boys tumbled over in piles of autumn leaves. Somewhere far off, a girl in platform sneakers laughed a high, mechanical laugh that struck Tate as somehow geometrical in its design, like the scales on a snake.

Panic threw punches at, over and around Tate's guard, battering the side of his head, his arms, aiming for the floating ribs, where one heavy shot would make his body buckle.

Another punch jolted Tate's mind clear: he knew his thoughts were absurd, but they did not feel absurd. This felt absurd: his body had disowned him, it no longer bothered to report its pain. Tate was surprised that it could put up with so much hurt.

Tate hung on to Panic, stifling his punches with his tenacious arms. The referee pulled them apart and looked at Tate, who instinctively touched his gloves together and nodded.

At the bell, Tate went back to his corner knowing he had lost the round.

A ring girl in toffee-coloured tights and knitted orange hot pants held a number two aloft and smiled in the face of desultory cat-calls:

'Flop one out!'

'I love you!'

Tate felt a certain regret at the thought he was still conscious and his suffering would be prolonged. The cold sponge on his head and chest returned him to his body. Now he heard its mutinous chatter, the pleas of his nerve endings, wheedling, urging him to stop. Tate would not stop, but he felt an abstract pity for his body, as though for an elderly neighbour, a mother struggling with a push-chair and heavy shopping, a dog locked in a parked car on a sunny day. Loverboy was shouting at him:

'You're too old for this, Tate. You don't need it. Another round like that and I'm pulling you out. I don't mind you trading with him a little, but he's hitting you with stuff that shouldn't get through'

Isaac swilled the gum-shield for him. Loverboy wiped his face with the towel and went on: 'He's leaving you all sorts of ways in. He's dropping the right hand when he throws the jab, and he's getting sloppy with the jab as he comes forward. You can beat him to the punch. You can hook over the right hand just like you would with a southpaw . . .'

Tate let the words wash over him. Isaac put the gumshield into Tate's mouth. As he did so, the two men's eyes met, and Tate saw something in Isaac's face, something that he wanted to communicate but couldn't. 'What?' he asked. 'What?'

In Panic's corner, the fighter's trainer was congratulating him on having taken the first round, telling him to keep up the pressure, let the other guy keep coming to the right hand. And Panic nodded; sure, he said, sure.

At the bell, Tate shuffled towards the ring centre: he had Isaac's face in his head, that mobile, expressive face, the beady brown eyes, the soft, still unwrinkled brow that Daisy had sprayed with water and wiped dry a thousand times, pressing the towel to his head as tenderly as any mother did to her fevered child's – their child. All his nerves vanished. His heart lifted in a swoop of hope.

When Panic put together his first combination, Tate responded instinctively, pivoting 180 degrees off his front foot to leave Panic punching air. Two quick uppercuts to Panic's ribs and Tate was away again, floating around Panic on the outside, as uncatchable as a handful of sea mist.

No one was more astonished than Tate himself. Instead of pressing his advantage, he let Panic recover. What was going through Tate's mind was all those times in training that he had mentioned to Daisy, when Isaac had seemed sluggish and distracted, when his movements had been predictable. And Tate thought: it wasn't Isaac, it was me; he wasn't slower, I was reading him too well.

Panic moved towards him, but with less confidence, knowing that he faced a renewed opponent. There was a new vitality in Tate and he moved on the legs of a man twenty years younger.

Now all those times that Tate had played Panic – had inhabited his body so that Isaac could devise ways to fight him – began to pay off. Tate knew this man, had *been* this man, the man in front of him. He knew how he set his mouth just so as he prepared to throw a hook, how he moved his right hand fractionally wide when he jabbed, how he telegraphed his intention to go for the body. Tate hit him with clusters of punches, not setting his feet for big shots, but exasperating him, taking the heart out of him.

Valley Hall had fallen silent. Crowds go quiet for long periods at boxing matches, especially during dull contests where nothing much happens. You hear fidgeting, coughs, rustling and the sound of the gloves making contact in the ring, not the fulsome crack you hear in movies, but something more akin to a slap, to *squish*.

But this silence had a different quality to it. It was intense, the hush of collective awe as Tate delivered his masterclass. He was free, wholly alive, all fire and dance. Some other spirit moved in him: the things he had picked up from working with Isaac Plum, and the shades of other fighters too, famous and unknown – Ali, Herol Graham, Naseem Hamed, Sugar Ray Robinson, Jack Johnson – going back to God knows where, to the prize ring and before, to Molyneux and Cribb, to the *agon* of Homer, to the ceremonial challenges of prehistory that were not so much about victory and defeat, but a conscious echo of the endless conflict that generates life, that *is* life.

Panic visibly wilted. All that self-assurance had gone. Tate had succeeded in unloading all his self-doubt on to his opponent. Panic had become Tate. He looked awkward, worried, trudging across the ring towards his tormentor, knowing he was falling behind on points and needing to make up ground. But every time he got close, Tate rattled off combinations of punches, wheeled to the side, pivoted around him. So now Panic was looking to hold, because as soon as he stopped chasing Tate, Tate would come after him, stinging him with clusters of blows. Panic tried to grab him, wrestle, catch his breath, but there was nothing to hold on to. Tate had evaporated. Smoke.

Then, on the bell at the end of round six, Tate dropped his hands and Panic caught him in the face with a sneaky and obviously late punch, and then another. Panic claimed afterwards that he hadn't heard the bell. It was a lie. He hit Tate for the same reason that you might pinch yourself after a bad dream. He wanted to be sure that Tate was real and not a phantom. The referee cautioned him. The blows rocked Tate's head back. He rubbed his face with his glove, shrugged and went back to his corner. But it was clear from the look on Loverboy's face that something was wrong. Isaac saw it too: the flash of silver in Tate's eye. Panic's corner had seen it as well and told the referee with wild gesticulations. He called the doctor into the ring to have a closer look. The doctor shook his head. And the referee waved it off. Round six: RSF.

Of course, if the referee had known the truth about Tate, it would have meant instant disqualification, but no one guessed that Tate had been boxing with one eye through the entire fight. The referee assumed it had just happened. And under the rules of the sanctioning body, Tate's injury was treated as a cut. After six rounds, the decision would be awarded on points. So the referee called on the judges.

Loverboy must have thought it was in the bag, because he hugged Tate and Tate smiled.

The Master of Ceremonies was in the ring. 'The referee has stopped the contest at the end of the sixth round, having determined that one of the fighters was medically unfit to continue. Since more than three rounds have been fought, the verdict rests on the judges' score-cards. In a split decision . . .'

That phrase drew disquiet from the crowd.

'. . . the judges have scored the contest 57–57, 59–55 and 58–56. So the winner and still the undefeated . . .'

The rest of the sentence was drowned by a chorus of boos. Bottles flew into the ring. A chair-seat skittered through the air like a misshapen frisbee.

Ron Costello came to Tate's changing room afterwards, ostensibly to commiserate. He shook hands with Loverboy, but Tate was unwinding his bandages and just nodded at him. 'No hard feelings,' said Costello. 'Funny old result in some ways. It's all in the game, though, eh? Probably best this way. Imagine: if you was to be champion, they might uncover God knows what kind of medical irregularities. Aye, aye?' Costello winked at Tate. 'So the best thing, from everyone's point of view, is that you tell the press as losers – or, I should say, runners-up – that you're happy with the result.' Costello took an envelope from his jacket pocket. Tate shook his head. 'There won't be a rematch, Lynton,' Costello warned him. 'Not with the eye and everything. Not after the fright you gave Panic's lot tonight.' He offered the envelope to Loverboy. 'You take it for safe keeping,' he said. Tate shook his head again and Loverboy folded his arms against his chest. 'It's a loser's bonus,' said Ron. 'You're being very stubborn.'

'A deal's a deal,' said Tate.

'There's no need to be doctrinaire,' said Costello.

Tate stared at him, still high from the contest, still exuding the same silky menace that had so baffled Panic. Tate turned to look at Loverboy. 'You want it?'

'Not me.'

Ron slipped the envelope back into his pocket. 'What the fuck is wrong with you, Lynton?'

Tate slid off the massage table and went towards Costello, who instinctively shaped for combat. Tate pressed in closer until he stood nose-to-nose with him, so close that Costello found himself staring at Tate's strange blank iris and feeling Tate's breath on his face as the fighter spoke in a whisper: 'And Abram said to the King of Sodom, I have raised my hand to God and sworn an oath, that I will accept nothing, not a thread, nor a thong of a sandal, so you will never be able to say: "I made Abram rich."'

Ron was mystified. He looked from one man to the other, shrugged, then turned on his heel and slammed the door behind him.

Thirty-Three

Daisy passed Costello in the hallway. He didn't see her in the crush of people. She had been unable to stay away from the fight. In that first round, she almost left, but she stayed on, for the miraculous subsequent rounds, Tate's recovery and the crooked result.

There was still that misgiving that she owed him too much, but it was silenced by the euphoria she found him in. Tate was elated. His hands were swollen from the accumulated impacts again Panic's head, but he appeared otherwise uninjured

Daisy walked with him out of the building. So many people crowded round to congratulate him, to beseech him for autographs, to touch his swollen hands, that she got shunted aside by the press of people. She stood outside the ring of well-wishers, watching him. It seemed that for one instant Tate had experienced a kind of grace. For one transcendent moment, he had been not only better than Panic, but better than himself. It had been a moment by definition outside the powers of his anticipation, but one for which he had been preparing himself for years. Now he was free, as Daisy was, having laid the ghosts of the long-unburied dead, no longer crippled by the weight of the past, by the thought of what might have been.

Tate looked up from the programme he was signing. Daisy waved goodbye. He raised his hand and winked at her. It would be the last time he ever saw her.

Tate's losses didn't end with his points defeat on the referees' score-cards. Twenty-four hours after the fight – hours which he spent in a euphoric daze – his alarm clock woke him at eight a.m to a world of perplexing darkness, an obscurity that no amount of light could illuminate. When the doctor examined him, Tate recalled a faint ticking he had felt at the back of his right eye since well before the fight, that he had dismissed as a muscle strain. In fact, it was a blood vessel that had been haemorrhaging slowly for days. Some oblique knock, it seemed, had caused it. The structure of the eye, the doctor said, had been compromised from too many shots in training. No amount of surgery could save it. A lifetime of boxing was a lifetime of accumulated injuries. That was another of the sport's intrinsic cruelties. The arc of endeavour that made a boxer great was what destroyed him. Tate touched the summit of his craft only for an instant, before the effort he had expended to get there destroyed his sight.

Daisy went to the hospital as soon as she heard the news from Loverboy. She was afraid to find him bitter, but he was as happy as she had ever seen him and, in those days, still optimistic about the prospect of recovery. Daisy took him in her car to Regent's Park and they sat in the rose garden.

'What does it look like?'

She described it to him: the leaves and flowers looping over the trelliswork. He sat in silence, listening. 'I like hearing your voice,' said Tate

'Cleon told me about the money,' she said. 'I would have taken it.'

Tate shook his head. 'I told him to stuff it. I was flying, man!'

'Why didn't you take it?'

'*Why*. Aren't you bored of reasons?'

'I just wondered.'

'You're afraid it's to do with you?'

'I feel responsible.'

'You mustn't. I had my own reasons.' Tate leaned back on the bench, feeling the lightless warmth of the sun on his face.

'I should have figured it out a long time ago, when I was sitting in that hospital bed after the Sugar fight and Costello came, promising me this and that.' Tate was vehement: 'I don't want *nothing* that Costello wants. As long as you want what he's offering, you're stuck in his world. Nothing ever changes. Oh yeah, someone gets a belt, someone makes a bit of money. But deep down everything stays the same. Every time there's a winner, there's a loser. It just goes pinging round and round the world, each person laying it off to someone else, until someone says *enough*.'

'Enough,' said Daisy.

'That's right.' Tate looked in the direction of her voice and smiled. 'Otherwise when are you ever going to be free?' He was carrying a cane to guide himself with, and he shifted it to his left hand while he adjusted his dark glasses. 'It's not all bad, you know. I smell better since the accident.'

Daisy laughed. 'You don't mean that how it sounded.'

'You know what I meant,' said Tate. He leaned his head back and took a huge breath through his nostrils. 'The roses.'

'I can smell those.'

He pointed with his stick. 'Someone over there is eating a choc ice.'

Daisy looked over. It was true.

'See? It's not all bad.'

They pulled down Valley Hall in the end. Eighteen months into the new millennium, the bulldozers moved in. A wrecking ball smashed through the Victorian brickwork with a faint crunch, as if it offered no more resistance than pie-crust. It had outlasted the imperial certainties of the age in which it was constructed. It was two years shy of its centenary. Valley Hall was over, but not the boxing. Ron Costello was right: the fights would go on. People were prepared to tolerate anything better than ambivalence. Some other venue would continue the trade in certainties, supplying an insecure time with unequal contests. But neither Tate nor Isaac Plum would be part of it.

Isaac and Una moved out to Hereford, where she had family, and Isaac bought a little picture-framing business in the town. They had another child, a son, with fast hands apparently, but they wouldn't dream of letting him near a boxing ring.

Tate and Daisy went back at night for the last time before Valley Hall was consigned to history. It was bitter. The demolition men had packed up work at five on the dot, leaving the old building half-demolished. The 1950s neon sign dangled off the front of the building.

'What can you smell?' asked Daisy. She watched him tilt his head to one side and sniff, concentrating intently.

'Diesel. Brick dust. Plaster.' He paused. 'I won't miss it.'

The moon slipped out from behind a cloud, bright as a dentist's spotlight, shining down indifferently on the rubble that enclosed the memory of so many victories and defeats, and in the dim light, it looked to Daisy like the rocks of a new planet, a place without words or the burdens of history, whose inhabitants would be free to start afresh, absolved once and for all from the necessity of choosing sides.